Scarborough Fair
& Other Stories

Scarborough Fair & Other Stories

Elizabeth Ann Scarborough

Five Star • Waterville, Maine

First Edition
First Printing: February 2003

Published in 2003 in conjunction with
Tekno Books and Ed Gorman.

Set in 11 pt. Plantin by Al Chase.

Printed in the United States on permanent paper.

Library of Congress Cataloging-in-Publication Data

Scarborough, Elizabeth Ann.
    Scarborough fair and other stories : stories / by Elizabeth Ann Scarborough.
        p. cm.—(Five Star first edition speculative fiction series)
    Contents: Mummies of the motorway—Final vows—Whirlwinds—Worse than the curse—Boon companion—Long time coming home (with Rick Reaser)—Mu Mao and the court oracle—Don't go out in holy underwear, or, Victoria's secret, or, space panties!!!—The invisible woman's clever disguise—A rare breed—Scarborough fair.
    ISBN 0-7862-5053-4 (hc : alk. paper)
    1. Fantasy fiction, American.   I. Title.   II. Series.
PS3569.C324 S28 2003
813'.54—dc21   2002043068

Dedication

This collection is dedicated to Martin H. Greenberg, who has done so much to sustain and support contemporary science fiction and fantasy short fiction.

Table of Contents

Introduction

Writing for theme anthologies reminds me of what I liked to do best in school. When the teacher assigned us to write about a particular subject, I took perverse enjoyment in twisting the subject as far out of shape as I could and writing along the edge of it. I wanted to write something completely different from anything anyone else was doing. While that wasn't the height of literary aspiration, I suppose, it has stood me in good stead for the current market where anthologies are mostly based around themes: "write about monsters, witches, the occult, shape shifters," etc.

This collection consists of stories I wrote for such anthologies. However, each story also has another inspiration, rather than a simple theme, and for the benefit of those people who are always asking where writers get their ideas, I thought I might share those inspirations here.

"Mummies of the Motorway" and "Scarborough Fair" were both inspired originally by my own name, which indicates that I had a paternal ancestor who came from a seaside resort in England. I spent a few days in the town soaking up all the atmosphere I could, and it serves as the background for both stories. "Mummies of the Motorway" was also inspired by stories of the disrespectful treatment the Egyptian dead received in Victorian and turn-of-the-century England and by the personalities of my niece and nephew, with whom I had just been fortunate enough to spend some time. "Scarborough Fair" took its inspiration not only from the very old song whose most recent version involves my name and the name of the town where a hiring fair did indeed take place in Medieval times, but also from the Agatha Christie stories where the English go on "hols" and "take the waters," which is the sort of town Scarborough was in its heyday.

Ellery Queen once wrote that when writers get together they talk about their taxes. In my experience, authors talk about their animal friends and the veterinarians who keep them healthy. When my friend Carole Nelson Douglas, author of the Midnight Louie series, requested an animal detective story, I wanted to do one for my recently deceased cat friend of twenty years, Mustard. When I had to have Mustard put to sleep because he was in great pain from being poisoned, I was very moved by something said to me by Jeannette, Dr. Tony the vet's wife and herself a wildlife rescuer. She said that Mustard would not be left alone, but would be laid in a nice little box with candles and incense around him and someone staying nearby. Also, a man I had been seeing had turned out to be a career criminal who was nevertheless very good with animals.

"Whirlwinds" comes from my interest in folklore. I had just completed *The Godmother's Web*, a novel set in the Hopi Partitioned Lands in the middle of the Navajo reservation. The Navajo beliefs about the wind and whirlwinds in particular were fresh in my mind, and I was pleased to find an Irish belief that corresponded.

"Worse Than the Curse" and "The Invisible Woman's Clever Disguise" were both informed by my experiences as a once voluptuous sweet young thing turned, almost overnight, into an all too sturdy and stout middle aged woman (*when* did that happen?).

"Boon Companion" was originally written for an anthology about familiars, and I think it is a good example of that. However, the editor felt it fit better in an anthology on vengeance, although the vengeance is more of a "what goes around comes around" nature. My mother told me about the girlfriend (now wife) of my cousin's son who lost her mother and was promptly set upon by rampaging relatives who tried to take everything her mother left away from her. In that case the girl had my cousin to help her. In my story, it's a cat.

"Long Time Coming Home" was written for *In the Shadow of the Wall*, an anthology edited by Byron Tetrick. I wrote about my own experiences in Vietnam in my novel, *Healer's War*. However, my friend and sometimes muse, a fellow Vietnam vet named Rick Reaser, had some hair-raising combat experience in Nam and has the names of many fallen friends on the Wall. I asked Rick to co-author a story with me. Although Rick doesn't write, he is one of the best extemporaneous storytellers I've ever met. We tossed ideas back and forth, they mutated as I wrote them down, then read them to Rick, he suggested things, I made counter-suggestions, and so forth until the story was complete.

"Mu Mao and the Court Oracle" took its inspiration not only from a minor character in *Last Refuge*, my post-apocalyptic novel set in Tibet, but also from an experience I had at the animal shelter. The elderly inconsolable cat whose dying master wanted it to find a home broke my heart. That cat never did find a home, but in my stories I get to control things, so they come out somewhat better.

11

Probably the only story that actually took most of its inspiration from the title of the anthology was the one I wrote for Jody Lynn Nye's *Don't Forget Your Spacesuit, Dear*. It was supposed to be about bold space explorers and the things their mothers told them. My mom was very big on the clean and intact underwear, hence my story.

"A Rare Breed," written for Peter Beagle and Janet Berliner Gluckman's *Immortal Unicorn* anthology, takes place in the town where I live and has the town's New Age, er—sensibility—at its heart. It also has the unicorn's magic horn healing a heart singed by an old flame.

So that's where I got my ideas. I hope you'll enjoy what I did with them.

—Elizabeth Ann Scarborough

Mummies of the Motorway

Scarborough, UK
March 25

Dear Mom and Bro,

Just wanted to let you know that no matter what the kids write to you, I really have done my best to show them a good time over here. Please don't blame me if they tell you that next time I offer to treat my only niece and nephew to a trip to England, you should say they have come down with bubonic plague.

We had a great time in London, where there were more indoor activities and it didn't matter so much that it's been raining since we first arrived in England. The kids loved everything: Madame Toussad's, the museums, and especially the plays. Rain in England is part of the atmosphere, really. Just like it is in Seattle. Maybe we should have paid more attention to the news before we left London, but the B&Bs I could afford for us did not have TVs. We got on the last train coming or going before the mudslides washed out sections of both the roads and the tracks. With the roads washed out, and the postal service on strike again, I may have to send this via carrier pigeon relay but there's not a lot else to do under the present circumstances, so I am writing to you.

Needless to say, Monte, your offspring are bored. Jason was monosyllabic all the way up to Scarborough and Cindy could only talk about how much she missed her cats, which is of course making me really miss *my* cats. I can't blame them. There isn't much for an eighteen-year-old boy or a fifteen-year-old girl to do here, really. Or a fifty-three-year-old Aunt who's already been here, for that matter, and we did most of it today.

We seem to be the *only* nonresident guests in this whole heap of a hotel. The resident guests are more like patients—as in nursing home patients. Scarborough doesn't get enough visitors in the off-season to keep the hotels open. So apparently the large ones like this one, which *was* suspiciously cheap, take in people who spent happy holidays in their youth here back in the days when people still came for the mineral baths and played at the seashore.

It looks like there's just one couple that runs the whole pile, the snooty woman at the desk who took one look at us robust and sturdily built Scarboroughs and insisted we had to use the stairs, even though she stuck us up on the fifth floor. The lifts, as they call elevators here, are for the disabled only.

The kids took it pretty well. Jason got all macho and took the stairs four at a time. Cindy pretended to prop me up and reminded me that I had told her this was a spa. "And see, Aunt Annie, they give you the exercise class free with your room. Anyplace else we'd have to pay for a Stairmaster!"

We made it upstairs, lightened our knapsacks, strapped

on our bum bags and flipped our ponchos dry, then hurried back down for lunch. One look at what they were serving, again in deference to the residents, and we decided to risk being washed out to sea by walking down to the tacky little tourist traps on the beach and seeing if we could find a fish and chips joint.

I tried to call a cab, but because of the weather, even with so few visitors in town, none were available. So we slipped on our ponchos, opened one of the big front doors and took one step out before the wind, which had whipped itself into a gale, and tried to pick us up and carry us in the opposite direction from town. It didn't just whistle. It shrieked and howled and the ocean that had been so placid on my previous visit crashed and roared as if auditioning for a surfer movie.

I put my head down and splashed forward. The kids trailed behind at first, but once they could see the strand, as they call the beach around here, Jason plunged forward as the leader of the expedition. Of course, when he got to the place where the sidewalk ended at the cliff, he had to stop. Turning a streaming face to me, he shrugged and asked, "Where to now?"

"Aha!" I gurgled through the rain. "This is the first of the many wonders of your ancestral town, nephew." I led them past a couple of bushes to the little cage at the top of the cliff. "Behold, the funicular!"

Cindy rolled her eyes and Jason gave another shrug questioning my sanity and whether or not their aging aunt had begun speaking in tongues. But they were as glad to get in out of the wind and rain as I.

"A *what?*" he demanded.

"This little tram," I said. "It's called a funicular. They've had them since back in the days when people came for the baths, back before the wars."

"How does it work?" Cindy asked.

"You put a coin in here," I told her. Which I did. It had been fifty pence when I was there five years ago. Now it's a pound.

"Big whoop," Jason said at the bottom.

I peered through the rain at the straggle of fairylights bouncing above the beach, and the neon lights and cardboard signs proclaiming the wonders of each and every gift shack which was open. There weren't very many of the neon signs lit.

"Hold that thought," I told him. "That may have been your big thrill for the day."

We asked at the first souvenir shop if there was likely to be a chip stand open, and the fellow jerked his thumb and said it was two doors down. Cindy bought some candybars and pop and stuck them in the empty knapsack she had had the foresight to bring along. I found the notebook and authentic Scarborough, England pen with which I am writing to you now.

The man was a little cheerier when he saw we were after something besides free directions, and he chatted a bit with Cindy, who I suspect kept him talking to hear his Yorkshire accent. "He sounds like those guys in *The Full Monty*, Aunt Annie," she giggled behind her hand as we left.

The chippy, as they fondly call fish and chip shops hereabouts, was almost cheerful. Just about every person still working on the strand came and went from it or stood around talking. There was no place to sit except outside in the rain, so we stood around too and ate our greasy fish and French fries out of newsprint cones and drank our Cokes and lemonade, which is like 7-Up.

"So, you're here on holidays, are you?" the lady at the chip stand asked. I felt like saying no, we were all very frail and puny, obviously, with the three of us all looking as hefty as is the Scarborough clan legacy from Dad.

"Yes."

"Pity about the weather. It's generally much finer in summer."

"Yes, but the airfares are higher," I said. "And the kids had their Easter break, so I thought I'd bring them over."

"We don't get a lot of American youngsters here this time of year," a bearded man remarked, also in a Yorkshire accent.

"We have a special reason," Cindy said. "See, our last name is Scarborough. Our Grandpa Scarborough died last year and Aunt Annie thought we ought to come over and see where all our English relatives came from."

"Your grandpa was from here, was he?"

Cindy shook her head. "Oh no. Kansas City."

"My history teacher, Mrs. Martinez, says people usually only got named for a place after they left it," Jason volunteered.

"Did she now?" The man asked gravely. "Well, then, you'll be needing to see my place. I have a museum and historical exhibit of the history of this town from the time it were a Viking village. You can see the castle from my place as well."

"We don't have any kings in our family, do we, Aunt Annie?" Jason asked suspiciously.

"No, honey. They just named the castle after the place. A king or two stayed there once in awhile when they were passing through."

"Oh."

"But *my* history professor told me that a king once killed his son the prince's homosexual lover by throwing him out the window at Scarborough Castle."

"Cool! A murder!" Jason said with typical teenaged bloodthirstiness.

We toured the exhibit, asked questions, bought booklets and souvenirs and looked out the window at what we could see of the castle's ruins through the gusts and sheets of rain. The kids were really disappointed when the man said we couldn't visit the ruins. Since we had probably paid his expenses for opening that day though, he asked, "Where are you staying?"

I told him and he said, "I'll give you a lift in the tour bus then, half price! I'm needing petrol anyway. Name's Bert Hoskins."

Once aboard the bus, Bert turned on the radio instead of giving us the tour, and that's when we heard that the railroad bridge had washed away.

"Wow! We just went over that one."

"Do you think they'll get it fixed before we're supposed to leave tomorrow, Aunt Annie?" Cindy asked.

"I wouldn't count on that," Bert said. "Probably won't be fixed for weeks. I'm afraid you'll have to take the bus back."

Just about then we crested the hill in time to see one of the hotels that teetered on the edge of the cliff like a mudslide mansion in California do exactly what those houses did during heavy downpours—it listed toward the sea for a few moments while our driver, his brakes on, waited for it as if it were a dog crossing the road.

The kids thought this was pretty neat, especially when the five-story brick building began its slide, picking up speed as it toppled, eventually dragging a portion of road with it, shaking the bit we were sitting on so that the kids and I glanced nervously at each other. It was a huge crash, and Cindy covered her ears, even as we all craned our necks. However, we couldn't see much for the dust and smoke and little spurts of flame from the severed electric and gas lines. Apparently the staff had enough warning of their domain's eminent demise to disconnect the necessary and evacuate before the disaster. The staff, the old and disabled residents, and probably a good portion of the town watched from the swampy overgrown green quadrangle, formerly a garden, around which the hotels primly perched.

"The bus doesn't need to run on *that* road, does it?" Jason asked Bert. Jason had that skittish horse look in his eye he gets when his voice is perfectly calm but he is very worried about something.

Bert laughed. "This is a good one for these parts. We don't see much of our tax money going for new roads up here. Save all that for the cities, they do. During the war when asphalt was not to be had for civilians, me old Dad told me they ground up all them mummies the museums had dug up in Egypt and brought over here."

"Ugh!" Cindy said. *"Why?"*

"Well, the way Dad told me, the bandages the bodies was wrapped in were coated with something like pitch, and it worked almost as good as the genuine article. So, they recycled them, you might say. Used 'em as fertilizer too, and to fuel the fires in the trains."

Jason glowered. "That's horrible."

"Practical, more like," Bert said, and then added, slyly, "But they do say when you have these wet spells, washouts and the like, it's them mummies tryin' to bust their way loose from the roads so's they can drag their bandagedy arses back t' Nile." Jason rolled his eyes and made a spiral motion with his finger by his ear. "I'll be turning at t' square."

I thanked him and told him we'd get off. We spent the rest of the afternoon helping the hotel staff and a few other able-bodied people taking the now homeless old folks into the various hotels that had agreed to shelter them.

We finished up about an hour ago and the kids were both tired. They slept through dinner, and we had to make do with the candy and crisps (Brit for potato chips) we bought on the strand. Sorry, Mom. Since little British towns like this one roll up the sidewalks at five, the kids decided to go to bed early. I plan to get us on the first bus out if at all possible, so I'll go downstairs and call the bus station recording pretty soon to see when we have to get up. Our plane for home leaves day after tomorrow

Later.

When I woke up to go to the bathroom at about midnight, Cindy was gone. I had been having restless dreams of my cats crying for me to come home and seemed to still be hearing them as I woke up. Vaguely, I remembered hearing Cindy arising and the toilet flushing but now the bathroom was dark and her bed still empty.

I pulled on my own black leather jacket and the sandals and padded down the hall to the communal bathroom. Maybe she'd decided to take a shower or something, I was thinking. But there was no light down the hall and the doors to the loo and the shower room both were dark and empty. My heart stopped. I knew you were going to shoot me, brother, if I lost your little girl. She is so sensible and calm most of the time I forget she's just a kid and though we are all of us a bit large for anyone other than Hercules to drag off into the bushes, still there were a lot of creeps who prey on young girls, and Cindy is so friendly . . . I re-minded myself of your family's karate lessons all the way back to our rooms, where I woke up Jason and told him to get dressed, then shucked out of my jacket, pulled on my own socks and shoes and a sweater over my night shirt, and shrugged back into the jacket.

Jason, still wearing his sweat-pajamas, padded sleepily to his window, frowning as he gazed out.

"What are you *doing?*" I'm afraid I came very close to snarling at him as he returned to my room, still wearing the sweats he had worn to bed.

He gestured with elbows bent at the waist, hands extended, palms bouncing up and down, telling me to cool it. "I was just *checking* to see if I could see her out the windows," he said. "But you can't see anything out there. It's really foggy. Besides, she's probably not out there. She probably found someone to talk to." That was not unlikely, Cindy being your daughter, oh most sociable of brothers, and her garrulous grandpa's granddaughter. In which case, since except for the distinctly unfriendly staff here, there was no one much under the age of eighty, I hardly saw how she could be in any danger. But her coat was missing and, on closer inspection, I saw that her running shoes were gone as well.

Jason had on his jacket and his own unfastened shoes and handed me a flashlight. "Where'd this come from?" I asked him.

"I brought one for each of us," he said in that very matter-of-fact way he has, then added, "I decided we might need them more than I'd need my tuxedo. Cindy had one too. I was looking to see if she was using it a minute ago." Sometimes that boy actually seems to have a sense of humor. Not to mention that he seems to have learned what a tuxedo *is* since he turned down the girl who asked him to the prom because he thought she had to be joking.

We heard the wind howling and moaning around the corner of the hotel as we trudged down the stairs. That seemed funny to me because usually when the wind is high,

21

the fog gets blown away.

Instead it was as if kidnappers had pulled a gray woolly sack over the entire area; the only distinctions from the pervading dark fuzziness were the occasional wisps or blobs of white floating through it.

I unlocked the hotel's outer door (they always give you a key for after-hours) and we had only taken a few steps out toward the road when I glanced back. The hotel's looming bulk had been swallowed by the fog.

"Cindy?" I called, trying to keep my voice pitched so that if she were near, she could find her way back to us but I wouldn't be waking the old-age pensioners. I couldn't help feeling that if I had screamed my lungs out, the fog would muffle my racket as it muffled everything else.

Jason strode past me, cupping his hands to his mouth and bellowing, "Yo, Cynthia Dawn!"

Something scrabbled off to the right and I said, "Cindy!" sharply.

There was an answering "Rrrow?"

Though that is not, of course, Cindy's normal voice you will understand, brother, why I, cat-mother of Treat and Kittibits, instantly felt relieved. I understood Cindy's motivation for being out here. Obviously she had heard the cat crying and come out to investigate. I'd have done the same thing if I'd been aware of it. She was very possibly trying to find her way to the hotel kitchen to get it some fish or milk or something. I handed Jason the key to the outer door of the hotel and told him to go check out the kitchen and see if his sister was there. I would stay and try to entice the cat to stick around until the kids got back either with or without a tidbit.

"Here, kitty," I said, kneeling and rubbing my fingers together. "Kitty, kitty? Mrrow?"

Now, yes, Mother, I know that not even my animal loving

niece and nephew and I can save every stray cat in England, but what you don't seem to understand is how awfully lonesome I get for my kitties when I'm away from them for any length of time. I was not cajoling the cats for their benefit as much as my own and I can safely say that Cindy's motives were similar.

Jason had already turned away and I heard the key turn in the lock of the door. I didn't even look back, however, knowing that with the fog so thick it wouldn't do me any good.

"Kitty?" I asked again, since I hadn't heard it since that first time. "Cynthia? Are you out here too?"

"Yow," said another, higher pitched feline voice from the other direction.

I took a step into the fog toward it.

It's a good thing I was looking for a cat because I was looking down, hoping to see those coin-bright eyes reflecting the beam of my flashlight. Where the road should have been, blackness gaped. I shone my light directly into it. Water and rock, broken asphalt and jagged edges of earth and cement rimmed a hole so deep the beam couldn't penetrate the bottom.

The sameness of the fog and the depth of the abyss—I'm not exaggerating. It really was an abyss, not just a hole. I have never seen sinkholes in permafrost that deep—plus being jerked out of a sound sleep combined to give me a sense of vertigo. "Omigod!" I know I said aloud, and yelled, "Cindy, are you down there? Are you okay? Say something, honey? Make a noise!"

The pavement crumbled from under one foot and I stumbled backwards. As I did, my heel encountered something soft and yielding. An angry hissing and the scream of a cat pierced my shell-like ears. I almost jumped back into the hole again but instead tripped over my own feet and fell on my butt, which did not endear me to the invisible feline at my feet. Trust a cat not to come when it's wanted but to be right underfoot when it's sure to trip you up.

"Sorry, kitty," I said, falling on my rear. I tried to stand, but found my ankles wouldn't separate enough for me to rise. As I reached toward my feet, my hand encountered a strip of fabric, something that felt like rough cotton, snaking up my legs toward my knees. Now instead of the angry tea-kettle noise, a loud purring twined around my legs as the cotton strips did the same. "That's enough of that, cat!" I said sternly. "Naughty kitty!"

I swear I could hear it laugh, and maybe it was just the stars in my head from my fall, but looking around me, I seemed to see teams of golden eyes surrounding me in the fog, an occasional "mrrup" of encouragement punctuating the thrum of purrs.

And then, suddenly, something infinitely larger loomed out of the darkness throwing its huge shadow across the frail beam of my flashlight.

"Nope, Aunt Annie, she's not in there either," Jason said.

"Shine your light on my feet so I can get untangled here, will you?" I asked. He did. There was nothing around my ankles but little wraiths of the white fog, that trailed away as I got to my feet. "These cats seem to be practical jokers."

Jason started off.

"Watch out!" I cried, and he stopped. "There's a big hole there. I thought maybe your sister had fallen in . . ."

He shone his beam, considerably stronger than mine, into the hole. "Nope," he said and started off again.

"Where are you going?"

"To look for sister," he said.

"Well, yeah, but watch the ground. I bet that's not the

24

only new hole in the road."

"I *know* that, Aunt Annie," he said disdainfully, as if I were treating him like a baby.

We walked and walked, with only our flashlight beams to guide us. At first the walking was flat, then it went uphill and down, and though we walked slowly, my feet were getting tired. Despite my coat and the exercise, I began to shiver. I heard Jason sneeze and thought something was blooming which was no doubt bothering his allergies. That's about the time I realized my hair was blowing into my face and plastering itself over my eyes, and wind was cutting through my leggings. Then a big fat raindrop—the gulls weren't up yet so I hoped it was a raindrop—plopped on my nose, followed by a lot more of them.

The wind tore ragged chunks from the fog, revealing that the white blobs were not simply different colored foggy bits, but raggedy, lumbering, forms that looked as if they were the heavily bandaged victims of terrible accidents. As the rain moaned it seemed that these bandaged forms did too, their gauzes bannering like dirty, tattered ribbons away from what was no doubt their corrupted bodies underneath. Although, hadn't Bert said they were ground up?

"Aunt Annie?" Jason asked.

"Huh?"

"How come the mummies of people and cats we saw in the museum had their legs tied together but these guys are walking and the cats are even waving their tails?"

"I don't know," I said. "Don't ask me. I'm no special effects expert."

Most of them *did* look fairly indistinct, and then the fog before us also got blown away and we saw a larger mummy, taller than me, and under its bandages the pale triangles of orange reflector cloth winked back at us from its jogging shoes.

"Cindy!" I yelled. Jason yelled, *"Cynthia,"* at the same time.

This is the point at which many of my students would write, "and then Cindy turned around and we saw that the bandages were just wisps of fog wrapped around her, as were all the other things we thought were mummies. She lowered her hands, blinked her eyes and said, 'I must have been sleepwalking!' and I hugged her and said 'Yes, it was all a dream.' "

But at any rate, that is not what happened, though she did seem to be sleepwalking. However, contrary to what they say in the movies, waking a sleepwalker is not dangerous to his or her health and it certainly doesn't kill anyone.

Cindy simply blinked at us through very sloppily applied bandages, which she brushed from her face like cobwebs when she stretched and yawned. "Aunt Annie, Jason. Hi, what are you guys doing here?"

"You go first," Jason said. My sentiments exactly.

Cindy said, "I heard a little cat cry and I came out to find out where it was and if it was hungry. Then a bunch of bandaged kitties came out of the fog to play and wrapped me all up. Then they wanted me to go someplace with them."

"Where?" I asked.

As if in answer, the wind roared itself into a gale and blew away the last of the fog. We were standing on a lonely stretch of road beyond the strand, beyond the main part of the city. The road gaped with holes and in one of these was lodged the front wheel of the bus that had driven us back up the hill that afternoon.

"That's Bert's bus!" Jason said.

It was indeed and Bert himself, albeit Bert looking like a refugee from a casualty ward, swathed in bandages as seemed to be the style, tottered forward with his hands out-

26

stretched. "I am the ka of the Pharaoh Hamen-Ra. Woe to those who disturb my rest."

"*Us* disturb *your* rest?" Jason complained. "We haven't slept all night because of all you Band-Aid guys and cats."

"Izzat so?" demanded Bert/Hamen-Ra. "Well, maybe you'd like to have what was s'posed to be your immortal body ground up and put on the road for lorries and tourbuses to lumber over, eh? See how well you'd sleep then, my lad! Not to mention the sacred moggies ground up for some-body's rose garden. We've had a rum deal since we was taken from our tombs and brung over here! We demands to be took back t'Nile right away."

"Bert, this is all very funny," I told him. "Cut it out. The Nile is definitely not on our itinerary. And listen, if you're going to play at channeling ancient entities, you're not doing it right. You're not supposed to use your own accent. I live in Port Chetzemoka, where there are lots of channelers and past life relivers and all that stuff, and I can tell you for sure you have to use the ancient spooky voice the whole time you're channeling or the effect is just ruined."

"Silence, mortal woman!" Hamen-Ra said, continuing in the same mixture of stage-mummy and Yorkshirese. "If you'd been lying in the road, listening to kids squabbling in back seats, old folk nattering about the plumbing and com-plaining about the food gives them gas, or talking about what was on telly last evening, you'd not have a posh accent to channel with either. You're just lucky I've deigned to learn your bloody tongue so's I can make meself understood through Bert here."

"He's not kidding, Aunt Annie," Cindy said urgently. Maybe it was the rain dripping down my face, or maybe it was the rain dripping down her face or the fading beam of the flashlight, the batteries of which had put up a valiant but now

27

losing battle, but Cindy's eyes still looked a bit strange to me.

"Oh yeah?" I argued. "Surely you've had enough theater to recognize the amount of ham in Hamen-Ra."

Then *she* started speaking in a deep spooky voice, claiming to be a priestess of Bast's shrine at Memphis, reciting her lineage, Hamen-Ra's lineage, and the lineage of the dynasties and so forth leading up to her time of life. That was when I knew we had a real supernatural manifestation on our hands for sure. Cindy and Jason are, as you've often told me, Mom, both great students, but Cindy is not really crazy about history and the movies don't go in for that sort of boring "begat" detail.

I inquired again if the *kas* of the pharaohs, cats, and courtiers wouldn't like to come home with me to Port Chetzemoka in America, where we had a nice seaport and lots and lots of nutcases who would be thrilled to channel their immortal essences, but they stubbornly declined in favor of the Nile.

Well, I was sympathetic of course, and certainly didn't want to bring Cindy home with an ancient cat priestess cohabiting her body, so there seemed to be only one thing to do. The family build came in handy for us Scarboroughs then because between Jason, Cindy and her priestess, and Bert/Hamen-Ra and me, we managed to get the truck's tire out of the hole, and turned around. Hamen-Ra wisely let the inner Bert take over the driving, since he knew the back roads out of Scarborough heading south.

Which is why my writing is a little bumpy as I sit here between the sleeping kids, bumping along in Bert's tour bus with piles of bandages and scraps of bone and pitch swept into lots of paper marketing bags taken from Bert's newsagent friend. We should be making our delivery in London and then hopefully the priestess of Bast will vacate Cindy at that time. If not, I hope the Church Camp she was going to attend when she comes home is multidenominational.

March 26, Evening

Dear Mom and Bro,

You'll be pleased to know we are sitting at Heathrow waiting to board our red-eye special, having made it to the British Museum by noon today. Other than Bert having a hell of a time finding a parking place outside the museum, we had no real trouble, much to my surprise.

I was very much afraid the museum people would think I was a nutcase, even with exhibits A and B, Bert and Cindy and their respective guest entities, but when I told the security guard that I had somehow inadvertently become the head of a Motorway Mummy Liberation Front and we wished very much to speak to the acquisitions director for the Egyptian exhibits at the museum, he simply grumbled, "Oh, yeah, we get a lot of that sort of thing with this wet weather," and led us to the rather tacky steam-heated office of the director.

I had been hoping for an Indiana Jones type perhaps, or at least a Sean Connery type, someone with distinguished strips of gray at the temples and maybe a slight foreign accent. Instead, the director was a very earnest and nerdy young man with rabbity teeth, and scant hair pulled into a ponytail. All of that was forgiven because his manner was most sympathetic and his eyes understanding and full of apology as Hamen-Ra and Cindy's priestess poured out their stories, with a few interjections and explanations from me. Jason just looked disgusted but helped the security people and the grad students interning at the museum haul the bags of mummy material into the museum.

"It was very good of you and the children to come forward, Mrs. Scarborough," he said to me. "Most conscientious, especially since you are not, ahem, British. We are, in the interest of international harmony, religious tolerance, and respect for the customs of others sadly ignored in former times, attempting to repatriate many of the mummies and have them returned to their tombs. I don't suppose your niece or Mr. Hoskins would care to come with us to interpret for us the original location of the remains you've brought?"

I said absolutely not, and if that priestess didn't get herself out of Cindy this instant, the deal was off. At that point, Cindy had a little coughing fit, and one of the female grad students, a girl who looked Indo-Asian, stood a bit straighter and got a weird look in her eye.

Cindy glanced at me a little regretfully and shrugged.

"We at the British Museum certainly appreciate your efforts on behalf of the offended parties and, to show our gratitude, would like to offer you a gift certificate for the postcard of your choice at our gift shop," the director said.

I chose this one of the mummy I'm enclosing with this letter.

Should be home well—today, by your time, about five in the evening. See you then!

Port Chetzemoka, WA

Dear Mom, Bro, Cindy and Jason,

It's very nice to be home again after the trip to England. The cats are glad to see me. I'm sorry, Brother, that every cat in five miles has flocked to your house to see Cindy, but I don't know what I can be expected to do about it. As far as I know that priestess is back home again in good old Memphis, maybe enjoying a new incarnation as kitty litter for the descendants of her former goddesses.

I am very happy to hear, however, that Wizards of the Coast is considering adding Jason's new deck, The Eyes of Hamen-Ra, to their pantheon of Magic Cards.

Egyptian-ness seems to be quite the thing these days. Several of our local channelers have added—uh—new stations, with Egyptian entities as their guides or whatever the heck they call them. Makes me wonder what I brought back in my coat pockets and shoes when I came home.

But on a more practical note, Mom, you'll be glad to hear I've become more active in city government. I am our neighborhood's liaison with the public works department for having potholes on our street filled. Can't stand the damned things. Guess this wraps it up.

Love, Annie

Final Vows

At first he thought the candle flame above his ears was the white light he'd been chasing, trying to get within pouncing range. But now, as he pried his encrusted eyes open, he saw it was just a candle.

He lay there dazed, among the waxy smoke of candles and the tinkle of wind chimes, a cool breeze rippling his matted, fever-soaked coat.

Hmm. He no longer felt too hot or too cold. Stiff though. He could barely sit up, his muscles were in such a rictus. He took a long horizontal stretch, avoiding the candles and keeping his tail well out of the way, then stood on his hind paws and stretched upward, batting with his front paws at the curling candle smoke before dropping again to all fours.

Wherever this was, it wouldn't do to lose his self-respect, and he began setting in order his striped saffron coat, white paws and cravat with short, economical licks. He wrinkled his nose and lifted the outer edges of his mouth at his own smell. He had been to the vet. Dr. Tony and his wife Jeannette were lovely people and really knew how to pet a fellow, but their establishment reeked of antiseptic and medicine and Mustard did not like medicine.

When he looked up from cleansing the underside of his tail, another cat sat there, a female, surgically celibate, as he was, clad all in black from nose to tailtip, ear points to claws. "Finally awake, are you, lazybones? About time. Come along now. It is high time you met The Master."

"I do not have a master," Mustard said. "My personal attendant is female." He looked around him and considered the stone walls, the tiled floors without so much as a rug to warm the belly on, the ceiling so high birds tantalizingly flitter through the rafters, cheeping and leaving droppings on the floors and furniture. His home was a log cabin with his own private solarium (though his junior housemates had made free of it as he couldn't always be bothered to run them off. Besides, they were bigger than he was, all except the kitten. She had been a rather sweet little thing who begged him for hunting stories and when he growled in annoyance, would flop purring beside him.). His house was set in a large yard with a strip of forest in the back where he caught many tasty adjuncts to his the healthful but monotonous diet of low-ash kibbles his attendant provided. His last happy memory was of sitting at the picnic table being petted by his old friend Drew, who had stopped by to visit.

"Don't look now, but we're not in Kansas any more, Red," the black-robed female told him.

"My name is not Red, it is Mustard," he said. "And I do not live in Kansas. I was born and raised in Fairbanks, Alaska but for the past ten years have resided in the state of Washington. It is warmer there and I may go outside and it is altogether more congenial. Are we there still?"

"Your questions will be answered at length," she said. "When you've met The Master. And don't fret about a little nicknaming. You'll have to take a new one when you join the Order. I was formerly known as Jessie Jane Goodall but now am known simply as Sister Paka, which is in the Black Swahili tongue the name of our kind."

"Humph," Mustard said. "Affected. I've fallen into some cult, haven't I?"

She turned her new-moon dark tail to him and she waved it for him to follow. Since he wanted answers and had nothing better to do, he graciously obliged.

He was not, however, prepared for how weary he would be or how long the corridors were—miles and miles of them, stone walled or pillared, lined with trees and bushes—his favorites, roses. He was mortally shamed and self-disgusted to have to pause to rest from time to time on their journey, which felt more like a quest of many days' length from the way it taxed his strength. Normally he was light and spry, even though well advanced in years for one of his kind. He considered himself merely seasoned, toughened, tempered, but today he felt every second of every minute of every hour of every day of every week of every month of every year of his life.

He expected impatience and jeering from the so-called sister, but instead she simply squatted on her haunches, closed her eyes and wrapped her tail around her front paws until he pronounced himself ready to carry on once more.

At last they padded up a long, long flight of stairs, high into the rafters, by which time even the flitting birds could not hold the exhausted orange cat's attention. The lady in black scratched at an enormous wooden door, partially open, and from within an unusually deep and sonorous voice, a voice like the rumbling growl of a big cat—the kind Mustard had once seen in a television movie—bade them enter. Mustard straightened his white cravat and remounted the three steps he had backed down upon first hearing that echoing tone.

Sister Paka pawed and pawed at the door but couldn't get it to swing further open. Mustard meanwhile had regained his breath, and with a deep sigh walked to the door, inserted first his nose, then his head, shoulders, and upper body, and walked in. She entered grandly behind him, tail waving, as if she always sent her messengers to announce her entrance. She bumped into Mustard's behind immediately.

He could go no further straight forward, because a big hole took up most of the floor space, about an inch from his front paws. Hanging above the hole was a gigantic metal thing, a bell, as he recognized from the tinier versions he'd entertained himself with on various overly cute cat toys. That had to be why the so-called Master's voice sounded so deep and sonorous—it was bouncing off this humongous piece of hollow iron. Cheap trick. Mustard repressed the urge to growl himself. That hole was so deep it made the sound of his breath and heartbeat echo back up to him. And the edge was very, very close.

Sister Paka sat back on her haunches and swatted at his rump. "Kindly move forward, please. The Master must not be kept waiting. Do you think you're the only soul he must counsel today?"

"Who said I wanted counseling?" Mustard asked, but proceeded around the hole and the bell, hugging the wall as tightly as he could, since his exhaustion made him tremble. He was far less than his usual balletic self. Fine first impression he'd make. He could not help but hope The Master was a cat-loving human with kind hands and some nice tidbit and a bit of sympathy for a cat as ill-used as himself. He would love to feel warm fingers stroke his fur now. He didn't actually like cats, if the truth were known. He was a people sort of cat. He called his own person a personal attendant, just to keep it clear to others that he knew she was probably an inferior breed—especially since she had always had more time for his housemates than for his own excellent self, but he had loved her touch nonetheless.

He could see the other side of the bell hole now. A chair— a plain, straight-back chair with a bed-pillow on the middle— was the only bit of furnishing in the tower. On the pillow reposed another cat. This cat was a male—an old male, even more orange than Mustard himself. The old cat was absolutely rusty around the stripes actually.

"Peace, my son," the old cat said.

Sister Paka put a paw on Mustard's neck to force his head down. He bit her hard on the right leg and she fell beside him. He could tell she wanted to hiss but instead she lay there, submissively, on her side, though he could have torn her throat out if he'd wished.

"Peace, I was saying," the old cat said again. "Paka, see that bit under his cravat? He missed a spot. Get it for him will you, my child?"

Sister Paka put the paw of her wounded leg onto his chest, and, carefully leaning forward, gave the spot a lick and a promise. "There now," she said. "Much better."

The Master purred. "Yes. And that is a nasty looking bite you have there."

Mustard hurriedly gave it a lick, causing Sister Paka's fur to partially cover his fang marks.

"Much better," The Master said. "And so are you, my son. We had nearly despaired of seeing you on your pins again. The damage to you was great."

"Damage?" Mustard asked. "I don't remember."

"You no doubt slept through much of it, as our kind tend to do. But when Tony and Jeannette brought you here, it was after they had put you to sleep to spare you pain. They thought certainly you were dead, but as they were readying your earthly shell to return to ash, you stirred. Already you were beyond their knowledge and your lady had been told you were dead. They did not wish to raise her hopes only to have her lose you again, so they brought you to us."

"And you are?" Mustard asked, tapping his tail against the edge of the hole. He stopped that at once. It hurt.

"*I* am Mu Mao the Magnificent, spiritual leader of this order. Sister Paka you have met. The order is the Spiritual Order of Our Lady of the Egyptian Bandages. We are an interdenominational feline monastery and convent for the spiritual enlightenment and growth of our kind. While the noncelibate may study here, only the surgically celibate may take vows. Otherwise—well, we *are* all cats, after all." He twitched his ears in a humorous way. "Any vow taken by a more corporeally unenlightened cat would be meaningless in the face of our natural compulsions. But once altered, we may concentrate on higher matters."

"So, then you yourself are—?" Mustard asked.

"Yes. You see, in many of my former lives I was a human being, a priest, holy man, shaman, what have you, until I finally was allowed to achieve my highest form in this incarnation and became a cat. But my corporeal urges interfered with my ability to concentrate, so I voluntarily left my littermates and my safe abode and as a tiny kitten walked to the veterinarian's to go under the knife so that I might help others."

"He's what's called a *bodhisattva* by Buddhists," Sister Paka said with awe.

Mustard was impressed. "I like Tony and Jeannette—my doctors—very much but I always complain when I have to go. It smells bad there, and I dislike needles and having

37

patches of fur shaved. I would never have gone for the surgery myself except my attendant forced it upon me. I admit, life has been calmer since. I have time to study and read many subjects."

Mu Mao purred approval. "This is good. And although you are now emaciated, it is clear that you have kept sleek and active under normal circumstances."

"I am a fine hunter of vermin," Mustard said without false modesty. "And chase down even the fastest horoscope scrolls, however they may attempt to roll from my grasp."

"You are versed in astrology as well?" Sister Paka asked rather breathlessly.

"Oh yes. From the time I was a tiny kitten such scrolls were toys my attendant procured for me and me alone at the food-procuring place. None of my housemates were allowed to chase them. I alone was deemed worthy." His white cravat stuck out beyond his nose with pride, so even he could see a few pale hairs without taking his eyes from the cat on the chair.

Mu Mao did not sound as approving as Mustard might have hoped, but flicked the bushy rust-and-cream tail shielding his paws. "Did you not seek to share with your housemates the knowledge you acquired thus?"

"Of course not! They were *my* scrolls," he said, baring his teeth and then, seeing the old cat's eyes, added quickly, "Well, the kitten asked about them once and I did try to explain a few of the rudiments to her but she was much too young to grasp much of it."

"But that is a good start," Mu Mao the Master said in a tone sage enough to reflect his apparently exalted status.

"A good start of what, please?"

"A good start on your new life."

"My new life?"

"Well, yes. You've passed through number one and are now heading into your second."

"Then I didn't—survive?" He looked down at himself, all around at himself, and began licking furiously to reassure himself that all parts were there and solid and working.

"It's amazing you survived intact long enough to be brought to us," Mu Mao said. "Your mouth and your entire digestive tract were ulcerated. Something caustic, Tony thought. Something sudden."

"Something," Sister Paka said, "poison."

"But how can that be? I always ate the same thing, and have not even hunted much in recent years."

"Apparently you ate something out of the ordinary. And that something may linger to kill your former housemates as it killed you. The young one would be in particular danger, I should think."

"The kitten?" he asked, remembering the way the fur on her belly curled like a sheep's wool and how fluffy her tail was and how, though she was cute, she had the taste to be black so that it wasn't all that obvious—and she never tried to take Susan's attention away from him.

"Yes. And the others."

"I don't care—" he began to say with a spit, but catching the slight hiss from Sister Paka, stopped himself. Mu Mao gave him a warning look.

"Yes, well. I understand you have made that evident over the years. If you are to join us here, you must give up your greatest vice."

"I told you I've *been* neutered."

"A natural function is not a vice. You must abandon the baser instincts of our kind in search of enlightenment."

"I never said I wanted to be enlightened, though I like a sunny patch as much as the next cat. Why would I want to stay here? You're all cats. No human petting, and I've yet to see a food dish."

Mu Mao said, "Well, we shall see. You'll realize what this life is to be about soon enough. Sister Paka, you must take Mustard with you to the fish pond. A few more of those poor primitive spirits can be released from the bondage of their present lives in order to sustain his own, and then he may work in the garden while he regains his strength."

Sister Paka told him it was his duty to take the largest and fattest of the fish from the pond. "They've learned whatever lessons life as a fish can teach," she told him, "and are ready to move on."

He obligingly caught one and would have done more but she assured him they were always there for the catching and he didn't want to eat too much at first or it would make him spew. He felt tender inside and realized he wished to avoid that.

She then showed him his duties. "You will be the tender of the roses to begin with," she said.

"Oh, good. I *love* roses," he replied, and began nibbling at the petals of a fat red one.

"I'm told those that are a bit brown around the edges have the best flavor," she said casually. "Aged a bit. Not so green tasting."

"Oh?" he tried a slightly wilted one. It was good—had a slightly cheesy flavor. He tried another. Yes, she was right. Much better than the red one. And with the wilted ones gone, the bush looked nicer too.

"You may dig here," she indicated a spot where a new rose bush sat waiting to be pushed into place once a hole was prepared. "And here as well, though for other purposes." This time she showed him a spot in the garden where various humps of earth bore the scents of various brethren—this was

40

the communal litterbox.

When he had pruned a few roses, he slept in the sun, but his dreams were troubled and his feet pedaled, running to or from something. It was a shame that his daytime naps were so unsatisfying too, because as the sun set and the shadows grew long in the courtyards and the other cats disappeared from view, the night grew very cold.

He stood there shivering, looking about for some pile of still warm grass, some bit of fabric to nest in, but there was nothing. Finally, a somewhat familiar face, a slightly softer golden-orange than his own, poked into the courtyard from around the pillar.

"There you are! We missed you. How good it is to see you again, my old—uh—companion," the golden cat said in the voice that Mustard now recognized.

"Peaches! Are you here too?" He had almost disliked Peaches when he was alive, because Susan had loved Peaches best. Even when she was petting himself, Mustard always knew she would rather be petting Peaches and when his name was mentioned or he walked into the room, Mustard would hiss at Susan that she wasn't fooling him and jump down from her lap, often leaving her with scratches to let her know just what he thought of her taste. Of course, when she was gone, Peaches wasn't such a bad fellow. And now Mustard was downright delighted to see him.

"Not Peaches this time around, you know. Peaches died and when I was reborn I was sent here. Because I was already on my eighth life when I was Peaches, and an old soul, I do remember that time, and you, my brother. But now I am here among our kind as Brother Paddy."

"Oh, you would pick a name like that!" Mustard said in disgust.

Peaches/Paddy backed away from him and sat on his

haunches and washed his paw calmly. "The name was chosen for me."

"Sure, sure. Everyone always likes you best," Mustard said with his old bitterness, then, remembering his more immediate and practical concern, asked, "You wouldn't know where there was an extra bit of fabric to curl up in for the night, would you? It's cold."

His old acquaintance said simply, "Follow me. It is time for Ves-purrs."

Whereupon they re-entered the great building with the bell tower. To Mustard's amazement, it was now lit by candleglow and the floor was totally covered with cats, each with paws curled under it, tail wrapped around the body, purring so loudly the very stones of the building seemed to be—er—purrmeated with the contented throb. "What's this?" Mustard murmured.

"We are giving thanks to the Maker for creating such a wonderful form for us, for giving us a pleasant place to be and kind companions."

"There are an awfully lot of kittens here," Mustard said, noticing the young ones who occupied two entire wings of the building.

"That is because so many unwanted are dumped or killed. They are innocents and come to us to learn how to prepare for lives outside our walls, if that is their desire, or to take their vows."

Mustard was silent.

"I thought you would still be with Susan, until you died of your long years as I did," his companion ventured. "But I'm told you were poisoned. Susan must be beside herself with grief."

"Oh, you know Susan. She got a new kitten and another grown male besides the old girl and me."

"You must have been very distressed. I know you always wanted to be top cat."

"Well, yeah, but that didn't last for long. The old girl was bigger, you know, and she got bolder and started beating the living daylights out of me. I have to admit, I didn't like the kitten at first, but she's a nice little thing and very respectful. And Susan didn't really bond with the male, but he kept the old girl in line." He cried suddenly. "How can you stay here? I miss Susan so much. And she always liked you best. Can't you go back?"

Brother Paddy *nee* Peaches licked Mustard's face. "I taught Susan what she needed to learn from me. Now it is time for other lessons for all of us. Come. Join us."

He didn't feel like it, of course, but the thrumming purr relaxed him and he found himself joining in until his own purr lulled him into sleep, his body curling among four others whose warmth and softness made a better bed than Susan's comforter.

But though his body was comfortable, he began recalling the pain, the betrayal. And he saw the kitten, sniffing for him, calling for him, and at last trotting toward someone calling, holding out something attractive and deadly . . .

Mustard awakened and leapt from one small bit of floor to another, and bounded past the cats sleeping on the bell tower steps till he reached the landing. He scratched on the door.

The sonorous voice called to him, "Enter."

"Won't be but a minute, Mu Mao," he said, declining to call the old fellow "Master." "Just want to look out of your tower here and see if I can find my way home."

"So you have decided to attempt to rejoin the world, my son?" the old cat asked with his upper whiskers twitching.

"Of course. Susan is mine. I'm going back to her."

"Very well." The old cat hopped nimbly upon a window

sill. Mustard leaped up beside him. The leap wasn't as easy as it would have been before he came to this place, but it would have been impossible earlier in the day. This sort of thing was fine for cats who only wanted to be with other *cats*, he decided.

For just a moment it seemed to him that all the world was spread out below him, like the globe in Susan's office. And then he saw that it was just the Sound and the Strait surrounding his own little town, and there he saw the propane tanks beside Tony's office and farther off, Susan's red roof he had so often napped upon and the wide green yard of his home.

"Ye—oowwwt," he said to Mu Mao.

"In good time, my son. Do you see there? Dr. Tony and Jeannette are getting into their van with that bundle Jeannette is carrying. I sense we will be seeing them soon. You may save your strength by riding with them as far as their clinic, at least."

"I am still very tired," Mustard admitted.

"Then rest here with us," Mu Mao said. "There is yet time."

Time for what? Mustard wondered, but to his surprise found himself curled up in the bulk of Mu Mao's great belly, and falling into a deep and this time dreamless sleep until a lick on the nose awakened him again. "It is time, my son," the older cat said.

There were tears in Jeannette's kind brown eyes when she lay the bundle down beside The Master. "It's Susan's second loss," she said. "And there have been others in that neighborhood too. The woman down the street, Diane, lost one of her cats to the same thing."

"Looks like we have a serial cat killer on our hands," Dr.

44

Tony said grimly. He was gently opening the bundle. Mustard's tail lashed angrily, and his ears laid back flat against his skull. Would he see now that the kitten had been crying to him before her death, that her black curly underside would no longer vibrate with her purrs, her bright intelligent eyes that had watched so attentively while he told his hunting stories would be glazed with death before she had a chance to catch her quota of vermin?

He cried out as the tip of a black ear came into view. The eyes were shut, the whiskers stiff—her under whiskers were so very long they curled under at the tips. The black nose. His worst fears confirmed.

But then he saw that the fur was short and coarse and the body much larger than the slight little female's. As the bundle was further unwrapped he saw the once powerful muscles slack under the sooty fur and the long sleek tail, which had been so expressive, now hung limp. "Boston Blackie!" he cried. This was the grown male companion Susan had brought home from the pound with the kitten. Her protector, until she had charmed all but the old girl into loving her. With Blackie dead, or here, which would be all the same to Susan and the kitten, he could only hope the kitten would grow quickly and manage to keep out of the old girl's way in the meantime.

Mustard had resented Blackie, of course, but not as much as some others. The big black cat, so massive and tough looking, actually had been a decent sort who realized the kitten's play with him had convinced Susan to bring the adult cat home too. The big boy had looked after his small companion, protected her from the others, taken the heat for her, as if he were her mother. He also had been decently respectful of Mustard's seniority.

"Poor fellow," Mustard said to The Master, Paddy and

Paka. "A real softie for such a big palooka, you know? That must be why Kitten was sending me those dreams. She was mourning the big guy."

"Either that or she's next," Paka said grimly.

"Never fear, my son," Mu Mao said, giving Mustard's flat ears a lick. "He will soon be reborn into his new life, and a very good one it will be. He was a very old soul indeed and we have need of such a brother among our fold."

"That's great for *you*," Mustard said. "But what about Susan? And the kitten? And Diane? And even that cantankerous old girl? Are the little one and the old biddy going to come here too and leave Susan all alone and afraid to have any more friends for fear of the same thing happening to them? And Diane, who is so kind and comes to feed us or finds someone like that nice Drew fellow to come stay with us when Susan is gone, she's sick all the time, you know. She depends on her cats to be there when she's too ill to move and lonely and afraid. She told me so."

Mu Mao surprised him by flipping his tail and saying, "That may be, but our kind have problems enough to concern us. Until they come or are brought within our walls, the companions of human beings are not within our protection."

"You can't dislike *people?*" Mustard demanded. "What about Tony and Jeannette?"

"Both were cats in their last lives, and of our order," Mu Mao said. "That is how they know to bring others to us. Like myself, they are *bodhisattvas*, not the ordinary sort of person who abandons a cat who is no longer small and cute, or has become inconvenient. Why should you care? This male and others, like Brother Paddy's former self, take from you the attention that is rightfully yours. If you return to your Susan and find the others all dead, should you not rejoice? Surely you will not make the same error twice and die again of the same poison? With no competition, your Susan will love you and only you."

Mustard didn't argue. Master indeed! This old cat obviously didn't understand Susan. Mustard had always hated it that she was always bringing home other cats, true, but he had also licked away her tears for the cats she had to leave at the shelter. He never had to be in a shelter. She had picked him out of his mother's litter, still in a good home with loving people. He'd always felt entitled to love but he knew from what the others said they had no such hope and getting a home with someone like Susan was a big break for them.

He hopped in the van before Tony and Jeannette left and rode in back. He desperately wished to be petted, but felt too restless and anxious to lie quietly. They didn't seem to notice him. They got a call and drove past the turnoff for their clinic back along the route he recognized from his own visits to the vet. He thought maybe old Mu Mao had asked them to give him a lift, but no, they were stopping at another house, not too far from his own.

Mustard thought it interesting that they had a phone in their van. He liked Susan's phones. She sat still to talk and he could usually curl up in her lap for a nap. He was good at doing it and staying so still and relaxed that she didn't even notice until she hung up.

He jumped out of the van after Jeannette and trotted the single block to his house. No one was in the yard and he approached the cat flap so confidently that he nearly banged his head on the rectangle of board that barred entrance to or exit from the house. He scratched at the door and meowed until he noticed that Susan's car was gone as well. Of all the nerve. Here he had taken the trouble to return from the dead and she couldn't even bother to be home. Just like a person.

Then, from behind the front door, he heard an answering

scratch and a small mew. "Let me out! It's a pretty day. I don't want to be in here. Where's Boston Blackie? I want him to come and play!"

"Now now, young lady, this is no time for tantrums," Mustard said. "I don't think Blackie will be coming back but I dreamed of your danger and have returned to save you."

He meant to be reassuring but she gave a chirrup that was the kittenish equivalent of a giggle. "Uncle Mustard? Is that you? Where have you been? Do you feel better? Susan said those ashes she sprinkled on the roses were you but they didn't look like you. Weren't even orange."

"Stop prattling, child, and let me think. Why is the catflap closed?"

"Susan said so we wouldn't go outside and get into whatever killed you and Blackie." Her voice turned plaintive. "Is Blackie *really* gone forever? I don't like the old girl. She is not nice to me at all and I'm going to scratch her face if she keeps saying those mean things. I miss you and Blackie. I want to come too."

"That's just what you mustn't do," Mustard said. "My— er—illness, was long and very painful and far too much for a mite like yourself to bear. Or even a battleaxe like the old girl. About Blackie I can't tell you anything else. But we need to make the neighborhood safe for our kind again. Especially our yard. Have you noticed anything different?"

"No, nothing. And everyone has been looking out for us. Susan, Diane, Drew, Debbie and Dennis, Janice and Theresa, Mary and Michael Ann. Even Steinway barks very fiercely if he sees anything suspicious."

She was referring to Mary's and Michael Ann's dog next door. "Steinway must have a really suspicious mind then," Mustard said. "He barks at everything all the time."

"No, I think he's trying very hard to help. Merlin is very

scared." Merlin was the black feline in charge of Mary and Michael Ann and Steinway and Chopin, the junior cat of the house.

"Hmm. Merlin never struck me as a scaredycat. Maybe I should go have a word with him."

"Yeah, okay. I gotta jump now. The old girl is coming."

"Who is it?" the old girl's voice demanded in a growl. "Who's out there and who were you talking to, you little . . ."

"Lay off her and pick on someone your own size," Mustard growled back through the door.

"What the . . . ? *Mud Turd?* Is that *you?* You're dead, ashes, gone, kaput and you can't have the warm place on the video back. It's mine forever now."

The thump of paws came from inside and he could see through the lace curtain across the glass door panel that she had hopped up on a high shelf so she could, as usual, look down on him. He glared back up at her and shouted, "Yeah, sure, until you eat the wrong thing and end up with the grandfather of all belly aches and writhe in agony till you're a ghost too, just like me and good old Blackie."

"A ghost?" she leaned so far forward she fell off the shelf. He heard the kitten titter from somewhere high and the sound of a cat giving herself a brisk shake before coming to the closed catflap to sniff. "There's no such thing as cat ghosts."

"Oh, that's rich. A cat who doesn't believe in ghosts. Well, there are, and I've seen them. I R them in fact. And like it or not, you too can be in the same situation if you don't stop bullying and try to help out here. Do you know what killed me? How I died? Or what got Blackie?"

"Of course not. Can I help it if the dumb beasts around here eat any poison thing they come across? I survived loose in the neighborhood for two years on my own after those *people* went off and left me when I was only a little kitten, no bigger than Miss Burnt Poptart, here . . ."

"Yeah, yeah, we all know how tough it was for you out in the neighborhood, taking handouts . . ."

"Hey, smart guy. You asked. I'm trying to tell you. The point is, in my two years I made the rounds of all the neighbors and I tell you, there's not one of them, not even one of the kids, who would hurt a cat. In this neighborhood, kids and dogs are brought up to have the proper adoration for our sort. I could have had a real home any time I wanted but I didn't want any of them. I wanted my house back and the minute I asked Susan, she displaced all of you who came with her from her old house and invited me in. She *knew* this was *my* home."

"Sure it was, old girl," Mustard said with a comforting purr this time. She was right of course. The only people who had changed houses since the time the old girl was on the streets were the renters in the back, and they had been there a good year and a half and were wonderful people who loved cats. "Thanks. But listen, I know you want to be top and only but I gotta tell you, the other side, over here where us ghosts are, it's not what you think it's going to be. I miss you and the kid too . . ."

There was a huff of air as she sank to her chest onto the floor and she said grudgingly, "Yeah, I miss that terrified look on your yellow face when I chased you, and watching you stand on your hind feet to stretch. How in the world did you *do* that anyway?"

He didn't answer but just said, "I'll be back. Just take care of the kid, you hear me? Remember too that she's going to be a strong young adult by the time Susan brings in the next strays and you may need someone to protect *you*. It's never too late, old girl."

"Shove it, Mud Turd," she growled, but softly, regretfully. "It's dull around here without you. You're coming back, you say?"

"At least for a little bit. I have to figure this out. The kid thinks Steinway and Merlin might have seen something."

"I'm sorry I can't tell you more about Blackie. One minute I see him out rolling around like an idiot on the picnic table, the next thing I know the big galoot can hardly talk for the sores in his mouth . . ."

That was how it started with Mustard, he realized, though he hadn't known what was happening to him at the time. He tried to remember just when he had begun to feel uncomfortable but the whole experience was blurred by the fact that he had slept through as much of it as he could manage. He left the old girl to ruminate and sauntered next door to see Merlin and Steinway of course, who barked his few brains out when he saw Mustard.

"Cat Ghost at two o'clock!" he yelled. "Cat ghost! Cat ghost!"

Mustard put his face right up to the fence and spat his nastiest at the bouncing, barking black lab, who backed off, hunkered down and whined.

"Nice dog," Mustard said. "Hi, Steinway. Good to see you again. Can we talk?"

The dog whimpered and a black cat as sleek as Blackie, though not as well formed, suddenly appeared, followed closely by a gray and white spotted longhair prancing officiously behind. "Hey, there, you. That's *our* dog. If he needs spitting at, we'll do it," the black one said.

"Merlin!" Mustard said. "Just the guy I wanted to see."

"So, rumors of your demise were highly exaggerated, eh?" Merlin asked. For a musician's cat, he had a pretentious penchant for literary misquotes.

"No, I think I pretty well bought it, okay. I'm sort of—between lives at the moment, I guess. Can't seem to get on with number two until I figure out how I snuffed number one. Boston Blackie apparently died the same way."

"Not Blackie?" Merlin asked with genuine regret. "That is one fine specimen of my particular color. Poor guy. And he was so happy yesterday, just rolling on the picnic table, purring. I think he'd just had a visitor."

"Any idea who?" Mustard asked, looking from first one cat to the other and then to the dog, who covered his nose with his paws and whined. "Anybody unusual around?"

Steinway whined again. "You know how it is in your yard. Your mistress lets everyone walk through to get to the houses in back. Much too sloppy to keep proper surveillance on, though I try. A lot of thanks I get though. 'Shut up, Steinway,' people say, and uppity neighbor cats, who ought to be dead, hissing at me."

"You're breaking my heart," Mustard said. "You should know most of the people who go through the yard by now. Anyone you didn't know?"

"Nope. Just the usual residents and the usual guests. Of course, I think someone may have been through as I was chowing down—even I take a break once in awhile. Because right after I got back was when I saw old Blackie rolling on his back on the picnic table."

"Well, thanks, I guess," Mustard told them. "I seem to recall something about the picnic table too. Guess I'd better check it out. Could be the scene of the crime."

A recent rain had washed the table clean, but the sealant on the wood was old, and so maybe small particles of the poison might have sank into the cracks.

He trotted back to the door and asked into the room beyond. "How long ago did Blackie start getting sick?"

The old girl was just beyond the door. He could hear her scratching the bald spot on her head against the sill. "I dunno, let me see, I saw him rolling around yesterday afternoon. Susan noticed he was sick last night and took him to Tony's. Er—unless my memory fails me."

There was the sound of light, delicate paws landing on the floor beside the door. "No, that's right, okay. I asked him when he came in what was wrong. I could tell he wasn't himself right away. He was grumpy and kind of groggy and he smelled funny."

"Funny in what way, Kitten?" Mustard asked.

"Like that nasty stuff Susan sprinkled all over the floor at Christmas—that stuff that made you all act crazy. I was scared."

"You're always scared—" the old girl's growl began. At a warning hiss from Mustard she moderated it to, "or maybe I should say, overly cautious. That was nothing to be scared of. Just catnip."

Catnip! Of course! He raced to the table and sniffed—the rain had done a good job. And there might be fine particles of 'nip in the cracks, but he couldn't see them. He jumped under the table and put his paws on the supports and sniffed the undersides. His lips curled at the edges. 'Nip yes, and another smell, a smell he had not really noticed except as one of the subtle vintage differences in 'nip, but now that particular difference made him feel nauseous.

He streaked up the street to Diane's house, to the cabin at the back of it, the one Diane rented to Drew.

Sadie barked a warning, but Mustard ducked past her and over to a window where he scratched at the glass. No response. Then he looked through the pane. The inside of the cabin no longer contained Drew's books and bed, the little arrangements of Christmas lights he made, or Moonshadow's dishes. It was totally empty and almost odorless.

He was about to ask Sadie where his friend had gone when he heard the sound of Dr. Tony and Jeannette's van pulling into the driveway. Diane met them at the door and ushered them inside. Sadie kept bouncing and barking.

"Shut up!" Mustard hissed. "What happened?"

"It's Moonshadow. He's been laying in the cabin for the past two days while Diane was gone."

"Dead?"

"No, but close. Oh poor Moonshadow! He's been so lonesome since that Diane made Drew leave."

"Why did she do that? Drew was nice."

"I don't know. Maybe he peed on the rug."

"Has he been around the last couple of days?" Mustard asked.

"Yes, Friday the 13th it was, day before yesterday. He came to pick up his things. I heard him yelling it through the door to Diane but she wasn't here. He petted us, gave Moonshadow some catnip, and left."

"Catnip!" Mustard exclaimed, and bolted out of the house and back down the street again, to the front door. "Kitten! Old girl! Are you there? Where is Susan anyway?"

The kitten's voice answered in a plaintive mew. "She went to get Drew to come and stay with us while she goes to visit her friends in Copperton. She doesn't want us left alone with all this cat-killing going on."

Mustard twined back and forth across the ridges that held the cat flap. He was agitated and had no idea what to do now. Except to say, "Look, don't either one of you let him near you. Don't eat food he puts out or touches, or even water. And don't take any catnip from him."

"Ick," the kitten said. "That nasty stuff. I am not one of the youth with a drug problem, Uncle Mustard. I think that stuff sucks."

"Just keep thinking that way," he said, noticing she was already falling into the teenaged vernacular.

He was about to run back down the road to check on Moonshadow when Susan drove up. She got out of the car on one side. Drew emerged from the other. "Thanks for coming to get me, Susan. With Diane's car broken down again, and me taking that job out of town, I had no way to get here. But it will be good to see the kitties again. I'm sure going to miss Blackie and Mus—" he stared straight at Mustard, who walked calmly over and sat down in front of him and stared straight up at him.

"Returned to the scene of your crime, eh, murderer?" he asked, but Drew didn't understand that much. He did, however, recognize Mustard for who he was. Which was unfortunately more than Susan did.

"What's wrong? Oh, look at the pretty white cat. Hello, honey. You better be careful around here."

White cat? Was she nuts? He looked down at his own orange stripes and back up to her. Well, Mu Mao had said this was a second life and he wouldn't seem the same to Susan. But *white?* So impractical.

He returned his attention to his murderer, who certainly looked guilty enough. Mustard was certain that somehow Drew saw his victim for who he really was. There had always been something uncannily catlike about the big man—leonine, really. It was what the cats liked about him. Had he been a cat in his last life like Tony and Jeannette? But he was no *bodhisattva,* even though at one time Mustard would have said so. Drew was wonderful with animals, he had often heard Diane and Susan say. But Diane had thrown him out. And Mustard doubted it was for peeing on the rug. She must have found out something about him to make her run him off and hadn't told Susan yet. No wonder, really. Right after

Susan met Drew, she and Diane had had a fight, though they'd been the best of friends for years. But why would he poison the cats? His friends? Because now Mustard was sure it was Drew who did him in. You could still smell the tainted catnip on him. Probably had a bag in his pocket to feed the old girl and kitten.

Well, no way was that man going near them! Or any other cat, or Susan, not if Mustard had his way. He did the only thing within his power and sprang for Drew's throat, biting and clawing his way up as he went while Drew swore and tried to tear him off.

"The damned thing's rabid!" Drew screamed to Susan, who tried to pull Mustard away from his murderer. "Kill it!"

"No! I have it, see?" she said, pulling Mustard spitting from his victim. "But you need a doctor."

"No, I—"

"Don't be silly. I saw Tony's van up at Diane's. He can look at those scratches and test the cat for rabies. Just let me pop him into the carrier in the trunk. I still have it—" her voice broke and she looked very haggard. "From taking Blackie in, you know."

Of course, Mustard, white or not, was gentle with Susan and only hissed over his shoulder at Drew, who surprised him by sticking his tongue out at him and making a neck-breaking gesture with his big hands just before Susan tucked Mustard into the carrier.

They drove down the street in a split second, just as Tony was leaving. Moonshadow, bundled into Jeannette's arms, mewed plaintively and Drew pretended to make over her. "Don't let him near you, Moon!" Mustard cried. "He tried to kill you!"

As Drew stuck out his hand to stroke Moonshadow, she

crouched back against Jeannette, laid her ears back, hissed, spat, and tried to rip his hand open, despite her illness.

Drew pulled his hand back just in time, then hissed back at her, *"Traitor,"* he spat, and then tried to look wounded. "She must be delirious. Doesn't seem to know me," he said to the others.

It was Mustard's good luck that Tony and Jeannette were who they were. *They* didn't think he was white and recognized him too. Furthermore, they seemed to understand him. While Tony was examining Drew's scratches right there in the driveway, Jeannette called Susan and Diane over to look at his shirt. The pocket was ripped and a small bag of the tainted catnip sprinkled its contents down to mingle with the still-wet blood.

"Just what is this?" Jeannette demanded.

"A treat for the cats." Drew said, "OUCH," as Tony washed out a scratch.

"It smells funny. You don't mind if I analyze it, do you?"

"It's a special kind and it cost me a lot. But hey, nothing's too good for my kitties, huh?"

"Is that why Moonshadow is afraid of you?" Jeannette said. "Because you gave her this?"

"Afraid of me? Why should she be afraid of me? When *Diane* wouldn't let Moonie in the house because Rasta gave her too much shit, *I* took her in. But when Diane threw me out, did Moonie so much as catch me a mouse to get by on? Hell no! And Susan—she wouldn't even hold my hand but she treated those cats of hers like royalty and wanted me to do it too! She wouldn't even pay for me to go to a movie with her but she spent thirty bucks every two weeks on food for *them*." His eyes, which had always seemed blue, were now blazing green with jealousy. Yep, no doubt about it. The guy was one jealous dude—even of the cats. And if Mustard was right, he had *been* a cat himself. But then, cats were jealous of other cats. Mustard himself, for instance. He began licking his right front paw in embarrassment while the questioning continued. It didn't take long to wring a defiant confession from Drew.

As he had already said when he let the cat out of the bag, he had poisoned Mustard, Blackie and Moonshadow because he was angry with Diane for throwing him out and with Susan for breaking up with him—which Mustard actually hadn't realized happened. Human mating habits weren't of particular interest to him, after all.

Mustard told all of this to Mu Mao and the others later, as they kept vigil over the still body of Boston Blackie.

"But why did he hurt the cats he had taken such care to befriend?" Paka asked.

"Well, I guess he had a long record as a con man who got nasty when his victims turned. He was nice to us because that was a good way to get him close to single, cat loving independent ladies like Diane and Susan. He tried to go back on what he said about trying to punish them for rejecting him and said he was just trying to upset them so they'd turn to him in a crisis because they thought he was sympathetic to their love for us."

"And with your Susan, it almost worked," Mu Mao said.

"She's sweet, but not always real bright," Mustard admitted. "But at least the neighborhood should be safe from that particular danger now."

"You've done good work, my brother," Mu Mao said and Mustard noticed that he said "brother" instead of "son." "Will you be returning home to Susan again, even if she thinks of you as a white cat?"

"I've thought about it," he said. "But I'd like to know a little more about this place and there's a shelter full of kittens who've never had a good home. Susan will fall in love with some, the kitten will play with them and the old girl will have her usual tantrum. But she'll be okay."

"It isn't just that Susan didn't know you and it hurt your feelings, is it?" Paka asked.

"No, no," he said, though perhaps that was part of it. "I was never her top cat. I think I see why now. I always hated all of the others—even hated her for loving them. But, you know, it took all of us to figure it out."

"You're too modest," Mu Mao said. "You overcame your jealousy of your housemates to save their lives. You are evolving very quickly, my brother, and growing in enlightenment."

Brother Paddy licked Mustard's ear affectionately and, for once, Mustard didn't mind. "Not only that but he's smart. Mustard was always the smart one. Why, now he's a real detective, just like in those books of Susan's."

"Or on TV," Blackie mumbled, stirring and sitting up. The other cats surrounded him, licking and purring and he responded with a weak purr himself.

"The Mystery series," Sister Paka said. "That's right. Oh, Mustard, you have to stay now, won't he, Master Mu Mao?"

"If he wishes, of course. It's entirely up to him. But it would add very much to our order to have our very own Brother Catfael among us."

Whirlwinds

The old woman had carried Dezbah when she could no longer walk. The same one had told the frightened child stories of their people, of Monster Slayer, Born-for-Water, and Changing Woman, to make her heart strong. The same one had been the one to calm her when Dezbah was torn from the bodies of her murdered parents. This grandmother, this same one who had helped Dezbah on the twenty-day forced march from Fort Defiance to Hweeldi, or Bosque Redondo as the soldiers called it, now ran naked and screaming toward the fort. The soldiers gathered outside their adobe houses to watch and mock and throw things.

Dezbah was frightened, for herself as well as the grandmother. The soldiers weren't shooting yet; instead they made bets and tried to hit the old lady with clods of horse dung. The dung of their horses.

All the tame horses of the Dine' were dead. Dezbah, who was more commonly called Horses Talk to Her, had heard them screaming, and the wild ones too—wondering why? The Dine' treated them like brothers, like the valuable beings they were. Why had they died, and the other animals? A man who would do that to the animals, to babies, to elders, who would shoot a woman going into labor because she slowed the progress of the march, that sort of man would do anything.

"Awww, for the luvva Jaysus, wouldja lookit yez!" It was a funny sounding voice that rang out so suddenly, from within the group of soldiers. Dezbah should not have been able to understand what it said, but she did. A man with hair as black as her father's and skin almost as dark, pushed his way through the other men and stood with both fists on his hips. A blanket dangled from one hand and he turned almost absently and threw it to Dezbah.

She caught a thought with it. The man's face was a mask of disgust but his thought, urgent as it was, was kind. "Wrap it round her, girl, and away with you both." Ah! She knew him now, though she did not think she had heard him speak aloud before he began scolding the soldiers. She had heard his thoughts before, but this was the first time she knew who the thinker was. Perhaps it was because she saw, as much as heard, what he thought, that she could understand him, though he spoke none of her tongue and she had learned only some of the English the soldiers spoke during the Long Walk. He had been on the walk too. She had seen him before and taken no notice. When she heard his thoughts before, she realized she mistook them for those of a Navajo. Only the first time, she realized now, she would have known the thought for what it was, had she not been so sick from all of the other disasters striking like lightning into the canyon. Through all of the dying, his thought had fallen like a dead pine needle from among the soldiers lining the rim of the canyon. "My God, what are we doing to these people?"

Dezbah picked up the blanket from the ground while the

soldier made big movements with his hands and walked back and forth between the soldiers and the grandmother and her. He was yelling at the other men and said he would tell the white leader that the soldiers didn't have anything to do, that they made sport over some naked old granny. Better send away for their wives quick, he said. Better send them to town soon, because they were pretty bad off to act that way. She knew, somehow, that he was being funny as he said it, making himself look sillier than the grandmother, so the men would listen to him and let Dezbah take the old woman away. Dezbah ran after the grandmother, who was stumbling now on feet that had become very bad during the walk. Dezbah caught her and folded the ranting old woman in the plain green wool blanket. With one hand she tried to tuck the grandmother's straggling, dirty gray and black hair up into the traditional bumblebee hairdo at the back of her head. She was afraid to look at the soldiers but heard the man still scolding them in a lewdly humorous way about their own mothers and grandmothers.

"Go!" his voice said in her head and she didn't need to be told again.

Keeping her arms around the grandmother to hold the blanket in place, Dezbah bundled the old woman as deeply among their people as she could. Most made their houses, which were nothing more than holes dug into the ground, covered with whatever they could find, in the Pecos River Basin, on the eastern side of the river. Since the soldiers controlled all food except for the scarce amount the people could hunt or grow themselves in this desolate place, the people needed to stay closer to the fort than they would have liked. The soldiers' compound squatted in the middle of the forty-mile square of desert imprisoning the Navajos.

Bosque Redondo was far from their own lands and within

that of the Comanche. The Comanche raided the unpro-
tected Navajos, taking children and women since there were
no horses to take, and those raids made living on the outskirts
of Hweeldi even worse than living within constant sight of the
soldiers, who forced the people to build adobe houses that
were supposed to have been for themselves, but in reality
were built so that only the soldiers could use them.

At first Dezbah had tried to stay farther away, but when
the grandmother had begun acting in this way, the girl could
not stay away from her long enough to make trips to the fort
to collect their rations, take water from the river or gather
droppings for a fire.

When she returned with the grandmother to the miserable
pit house she had dug from the ground with her own hands,
she sat down outside it with the old woman, who began
picking up sand and flinging it hard at Dezbah, berating her
and calling her a killer.

People came out of their houses and looked at them.

"You should tie her up, maybe." The suggestion came
from Blue Bead Woman, who had been relieved of the beads
she was named for, along with her man and her two oldest
sons, before she took the younger children to Fort Defiance.
Three of them had perished on the great journey and Blue
Bead Woman, once prettily plump, was now wasted so that
you could see sunlight through the flesh between her arm
bones.

Dezbah said nothing, just shook her head. She ducked another handful of sand.

"I wish I had tied up that boy I had," Blue Bead Woman
said. Dezbah nodded. They all knew how, during the siege in
Canyon de Chelly, her younger son had gone crazy from the
thirst and heat and had suddenly run out of their hiding place
in full view of the soldiers. They had cut him down, wounded

him real bad, and when his father and brother tried to go out there and save him, the soldiers got them too.

They'd had lots of practice with their guns, killing the people's horses and sheep, their cows, even the dogs. And then they had chopped down and burned the beautiful peach orchard. It was that Kit Carson told them to do it, Dezbah had heard someone say. He used to be friends with the Dine' but the soldiers paid him a lot of money to betray the People. Because he knew all about them, he was able to cut the heart from them, their horses and trees. And their relatives.

Several other people were standing around watching and the children with enough energy left to play began making fun of the grandmother too. Dezbah threw sand at *them*.

"Don't be mad at them, little one," Hastin Yellow Horse told her. He was still young and handsome when they left the Fort but the soldiers shot his leg when he tried to protect his wife and baby and now he could only walk with help. He looked old enough to be married to the grandmother now. "This woman is not the one who helped you. A dark wind has blown through her and taken her away. It makes her do these dumb-ass things—the children are right to mock her. She is going to make more trouble for you and all of the rest of us if she keeps this up."

"She needs a sing," said a woman called Her Yarn Has Lumps. She was not from the canyon, but by now Dezbah knew almost everyone as if they were her own relatives. But no one knew the grandmother and it was not polite to ask names. Names gave you power over people. That's why she was never called Dezbah by anyone but her own family, who were now dead. No one would speak her name again, she realized suddenly, and tears began falling.

"Who will sing for her with our singer dead?" said Many Goats Woman, who now had only one skinny goat. Her others had been killed and rotted in the sun while she watched from her hiding place during the siege.

"Barboncito could ask Manuelito if maybe a singer could get himself caught," Blue Bead Woman said. She knew that the chiefs were in contact with each other, something the People were able to keep from the soldiers. Barboncito had purposely allowed himself to be taken so he might help his people and he had helped a lot. During the long walk he got the soldiers to sometimes let the little ones and the elders ride in the wagons. He had a good way of talking to the white men, and found whatever heart they had in them and appealed to it to get help for the People. Maybe the man who thought in Navajo was like that too, Dezbah thought. Maybe he could think at her old one and get her to act right again. Someone with the magic to make others hear his thoughts, even in a different language, who knew what such a one could do?

It didn't occur to her that she and many of the children she knew could understand perfectly well what the animals said and make themselves understood as well. She didn't like to think about the animals now, poor things.

She dressed the grandmother in the rags the old woman had worn on the trail, dirty and torn like everyone else's clothes. It was time to collect the rations then, and everyone had to walk to where the soldiers stood giving out the pound of beef, pound of cornmeal, pinch of salt that was supposed to last two days. The meat was maggoty, the cornmeal also afflicted with insects, but it was all that they had. They were to become farmers, the soldiers said, but the land was poor; there was no water except for the mud of the Pecos, and that was very scarce.

Dezbah's rations had run out two days ago and she was hungry but she didn't want to leave the grandmother when she was in such a state. Dezbah tried to tie their wrists together with her sash and get the old one to walk with her, but the grandmother slapped and scratched her and tried to bite her. Dezbah's stomach rumbled as she gazed sadly into those cloudy dark eyes, trying to find a trace of the wise and gentle woman who had saved her life and soothed her mind when none of her own relatives were alive to do it. Neither of them had anyone anymore, she guessed. It was one of the worst criticisms you could say of one of the Dine', "He acts as if he has no relatives." That was how the old woman was acting, as if there was no one who would be shamed by her behavior— but from its craziness, Dezbah feared the old one would be dead soon. And somehow that was even more terrible than the way she was now, when maybe, there was a chance she might come back.

The others returned. They looked away from her, and hurried into their houses. Dezbah knew the people were ashamed that they could not bring her rations to her as well but the soldiers kept very tight control over them. When the grandmother was not calm enough to go for her own, the soldiers would not give Dezbah both portions, even if she had two ration chits.

Many Goats Woman, Blue Bead Woman and the rest made their meals but each of them had children of their own to feed and the old woman sometimes threw food away. One child brought her a bit of corncake with a bite mark at the edge. She broke it to give some to the grandmother but the old lady knocked it out of her hand into the dirt, and it crumbled so badly that she couldn't separate the crumbs. By the time everyone disappeared into their hole houses to sleep, the sky changed from coral and deep pink to turquoise and indigo. The old woman would not go inside and Dezbah could not leave her. There was nothing to make a fire with now and they shivered, but at least they had the soldier's blanket to wrap around them both.

Her stomach growled again and she tried to sleep with her head on her knees and her arms wrapped around them. The old one fell away from her, taking the blanket with her, and snored right there in the open on the ground. Dezbah covered the old one with the part of the blanket she wasn't laying on. Her own belly felt stuck to her backbone.

And then she heard footsteps—not like the ones the people made, but boots, cavalry boots, and a man's heavy tread. She was on her feet at once but the thought-voice of the man who had distracted the soldiers spoke to her. "Aha! Didn't see you in the ration line and I figured you'd be hungry. Brought a bit of something for you and your granny. Couldn't get rations without a chit so I saved this from the mess hall."

He handed her a bundle and she unwrapped two good-sized pieces of mutton and two ears of roasted corn. He had a bag over his shoulder and from it he took two more items, which he gave to her—a can of peaches and even a knife to open the can with. "I'll need that back though," he said of the opener.

"I will have one peach and give one to the Grandmother," she said. "The rest we will save for the other people."

He shook his head and started to open his mouth then thought, "Better not. Word may get around and someone might think you stole them. When actually, I stole them. I'm riding picket at the northern perimeter for a spell, so I won't be here to catch."

"You aren't like the other soldiers," she said in Navajo. He seemed to hear it in his own tongue, as she did, catching the words from the thought.

"I'm entirely like them, except that I've been on the receivin' end of a great deal of the kind of trouble your folks are in and I didn't like the feel of it."

"Can you bring more?" she asked—thought.

"Not for awhile. I'll be up at the outpost. Can you keep your granny from getting you both killed until I get back?"

She sighed. "I am trying. They say that a dark wind has taken over her body now. It's very strong."

"Is that so? And what kind of wind would that be?"

She made a circle with her finger to show him the whirlwind, then pictured it in her mind.

He smiled, and she could see his teeth in the darkness. "Are you some kind of Indian yourself?" she asked.

"Me? No. Look it though, don't I? I'm from County Galway originally, in Ireland," and he showed her a picture in his mind of a small green country over a great water, an island country. "But me mam was widowed soon after I was born and remarried a man from Roscommon. When the Great Hunger came, I was seven years old and she and all my kin died."

"Just died? They didn't get shot?"

"No, but they were starved to death by the blackhearted devil of a landlord." And now she saw from him fields of blackened crops, people being put out of burning houses, much as her people had been.

"Lots of my people starved too," she said in her mind. "We're starving now, mostly."

"I know," he answered in the same way and though his face was lost in shadow she felt the clenching of his jaw and heard the bitterness in his tone. "I can see that. I've not enough rank to do much about it. At least your granny looked after you on the trail and though she's not much good to you now, you've each other."

"Yes," she said. "All of her people were killed too, she said. She's not from our canyon."

"Is she not? Just took you under her wing did she, and now you're repaying the favor?"

"Yes," she said, but sharing his thoughts took her away from her own problems and she wanted him to go on. "How did you come here?"

"The landlord had little use for seven-year-old orphan lads. So he took all of us who couldn't work as hard as he wanted and put us on a rotting ship for America. Not many of us survived that. I was sick for a long time meself but I had to work anyway. As soon as I was old enough, I joined the Army because they feed you really regular."

"But they shoot people who haven't done anything wrong!" she said.

"That's not what my recruiter said," he told her, smiling again as if he'd made a joke. "Too bad I couldn't read his mind like I can yours, the bleedin' whore's son of a—the bleedin' liar." He changed his thought because she was a girl, and young, though she didn't feel young anymore. She felt as old as the grandmother.

Poor grandmother. She had lost everything coming here, even herself.

"Maybe she didn't lose it," the soldier said. "Maybe it got taken from her. And I'd better tell you my name so you don't think of me that way . . ."

"Which way?"

"As a uniform with a gun in one sleeve and a torch in the other. I'm Pvt. Liam O'Malley at your service, young lady."

"I'm called Horses Talk to Her," she said. She would not tell a soldier, even this man, her real name. A real name would give him power over her and it was very possible he might be a witch since he could read her thoughts and she had never known any other human who could do that.

"Do they now? And do you talk to them too? As we talk?"

"I did," she said, curling her arms back around her knees. "But your people shot them all."

"Well, I'm very sorry about that, Horses Talk to Her. I'd have done it differently myself if the government put me in charge. If it makes you feel any better, when that was going on my shots went into the ground. No Irishman worth his salt would harm a horse. Too bad this company has a lot of that kind of Irishman. But never mind. You speaking of the wind reminded me of something I was told by me stepda's mam one time. She was a great one for stories, was Mrs. Donnolly. She was what we call a fairy doctor, was she. You'll be wondering what that is. I heard you thinking about witches just now, excuse me for intruding, but I couldn't help overhearing. We have witches in Ireland too but that's nothing compared to what the fairies do to folk sometimes."

"What are fairies?"

His mind produced many strange pictures and she couldn't see what he meant. Then he said, "Well, it's said that one time they lived above the ground until they fought the next race of people to come along and had to go live in the underworld. But they don't much like it, see, so they're always playing tricks on mortal folks."

"Like the Dine'," she said. "Here, living in our holes in the ground."

"No—well, that is, yes, a bit. Except folk in Ireland know better nowadays than to treat the fairies poorly—bad things happen to them as do. And sometimes, people will just be minding their own business and things happen." He showed her a picture of a baby sleeping peacefully in its cradle being stolen away by one of the people he called fairies, and another crying, angry, sick baby put in its place.

"Don't the parents know?"

"Well, the fairies change it so it looks like their baby and

70

they only know by its squallin' that it's not normal-like. The new thing put in place of the baby is called a changeling."

The word didn't translate well and he kept showing her pictures. Finally she thought she understood. "Oh, they're shapeshifters. Like witches."

"A bit, yes."

"Do the parents ever get their real babies back?"

"Yes, but you won't like that bit. They have to hold the changeling over a fire until the fairies fear for its life. Then they come and get it and give back the real baby."

She nodded, "Barboncito says that when the white men wanted to trade captives, we gave back ours but they wouldn't give back our people. Maybe we should have held theirs over a fire . . ."

"Now there's an idea you don't want the captain hearing you speak of, young lady. The thing is, a fairy doctor now, like Mrs. Donnolly, they'll know different ways of doing things. And there's different sorts of changelings too. Sometimes the fairies will steal an old person."

"I guess they need their wisdom, huh?"

"It's true. Fairies have been called a great many things but I don't believe wise is one of them. The point is, Horses Talk to Her, that when they take the old people, they also leave changelings—querulous, battlesome, trouble-making things, and an embarrassment to the person they're supposed to be."

Dezbah was afraid. "Do they have to be put over a fire too?"

"No—no, they don't. There's another cure for that and what made me think of it was you and your dark wind. Because we sort of think the opposite, you see. If you want to get an old person back from the fairies, you must go to a crossroad and stand there until a whirlwind comes by, catch the dust in your hand and cast it on them, whereupon the changeling is taken away and the real person returns."

"Really?" She got a very clear picture of this from him and wondered if he had tried it before—but she saw then from the picture that he had not. This was just the picture he got from what his Irish old one told him. "But what if you get the wrong kind of whirlwind?"

He shrugged, "Your guess is as good as mine. But herself there could hardly be worse now, could she?"

Dezbah cast a brief glance at the old one who had been her friend and shuddered, lowering her head miserably so that her cheek rested on her knees. The man sighed. He wasn't completely serious, Dezbah knew, just telling her a story to comfort her and because he was lonely. But there was no comfort in anything now. She heard his boots crunch the sand, the old one moan in the dark, and in the stillness of the night, the halt of footsteps, the man's voice speaking to the horse, and the hoofbeats gradually fading to the north.

The hooting of a hunting owl awakened her, and she blinked in a darkness without stars. Her hand found the roughness of the sticks that made her shelter, the rags and mud that covered the sticks. She was alone. She sat up, crawled out. There were the stars, the sand, the scrub, the blanket, but there was no old one.

Dezbah crawled completely out, stood and looked around. She saw the trail of rags leading across the sand, the footprints, all heading moonward, to the west now, and far off, she could see the movement of moonlight on skin that had not seen the sun and hair touched with silver.

She hurried after, scooping up blanket and rags as she ran, her young legs not as strong as they had been, because of exhaustion and poor food, but better than the old one's.

As she ran she realized she was sending her thoughts out, hoping the soldier might hear, "She's doing it again!" but no voice answered at all. He was too far away to hear her, she thought, and she could not hear him.

So she kept running after the old one herself.

Though the soldiers had little outposts scattered around the perimeter and sent pickets out to patrol for fifteen to twenty miles around them each night, they let the Comanches do a lot of their patrolling for them. Fear of those people kept the Dine' inside, close to the fort and the food. But not all of them. Some escaped across the desert. The messengers from Manuelito had reported that two of the ones who escaped made it, both strong boys who joined Manuelito's people in the hills.

The old one would never make it in the desert. She didn't remember what she knew about how to stay alive, Dezbah knew this. She knew that the grandmother's mind was confused, though she could not read it as if it were a horse's, or the soldier's.

She walked all night, it seemed. Sometimes she saw the old one just a little ahead of her. Other times she was afraid she lost her altogether. In the morning, as the sun rose and cast long shadows across the ground, Dezbah stumbled and found it was the old one over whom she had stumbled. She was lying there, face down in the dirt, her hair all straggly and with no clothes on. Dezbah covered her from the sun and did up her hair. She should have brought water, she knew. She found some brush and made a shelter for them with the blanket. Found a saguaro and used another stick to drill a hole in it, get at the juice from the inside. They drank this, she forcing some through the old one's lips.

So they were free of the fort but they were also free to starve, die of hunger, burn under the hot sun if she didn't take care of them. She couldn't hunt for food and leave the old one to wander off. There were not even the berries, grass seeds, yucca fruit, and pinon nuts they used for food at Hweeldi.

She slept till twilight, her arm tethered to the old woman's by a strip of rag from her skirt. She felt the rag twitch and awakened, in time to see the old one running off again. At least this time she was not removing her clothes. Dezbah grabbed the blanket and followed once more, further from the fort, toward the setting sun. She found the grandmother just as the darkness came. The old woman had found the river once more, and was sitting on its western bank. This was the river the soldiers called the Pecos, the same one where, further south, she and the other captives lived beside. Here, as further downstream, it was during this time of year little more than a collection of muddy pools. The old one yelled nothing, said nothing, didn't move. She was exhausted, despite her long rest.

Dezbah led her down into the river bed and the old one drank. But when Dezbah would have turned her back in the direction of the fort, she took off down the riverbed, heading north, toward the mountains.

Dezbah was heading after her when she felt a sudden pain in her head, as if someone was shouting at her.

She didn't try to answer. The soldier was a soldier and though he had seemed friendly and could thought-talk with her, he had not helped when she needed him.

She caught up with the old one easily this time and, following the riverbed, they walked all night.

At dawn, in the distance, far across the desert, too far for hoofbeats to be heard or a voice to carry, low gray shadows traveled eastward in a line that lengthened as the sky grew brighter. A rider then. Not a soldier. The rutted track the army traveled ran along the river for much of the way between the last two towns to the north. Dezbah could just make out some of the smoke from the cookfires of Puerto de Luna, the village called Door of the Moon, a bit to the northeast of them.

The dust cloud was coming toward it, directly from the east. One of Manuelito's men, coming to his people with encouraging news of their relatives in hiding.

Dezbah was not cheered by the dust cloud. It was so far away, it might never have been, for all the help she would have because of it.

They trudged onward through the heat, and watched the heat lightning in the sky. It brought no rain but occasional hot gusts that stirred the dust and agitated it into the little whirlwinds the soldier had called "dust devils."

At a crossroads, he had said. If you caught the dust of a whirlwind at a crossroads, and threw it on an old one who was witched like the grandmother, the spell would be broken.

Where the Navajos' secret trail came to the soldiers' road, would there be such a crossroad?

It would be dangerous to go to such a place, so near the village, with the soldiers watching for escaped prisoners. But she was not trying to escape. She did not think she could return to her own country so easily. She only wanted the grandmother to regain her own spirit. If the soldiers came, she would tell them she had become lost while following the grandmother. That was true.

One more day they slept and one more night they traveled until they were so close to the town that she could see it. She would never see the hoofprints of Manuelito's rider, she knew, for the ground in most places was too dry. But as the sun was rising once more, she saw something in the riverbed and, looking over her shoulder, could see the smoke curling from the chimneys of the town. The old one was tired and she made her a shelter once more. Then, instead of sleeping, she made her way to the edge of town where the soldiers' road would have crossed that of the rider. There was little cover there, but she was small and it was very early yet.

As if it knew what she wanted, the wind twisted itself into many cylinders. But one spiraled off to the right, one to the left. One came straight for her but she saw that the rotation went against the movement of the sun and she jumped aside at the last moment.

A dark wind could not hurt the old one, but it could still steal her own spirit.

Time passed and more time. The morning drew on. Three more of the dark twisting winds came whirling in their unnatural way toward her, taunting her by blowing up the dust and sand from the crossroad so that she had to run to keep it from blowing into her face and infecting her with its evil.

They came so quickly, one after another, that she felt evil spirits had been sent to take her. She had not eaten since the night the soldier brought her a meal, except for the few small edible things she could gather while the grandmother slept or was calm. She was shaking with hunger and her vision blurred by the hot shimmer of the Illusion People dancing before her eyes.

Their dance was very subtle, their feet lost in mist, their heads bobbing only a little as their bodies shimmered with the heat. Sweat poured into her own eyes and down her neck and arms. It blurred the sight of the next whirlwind until it came rolling out from behind the dancing Illusion People, and spun so rapidly it was almost upon her. She jumped up to run. But then she saw it was different from the others. This one twisted sunward. But now it was passing her, passing the crossroads.

She dove for it, her hands outstretched, and clutched them into fists. Her fists filled with hot dust and dirt, gritty and too agitated, for a moment, to lie still within her fingers.

And then the wind was gone.

Now she had what she needed and she walked quickly back to where she had left the old one. If this Irish magic worked, perhaps they would intercept Manuelito's rider as he returned. Maybe he would even take them home. Dezbah's heart lifted at the thought.

"But I'd be that sorry to lose you," another thought answered. Oh no! Not now, when she was so close. Her thoughts would betray not only themselves but, if she was not careful, the messenger who had been sent to report back to the Navajo leaders.

So she thought instead of the story he had told her, and of the journey she and the old one had just made. "We're very hungry—she's almost worn out, I think," she thought to him. "But I have the dust! The magic dust, just like you said."

And then she saw from his thought that it had only been a story and he didn't believe it himself, and that he was sorry to have encouraged her to have gone to such trouble for its sake.

"No matter," she thought. "I will not let go of this dust until I can throw it onto the old one, so that her spirit may have that chance of returning."

"You're a fine lass and a credit to your people," the thought came back.

But here was the place where the old one should be resting and she was not there. Dezbah wept dust, having no water with which to make tears.

And then she heard the hoofbeats again and saw the tall man in blue and felt strong hands lift her onto the horse. And she could not form the thought to wonder whether to be thankful or worried, but let him follow the trail of clothing and the bare footprints of tired old feet.

They found her lying face down, an hour or so from the river. At first it seemed she wasn't breathing, and Dezbah was afraid to approach her, lest she be dead. All ghosts were evil and dangerous, but the one that had taken this grandmother before she was dead would be an especially bad ghost, Dezbah thought. The soldier put his hand to her neck and said, "She's alive."

Dezbah, still clutching the dust, jumped down from the horse. The soldier, sensing her intention, stood aside and she flung the dust over the old one, adding the precaution of doing it to the four directions, clockwise, east, south, west and north.

The old one's wrinkled back heaved and she coughed out dirt. And saw the soldier and screamed.

"I beg your pardon, ma'am," he said, closing his eyes and turning his back.

Dezbah began helping her cover herself with the rags.

"Are we home yet?" the old one asked. "I dreamed we were going home. I was just about to see the peak of the first sacred mountain when that *biilaganah* woke me up."

"You've been sick, grandmother. But you're better now."

"Now that the Navajo fairies have returned her," the soldier's thought intruded.

But it was overlaid with another thought. This was not a human one. It was the familiar and beloved thinking of a Navajo pony.

The soldier caught the thought entering her mind and looked down at her with one raised eyebrow. "So. That's yer man from Manuelito and his people, is it? The general knew someone was coming in, but they've never caught him."

"Please," she said. "Go away. Just a little way. Don't try to catch him. Don't let him see you. I must speak with him."

"Would be a feather in my cap to take him," he said with a sigh. "But I think I feel a call of nature anyway."

A short time later the messenger arrived. He was traveling

fast and light but he could see the old one was all but dead. He took pity on them and held the old one before him while Dezbah rode behind.

It was a long journey, and food was still not plentiful, and the old one faded more and more, though she was always within her own senses. Suddenly she cried out, "There it is! The sacred mountain! Oh spirit of the mountain, I am home!"

She was so excited she fell off the horse. She was never able to climb back on and soon after died, wholly herself and very satisfied. Dezbah and the messenger buried her quickly and the messenger offered to take Dezbah with him back home. But she shook her head.

In a few more days, with the little food she could find on the way, she was near once more to the place where she had captured the whirlwind. A blue clad figure sat tall on a horse. He sat even taller as she approached, and she heard his thinking and knew that he was very glad she had come, and felt some burden that was his lift from his mind like a rock to reveal the happiness below it. He gave her a hand up onto the horse's back.

"I wasn't sure you'd be returning," he said.

"I did," she said. "The Grandmother died, but she had her spirit back and she saw the sacred mountain and knew she was home. Your magic was a good one. But this is not your Ireland. Magic works different here. You can't go catching just any whirlwind without danger. I will help you use what you know the right way, to help the People."

"My thought exactly," he said, and she realized that it was.

In the years that followed, the two of them worked with her people, helping them learn that which would benefit them in dealing with the Americans and the New Mexicans.

Dezbah herself learned to weave and work silver, and to wear dresses like the few white women at the fort. She helped others learn these skills as well. The soldier showed the men some skills too, and they worked in a way that was pleasing to the soldiers, who thought the Navajo men were doing it for them, when really they were doing it to learn how to improve their crops when they returned home.

And when the time came when the general and the Navajo leaders made a talk about sending the people home, the soldier watched from his duty station and Dezbah watched from among the crowd and both gave a little "push" of their thoughts at the general, who finally agreed to let the people go home.

This time too, the soldier accompanied the Navajos on the long walk. But it was not as a captor but as Dezbah's husband, known to the People as Catches Whirlwinds, though Dezbah had done the true catching, that Liam O'Malley, formerly of the U.S. Cavalry, went with them. He and Dezbah were married and began a trading post specializing in fine horses and with it, they helped her People start another long journey—that of rebuilding their lives, their homes, health and prosperity.

Author's Note: This is not a true folktale, but a made-up story about made-up people set against the true background of the Navajo's Long Walk and captivity at Bosque Redondo. The stories about whirlwinds, both the Navajo belief and the Irish, are found in books of such magical beliefs. I hesitate to call them superstitions, as I have never personally attempted to intercept a whirlwind, so how would I know?

Worse Than the Curse

In the old days, the crowd of suitors at the palace gate had been downright unmanageable. Knights and princes and even a king or two, each trying to pull rank on the other, had clamored for a glimpse of, a word from, a moment with the beautiful Princess Babette. Princess Babette was, as was *de rigeur* for one of her station, the fairest of the fair. The gold of her hair put that in the royal treasury to shame with the brilliance of its luster, the blue of her eyes was as guilelessly clear and deep as a cloudless spring sky, the rose of her cheeks and lips put the sunsets and dawns to shame, and her complexion was dewy and creamy.

As if the fine coloring wasn't enough, her very bones were beautiful: high cheeks, a firm chin and a wingcurve of jawline sweeping above a swanlike neck. Her figure was a symphony of slender, willowy grace, amply but not over-generously curved at breast and hip.

And all of that beauty went to he who won her hand in marriage, along with the aforementioned treasury (which was far more substantial if not as lustrous as Babette's tresses), a great deal of fertile land, a large and competent army—in short, a kingdom for which many of the noble suitors would have been happy to marry a far less beauteous princess.

Every day the royal audience chamber was choked with petitioners for the hand of the princess. Babette's royal mum and dad lay awake nights thinking of impossible tasks for the fellows to do, impossible things for them to fetch, to prove themselves worthy of the princess. Babette herself loved dreaming up and suggesting little embellishments—the mountain to be scaled by the king with the unfortunate wart on his nose should be made of glass, for instance. That would keep him busy. He'd have to find the thing first. She herself would have given less difficult tasks to the younger, better looking princes, but often these did not have fortunes that matched her own, and the King her father sent the poor dears off to claim the single eyes of fire-breathing dragons or clean the stables of giants.

Fortunately, unlike the impractical suitors of princesses in stories, most of the kings and princes and knights understood such tasks for what they were—a way of being told they were basically unacceptable unless they proved to be more than human. They were gently-born humans, it was true. Noble, even royal humans. But when it came to fire-breathing dragons, again unlike the hapless princes in storybooks, the suitors showed a streak of self-preservation and common sense that, had Babette's father and mother thought about it, were quite desirable characteristics in a son-in-law. Though they sighed and pined and cast many a backward look at the beautiful Babette as they slunk away, most of the suitors de-clined to die for her and decided instead to fall in love with someone a bit more accessible.

Not so with one candidate, however. King Vladimirror I was very tenacious. He was actually a wizard, the former Grand Vizier of a mighty kingdom, and by his wizardry he had overthrown the rightful monarch. He had no scruples about using that same magic to climb glass mountains, clean giants' stables, quench fire-breathing dragons, and whatever else was required to win a suitable queen.

Babette's problem in this case was simple. She didn't like him. Didn't trust him. As he crawled up one side of the glass mountain, atop which she perched, she could feel her skin wanting to crawl down the other side.

"Now!" he announced, when he stood on the pinnacle with her. "I am ready to claim my prize."

"Not so fast," she said, hastily dreaming up another embellishment. "You've only passed the first part of the test."

"What do you mean the first part?" he demanded. "I've done more than any of the other candidates."

"Yes," she said, "but *they* didn't even finish the first part. There's more."

"Very well," he said. "I will do anything to win you."

"Why?" she asked.

"I beg your pardon?"

"Why will you do anything to win me? The obvious answer is my dowry, but I'm told you live too far away for us to consolidate our lands, and that your kingdom is far wealthier than ours. Are you a very greedy king, that you want the little wealth I could bring with me?"

He was actually a very greedy man indeed, but his greed had never been confined to gold. His eyes roamed over the territory he currently desired and he thought of the pleasure of owning something—someone—other men had coveted, of the power he would have over her to do his bidding. "The answer should be obvious every time you look into your glass, Madame. You are very beautiful."

"True. But you're not. So my next question is, why should I be won by you?"

"I have braved the dangers set before your suitors and I alone have prevailed."

"Yes, but you used trickery."

"Magic, madame. I am wise in the ways of magic."

"Wise? Learned perhaps, which is not always the same thing. And I have never heard that a tricky husband was necessarily the best one. No, I think you have used an unfair advantage and besides, I don't wish to travel so far from home. So sorry. Wrong answers, but thanks for playing. Next!"

Vladimirror was angry. Vladimirror was wrothy, in fact. Foaming at the mouth, in fact. No upstart princess, be she more beautiful than the dawn, was going to humiliate him in that fashion. Or any other fashion, for that matter. "If I can't have you, my proud beauty, no one will," he fumed. Even to him, that sounded a little trite but then, he was a wizard with spells, not a wizard with words. Nonetheless, he added, "Not even yourself."

"Fine," she said. "Do you mind? It's getting hot up here and I want to get down," and with that she slid down the mountain on her shapely satin clad rump.

Vladimirror was very unhappy about all of this but he had not overthrown a monarch because he wore his heart on his sleeve or said what was on his mind. He had cast a curse upon her, though she hadn't noticed, and he left the kingdom smiling, anxious to return to his own kingdom and watch in his scrying glass as his revenge against the haughty princess manifested itself.

"You put the wind up that last one, m'dear," the King said, as he and the Queen joined their daughter and a few hundred of their closest courtiers in sampling the sweetmeats and candies the various suitors had brought in tribute to the princess.

She didn't answer. She was concentrating on the sweetness of the marzipan she had just slipped between her lips. Sweet somethings on the tongue were ever so much nicer than sweet nothings in the ear, she mused.

Unbeknownst to her, the wizard's spell had the effect of multiplying the effect of the food she put to her lips. Every morsel added girth to her lissome body. She didn't notice that night, when she slipped under her velvet counterpane and pulled the jeweled midnight blue draperies surrounding her bed. But the next morning, when her handmaidens tried to help her into her gown of white samite, trimmed with little seed pearls and white diamonds, the gown did not fit. She could not even pull it on. Fortunately, all of the handmaidens for fashion-conscious princesses had to be expert dress-makers and designers, and they were able to slit the seams and piece in new fabric. Still, the effect in the mirror was less pleasing to the princess than it had formerly been.

Babette decided white was maybe not her best color. But laborious changes of garment revealed that blue was no better, nor red, green, yellow, violet, lavender, fuchsia, cloth of gold, or silver. Black, the handmaidens informed her, was slimming, but it made Babette feel like a widow.

Oh dear. And she hadn't even married yet. She supposed she had better look at some of the young men more closely.

She didn't get a chance. As soon as the next lot of princes saw her, most of them made their apologies and left. The rest waited until they heard the tests, then they left too.

Babette felt strangely light, despite her increased weight. She was suddenly left alone—relatively speaking. No suitors waiting. No glass mountains to perch on. No one seemed to care what she was wearing or how she wore her hair. In fact, everyone, including her parents, seemed to be looking the other way when she approached. It made her feel invisible. That was annoying, but also something of a relief. The truth was, no one seemed to recognize her for herself. It was as if Princess Babette was someone else entirely and she was just—this largish girl, who was actually rather hungry.

This proved to be a bit of a problem for everyone else though. Now, when Babette reached for the sweetmeats the princes had left behind, her father sighed and her mother gave her a Look. The closest lady in waiting said, "Your Highness, perhaps you would like to wait until we can order more rare and lustrous fabric from the importers?"

And though she took no more at mealtimes than she was accustomed to taking, she felt eyes watching each morsel she put to her lips, and found she had quite lost her appetite until she was alone, back in her rooms again.

She was, as one wit put it, "the mock of the town." From being a proud and beautiful princess surrounded by suitors, she had gone almost overnight into being plump and ignored, even by those who she was quite sure loved her.

It was as if she were a ghost in her own castle. Her own servants snubbed her and when she reacted angrily, her mother, passing by, overheard and took her aside. The Queen searched her daughter's face, her eyes full of pain, and said, "You must not blame your maidens, daughter, or anyone else if you are not as well treated now as in your slimmer days. Wrath will not restore your beauty, nor the power it lent you. With your slenderness, you have lost something of your character."

"But Mama, that's ridiculous!" Babette stormed. "I haven't lost my character at all. I'm still a virgin!"

"Of course you are. And likely to remain that way unless you take yourself in hand." The sad thing was, Babette could see that the Queen thought she was being kind and giving wise advice. Part of it was wise. Babette never again took out her own frustration on her handmaidens or other people. She learned to get what she needed from them by looking them in the eye and getting them to stick to their jobs. If she saw in their expressions some pain or worry unrelated to herself, she got them to tell her of it, and relieved it if she could. Otherwise she would never have got anything done.

But still, without hours to fill dressing and dancing and entertaining suitors, she had a great deal of time on her hands. She drifted quite by accident into the great hall where her father was teaching her elder brother, the Crown Prince, about ruling and making good decisions and passing judgments. She sat on the sidelines and listened, day after day, as her father heard each case and spoke to his advisors and listened to them; then he and her brother weighed each fact until they came to a verdict, issued a decree, upheld or struck down a law, granted an exemption or a punishment, as the case required. Her father, she realized suddenly, was a very good king. Her brother would be a good king too, she could tell. They were both fair, listened well, and truly cared about the fate of the people in front of them. They understood how other problems within the kingdom would affect the welfare of those same people.

She came to feel extremely humble, and saddened. With such an example she could have been a good ruler too, at the side of one of those princes. Even one of the ones who wasn't really handsome or daring might have been good at kinging with her help.

Vladimirror watched her from afar and saw her bursting and bulging in her dresses, looking bewildered and shocked at how people treated her, and then sad and whipped, sitting alone in her chambers. He sent a message by carrier bat and it came in the night and tangled in the hair of her chambermaid.

"What does it say?" the chambermaid asked, when the princess had quieted the servant's shrieks, disentangled the bat, taken the message vial from its leg and was reading.

"It's from that wily wizard of the East," Babette said, frowning. "He's taking responsibility for my current—condition, and offers to give me back my figure if I pass three of HIS tests. It requires me to travel incognito, I'm afraid. You'll have to change clothes with me."

"*How* incognito?" the chambermaid asked. "You may need to travel in something a little rougher than the gown I'm wearing. It used to be yours, remember?"

Babette eyed the pink samite gown with the little ruby insets thoughtfully. "You might have a point there. If you would be so kind as to go to the kitchen and fetch the cook. Her gown should fit me. And I will need some food for the journey as well."

The chambermaid rolled her eyes, as if her plump princess *would* be thinking of food and cooks even at such a time, but obeyed. The cook took a long time coming and when she came, it was with a gown over her arm as well as her own.

Babette cocked an eyebrow and the cook said, "I brought you me other gown, 'ighness. It wouldn't do, me cookin' in your finery, and it'll bring a good price at the market if I don't get it all stained with grease and such. That silky stuff stains right through the apron, it does. So you can 'ave this 'un and I'll keep yours nice and clean. Might be I can wear it to me daughter's wedding before I sells it."

Babette nodded, thanked her, slipped out of her dress and handed it over. When the cook departed, the chambermaid tried to help her mistress on with the old roughly woven brown garment, splattered with gravy stains across the bosom. Babette shook her head. "I'll have to get used to dressing and undressing myself if I'm going to be incognito." The princess was appalled to find that the cook's frock fit her perfectly, and without too much room to spare. The cook had always been the largest woman in the palace.

The chambermaid clucked her tongue, "I wish your Highness could find it in you to go incognito with two or three of the palace guard anyway. It's as much as my job's worth to let you go haring off like this."

Babette spoke with the haughtiness of her thinner days, "You forget your place, Madeline. I am still the princess, gravy stained gown or no, and you are still the chambermaid. You have no authority to stop me. Besides, I very much doubt anyone will notice, or care all that much." She added with a tear of self-pity rolling down her cheek and chins.

Rather to her surprise, Madeline patted her hand consolingly. "Here now, ducks, I mean, Your Highness, don't take on so. That's not true, though you may think so. Your people will come around once they gets used to you. Same thing happened to my sister Sophie after the twins was born. She was afraid her man was going to leave her but he got used to her, didn't he? Now he just says there's more of her to love and meanwhile Soph's had our Wat and our Alice born, hasn't she?"

"Kind of you to say so, Madeline," Babette said, though actually it didn't give her, still a virgin, much comfort to think that she had the same weight problem as a mother of at least four.

"Here's your food now, ma'am. But cook says as how if you should come back after supper, she'll leave the makings of a cold meal for me to fetch for you in the kitchen."

"You and cook are both very thoughtful, Madeline," Babette said. She had never noticed that before but then, servants were expected to be thoughtful, weren't they? It was their job. "I'll just be off now."

"Aren't you going to take off your crown and bind you your hair, ma'am?" Madeline asked. "I mean, if you want to disguise yourself as a common woman. Just a suggestion."

"Oh, silly me," Babette said, "of course," and put the crown in her jewelry box and allowed Madeline to braid her hair into two long braids, then loop each of them up and tie her own kerchief around it. "How do I look now?" Babette asked.

"We-ell," Madeline giggled. "I reckon it's not that easy to make a sow's ear from a silken purse either, if you don't mind my saying so, but them little embroidered shoes don't seem like the right accessories to me."

"Oh dear. I can't go barefoot! I'd be lame in no time!"

"Be back in a tic, ma'am," Madeline said, and returned with some wooden clogs. "These will protect your feet and help you look your part as well."

They were not, however, very comfortable, inflexible and clunky. Babette had to remember to pick her feet up off the floor and put them down again rather than gliding heel and toe as she was accustomed.

But Madeline was satisfied with the disguise at last and saw her to the castle gate, handing over her cloth wrapped parcel of food at the last minute before waving goodbye.

Now then, Babette thought, what tests are these that the wizard had for her before she could resume her rightful shape and place in life?

From his palace tower, the wizard looked into his scrying glass and saw the humbly dressed princess, her wealth of golden hair braided up like a goose girl's, and chuckled happily to himself before releasing another carrier crow.

The crow dive-bombed the unsuspecting princess, who ducked and swung her arms, frightening a horse pulling a wagonload of dung. The horse reared and the cart upset, and Babette slipped on some of the contents and fell onto her backside in the ordur.

She said something very unprincesslike as the message tube dropped into her newly fragrant lap. "You must walk seven times seven leagues in seven times in seven months. You must climb seven mountains, ford seven rivers, and cross seven seas."

"Right," she said, though she couldn't help wondering why wizards were always so preoccupied with sevens. He would have been very tedious to be married to, she thought. No wonder she had disliked him on sight. But she set off briskly, avoiding the curses of the dung-wagon driver. A swim in one of seven rivers sounded well worth walking seven leagues for at this point. In fact, she thought of turning back to the palace to have a wash before she started but she doubted the guards would recognize her, which was rather the point, even if they let her get close enough, stinking as she was, to see her properly. Oh well, the sooner she started the sooner she'd be there.

Walking in clogs had very little in common with walking in seven-league boots, she realized after half of the first league. The clogs did not offer much in the way of striding ability. Finally once she was walking on the road that wound through meadows, she removed the offending footwear and walked barefoot in the grass, which was quite nice except for the occasional sticker patch.

She was also plagued by insects, drawn to her new perfume. She swatted them with her food bundle and used some very ignoble language in her attempts to discourage them. Unfortunately, the mountain she had to climb that day was not high enough to be cold enough for the insects to fall away from her. When at last she reached bottom of the mountain she found a stream and, though not the first river, and, carrying her food packet and her clogs above her head, began to wade.

At which point she became the object of aerial attack by seven crows, who tore the food packet from her hands and knocked away the clogs. They scattered what food they did not steal into the water, though she was left holding half of one of cook's best roast swan sandwiches.

When she bit down on it, she almost broke one of her teeth on another message tube. "You must travel through seven forests, sleeping on the ground among the beasts, finding bee pollen, chickweed . . ." and a long list of herbs, which she wouldn't know from ornamental ivy, followed. Contemplating the soggy half of her sandwich, she wondered how these herbs tasted, preferably fried.

"Share your food with a poor old woman, dearie?" a shaky voice asked.

"All I have left is half a roast swan sandwich," the princess said. She was hungry—very hungry really, but the sandwich didn't look like much. "It's rather soggy."

The old woman, who was very ugly indeed, looked anxiously from the sandwich to her face and back again, licking her chops.

"Oh, all right," the Princess said. "I'll split it with you, how's that?" She tried not to sound as reluctant as she was. After all, she may have until recently been a beautiful blonde, but that didn't mean she was stupid. She knew the fairy tales. She knew the score. You didn't ever, ever, refuse food or help to little old ladies you met on the road because they would A.) turn you into a frog (though that was usually for arrogant princes rather than hungry princesses), B.) make something nasty fall from your mouth eternally or C.) refuse to share with you the knowledge of herbs and simples all old biddies supposedly had.

She was a little surprised when the old lady did none of the above, instead, snatching the entire half a sandwich from the princess's hand and flinging it in the stream where it was carried off.

"Wh—" the princess began. But the old woman was flinging off her rags and lifting her ugly mask to reveal the face and robes of the wizard Vladimirror, who giggled evilly at her.

"No roast swan for you, little glutton. In fact, no sugar, salt, wheat, corn, fruit, bread of any kind for the duration if you ever want to look like a proper princess again."

"But that's everything!" she wailed. "What will I eat?"

"Crow, Your Highness. You can eat crow. That is, if you can catch one. You are truly pathetic away from your parents, you know. By the time you slim down again, you're going to be wanting a spell to get your youth back along with your recovered waistline."

"If I do, it certainly won't be so the likes of you will want to marry me," she snapped. "You are a horrid beastly man."

"And *you* are a thoroughly lost and very fat princess and will remain that way if you don't start moving," the wizard told her. Then he turned into a crow and flew away. She was mad enough that she thought if she could catch him she *would* have eaten one crow.

Still hungry, she kept wandering, and frankly had no idea how many leagues she had gone, though she did have to cross a river. By the time she got across it was night. And cold. The leaves were turning. Actually, she hadn't seen that too many times. Where she lived it was mostly farming country, good farming country, and beyond the castle was the village and beyond the village the fields. Not a great many trees any longer. The leaves were quite pretty and piled up nicely for her to lie down on, once she realized she was going to have to actually sleep IN the forest ON the ground with no blanket and nothing but what she was wearing. Very shortly she discovered that if she burrowed into the leaves and covered herself with them, they added a little warmth. Picking leaves beside a very large tree was helpful as a windbreak too. But when night fell and she heard footsteps, snuffles, and cries all around her and when she dared peek out, saw eyes glowing in the darkness . . .

Well, needless to say, she didn't sleep late that morning, lest she wake up just in time to find herself breakfast in bed for some bear or lion or dragon or boar or goodness only knew what else. She walked much faster the next day, but did not leave the forest, and after another night in the leaves, crossed another river and climbed another mountain without leaving the trees. This went on for a week. Seven days, actually, when she had nothing much to eat and felt in grave danger of being eaten.

So she was understandably very hungry, footsore and weary when she saw smoke rising from a chimney and came upon what looked like a woodcutter's hut. Woodcutters were always very handy in fairytales too. Except this one wasn't home. There was, however, another ugly old lady there, along with a calico cat.

Seeing the old woman sweeping at the door, Babette very nearly turned and ran but the old woman called out to her. "Who's there? Whoever you are, could you help me a moment please?"

"Oh, no, you don't," Babette muttered. But since she was still only a fat young princess and not a toad, she figured she still had something to lose so she cautiously turned back to the hut.

"Excuse me, beldame," she said with all the courtesy she could muster, "but I haven't had very good luck with pathetic old ladies lately. Would you mind taking off that shawl and tugging at your face so I can see whether or not you're this evil wizard who tricked me before?"

The old lady gave a reassuringly elderly cackle not a bit like the wizard's giggle. "Certainly, my pretty," she said and accommodatingly made faces with her face and whirled her shawl in the air like a flag.

'My pretty,' eh? Babette decided she liked this old girl, who was evidently not the wizard. "So what can I do for you? If it's food, I'm sorry, but that wizard I mentioned tricked me out of my last morsel."

"Oh, no, my pretty, nothing like that. In fact, I was about to invite you in for some nice crow stew I've made up fresh today. But first I wanted you to see if you can reach behind the stove. My cat brought a mouse in and the wicked thing hid behind the stove and died. Can you fetch it out? It's stinking up the house."

"Ewwww," Babette said.

"I wouldn't ask it of you except I'm blind, which as you probably know from the stories makes all of my other senses extra keen, so the smell is driving me mad."

Blind, huh? Hence the "my pretty." Oh well. She seemed nice enough. And though the house smelled ripe with dead mouse, it still didn't smell as bad as Babette herself had smelled until recently.

Whipping off her kerchief, Babette put it over her hand and groped until her kerchief-shielded fingers squished into dead mouse, which she pulled out, without looking, and flung into the woods, along with the kerchief.

The crow stew was a little bitter. "It's better with extra salt," the old woman said. "I don't normally have it but there was a whole flock of crows in front of the house today and my cat here is very, very fast."

The cat licked her front paws, one red and one white.

Babette looked longingly at the little dish of salt but shook her head. After all she'd been through, she supposed she could do without. "I'm not allowed salt."

"What? Whyever not?" the old woman asked.

"I'm having a curse cured, you see, and it's one of the magical formulas for curing it." She dug into Cook's pocket and read her the wizard's message. "Have you any idea where these herbs and simples can be found, beldame?"

"I wish you'd stop calling me that," the old woman said. "My name is Fifi. Fifi La Fey."

"Sorry, Mistress Fifi. I'm Pr—uh, precisely who you think I am, a young woman from town who got lost in these woods trying to fulfill these idiotic instructions from a wizard. My name is Barbara," she said. The old woman was an unlikely Fifi and the princess suspected she was an even more implausible Babette at this point. "Barbara—er—Cook."

"Well, Barbara, as I've mentioned, I'm blind, but my adopted son Pr—presently will be home. I call him Burl. Because he works with wood. Get it?"

Babette laughed. Now that she was comfortable, she found relief made her easily amused. "And does he know more about herbs and simples than you do?"

"No, of course not. I know all about them. I just can't see them any longer. But when he gets back, I can tell him where they are and he can help you find them. He's gone off to fetch Hamlet to us."

"Who is Hamlet?" Babette asked.

"The minstrel who comes by now and then. Specializes in long gloomy battles and dirges and laments. But being a traveling man, he is also very up on current events. Can you write that down? Laments? Events? He might want to use those lines in one of his songs."

"I'll try to remember," Babette promised.

"Would you be kind enough to fetch some water from the stream?"

Babette did. It was very heavy and she was very tired. Worst of all, there was a quiet little pool off to one side of the stream and when she looked into it, a fat girl with disheveled blond braids, a dirty face, and dimples looked back at her. All that hunger and walking and crow-eating and she was just as heavy as ever! She hauled the water back and was going to ask if there was a place where she could sleep.

But Fifi started to heat the water, at which time they discovered the fire had gone out and the last of the kindling was gone. So Babette had to quickly take verbal instructions on how to chop wood without chopping off her feet or hands. Then she learned to build a fire, after filling the room with smoke. When the water was heated, Fifi started to load a basin with dishes, but missed and dropped the plates to the floor.

"Oh, dear," Fifi said. "And these few are the last ones I made before my eyesight went. I don't suppose you're a potter by any chance are you?"

"No," said Babette, yawning. "And I don't think I have time to learn before I completely fall asleep. Why don't I finish the washing up?"

Babette stayed with Fifi for seven days. Babette did all the fetching and carrying and cleaning under Fifi's direction. It was hard work, but the Fifi was good company, and Babette was fed regularly, even if it was only crow stew, and she was most grateful not to have to sleep by herself out in the freezing nighttime forest waiting to be gobbled. She never in all her royal life would have imagined it, but she actually was enjoying herself a little. It was nice having *one* person to talk to who wouldn't go right behind your back and start some nasty story about you and who couldn't see you and didn't care what you looked like.

Then one day, as she was peeling potatoes for the crow

stew, Fifi asked, "Tell me something, Barbara. Why you?"

"Excuse me?"

"Why did the wizard put the curse on you that you must wander around eating crows and doing all of these strenuous things?"

"Well, he wanted to marry me," Babette said. "And he *did* pass all the tests and things, but I just didn't *like* him and when I asked him questions the answers he gave made me feel—well, let's just say I didn't want to marry him, tests or no tests. So he left and then all at once everything I ate started making me bigger. And then he sent a message with one of his crows telling me *he* was the one making my food do that to me and if I would follow his instructions and pass *his* tests he'd reverse the curse."

Fifi's expression grew shrewd and calculating but her voice was light as she asked, "Do you think he will? I mean, is crow particularly unfattening or is it just that he wants you to eat it because it, of all birds, doesn't taste much like chicken and he wants to avenge himself on you?"

"That had crossed my mind," Babette admitted. "Almost as often as I crossed my own path while I was getting lost. The truth is, I don't know. But I had to try. I'll never get a husband looking this way and my parents and all the courtiers act like I've become invisible, because they don't want their disgust to show in their faces." She realized she shouldn't have said anything about the courtiers but Fifi didn't seem to notice.

"Disgust?" she asked instead. "Are you very ugly?"

"I don't *think* so," Babette said honestly. "Just very heavy and consequently, well, it's hard to tell because I meant to look like a peasant when I set out, but very—*ordinary*. Whereas before I was beautiful. It makes a big difference."

Before Fifi could comment, a voice called from the outside, "Mother, I'm home! Sorry it took so long. You must have had warm weather here, the wood seems to have lasted . . ." The voice broke off as a large, solid man blocked out the sunlight coming through the doorway. His face was in shadow.

"Burl! You're home! You *were* such a long time I thought you'd found yourself a nice girl out there, settled down, and would bring grandchildren with you when you came. No, the wood didn't last that long," she said. She had arisen and given the big man a hug, warmly returned, as he followed her inside the hut. "But my new friend Barbara here has been a big help."

"Much obliged, Mistress Barbara," Burl said, ducking his head so that she *still* couldn't see his face.

"Where's Hamlet?" Fifi asked.

"That's what took me so long, Mother. He got a gig and he thought it would be over with the first day, but then one disaster happened after another and he has to make it into an epic ballad and then he'll have to sing it throughout all the local districts. After all, someone might have spotted her."

"Spotted who?" Fifi asked.

"The missing princess. Of course, you don't know but— say, is that crow stew ready yet?"

"Barbara was just adding the potatoes. I imagine the bread should be coming out of the oven now, don't you think, Barbara?"

But before she could turn, Burl was pulling the loaf from the oven and putting it on the table to cool.

"What missing princess?" Fifi asked.

"Oh, well, it's a long story. But the royal house as this kingdom has known it is not in power at present."

"*What?*" Princess Babette asked.

"Yes, shocking isn't it?" Burl asked. "First the Princess

was said by the palace to have some kind of health problem and the next thing everybody heard, she had disappeared. The cook was found with one of her gowns and the King had the cook and one of the chambermaids who was supposedly an accomplice locked in the dungeon. They had some strange story of crows carrying poor Princess Babette away, I guess. The King and the Prince immediately got on their horses and went looking for her high and low but according to the lords who were with them, as they were crossing a particularly tricky bit of stream, all of a sudden thousands of crows flew out of nowhere and dived at the heads of the King and Prince. The Prince fell off his horse and would have been swept downstream and drowned but the King plunged in after him. They both went over a slight cataract. Their attendants were able to drag them out at the bottom but both were unconscious and have remained so. Meanwhile, the cook's replacement was not a very good one and the Queen is ill unto death with food poisoning."

"Oh, poor mother!" Babette cried. Then covered by saying, "My mother would never do anything wrong on purpose."

"Oh, that's *right!*" Fifi said. "Your name is Cook. So your mother is the palace cook who's in the dungeon? Oh dear."

"Yes, I must get back to the palace at once and see what can be done!" Babette said. "Oh, Fifi, you've been so kind. And I have no idea how I'm going to find my way back there but I just have to. Poor f—poor King and Prince too. And the whole government must be a shambles with everyone so ill."

"Oh, it is, Mistress Barbara," Burl said. "And the poor princess missing and no one in her family to organize the search either. If she is still alive, she must be beside herself."

"She was—is, I suppose she must be, I mean," Babette said.

"We can't let you go alone, child," Fifi said. To Burl she confided, "Barbara had been wandering in the woods for days when she found the hut. She needs help getting back to the palace so she can see about her mother."

"I'll just chop some more wood and haul some more water for you before we go, then I'll take her back, Mother."

"No, I think I'll go too. It sounds as if the capital is in turmoil right just now. I could do with a bit of excitement."

And so once they had filled themselves with more crow stew, the three of them set out through the forest. They didn't take any food, because Burl was a very good hunter and trapper and could always find more crows—the birds flew in circles around them, but never once approached Babette, which was fine with her.

They brought extra blankets and all slept close together, Babette feeling safer than she'd ever felt in her palace bed smelling the woody scent of Burl's skin and feeling the warmth his big body generated. His mother slept between them, very snug indeed with a substantial person on either side of her.

When they were within sight of the palace and the village, Babette had come to a decision. "You are the dearest friends I've ever had and good people," she said. "So I cannot lie to you. I am Princess Babette."

"Of course you are," Fifi said. "I knew it all along."

"You did?"

"Yes, and so did Burl. He's met you before."

Babette lowered her eyes and felt warm and fluttery all over. "He did? I can't believe I didn't remember."

"There were a great many folk about then, Your Majesty, and I couldn't get right up close."

"No, probably not, but you will now, and you too, Fifi. I will need your help getting into the palace so I can help my family, get Cook and Madeline out of the dungeon, and get the Kingdom back on an even keel again. But the guards will never recognize me."

Burl nodded. "You've changed a lot since I saw you last."

"I know," Babette said, remembering for a moment her misery at her lost girlish figure and all of the admiration she had likewise lost, especially from males. Knowing that Burl had seen both her before and her after self made her feel strangely awkward and sad. She didn't mind it so much with Fifi, but for Burl to think that she was less than she had been by being more than she had been embarrassed her.

"You're more like a real person now. You've got dimples and you laugh a lot and worry over people who've been hurt and you're—well, I don't know how to put it and maybe it was because of the stress you were under before but frankly, I left without—uh—doing what I came to do after I saw the princess—I mean you—ordering all those princes around and picking through their gifts and pouting. You don't seem like that princess. You're a much kinder person than she was."

Suspicion began to grow in Babette's mind. Burl was very well-spoken indeed for a humble woodcutter, and his features had a noble cast to them. He was, in fact, very handsome, in a rugged, honest sort of way. He looked just the way she thought a real man ought to look. But all of that had to be set aside while she convinced the guards to let her in to the palace.

"We're here to help you, my dear," Fifi said.

And they did too, more than Babette anticipated.

Help came from another unexpected and unintentional source as well.

When the three of them were near the palace gates, they were once more suddenly surrounded by crows.

"Look," Babette said, looking into each and every pair of

beady black eyes as if thinking to confront the wizard, "You birds tell your master he can do whatever he likes but his cure is worse than his curse, at least so far, and I have a family emergency here and a kingdom to run. Now scat before we cook you!" she said, flinging her hands up and scattering crows.

As she brought her hands back down again she saw that they were A.) clean, B.) bejeweled and C.) sleeved with white samite which matched the rest of the gown she now wore.

"What in the world?" she asked, groping at her long and perfectly coifed golden hair to find her royal circlet in place.

Fifi, no longer an ugly old woman, but a very lovely and stately silver-haired, well dressed lady of indeterminate age, fixed keen eyes (no longer blind) on the palace guards and asked, "What are you waiting for? Prince Beauregard Burlingame the 54th and I have come to see Her Royal Highness Princess Babette home to the sickbeds of her family. Please open the gates."

They did. Fairytales were supposed to have happened "Once Upon a Time" but that time was recent enough that even palace guards knew an honest-to-goodness fairy godmother when they saw one and they weren't about to risk her wrath. If she turned princes into toads, think what she would do to a common soldier for disobeying her? Besides, that *was* most certainly Princess Babette—at least, the most recent, chubby version of the princess. And she wasn't whining or pouting either, like they remembered. She might be large, but she was definitely in charge.

She was too. Cook and Madeline were released from the dungeons, whereupon Cook immediately whipped up, under Fifi's direction, some healing broths that she and Madeline helped the other servants administer to the ailing royals.

Meanwhile, Babette strode into the audience chamber just

in time to keep the ministers from surrendering to the neighboring kingdom of Heinzland threatening war. Further investigation by Burl, who questioned the messenger delivering the surrender terms, revealed that The Pasha (formerly Grand Vizier) Vladimirror of distant Goblestan had offered to trade lands he held to them in exchange for hegemony over Babette's father's kingdom if they would annex it for him. The Pasha had guaranteed that Babette's country could be taken without bloodshed, since Vladimirror had already won it with trickery.

Babette's mother recovered slowly, a bit day by day, but she wasn't up to ruling, and by the time Babette's father and brother were able to speak again, Babette had lowered the taxes, made sure the excess harvest was stored for the winter, distributed some of the land to the peasants who worked it, promoted Madeline to Lady-in-Waiting, seen to it that the dung-wagon driver was reimbursed for his lost cargo, and generally promoted peace and prosperity throughout her land with all possible dispatch. Occasionally she would turn to Burl for advice or to ask a question, but most of the time he was out training with the palace guard, just in case.

Upon hearing that her father and brother were awake, Babette hurried to their bedsides—they were both in her parents' chamber, which had become a Royal Sickroom.

She had hoped her father would be glad to see her. She hoped he would approve of what she had done, preventing a war and the loss of the kingdom and all, and she told him all about it.

Her mother spoke up first. "Yes, but I thought I heard that you had been lost and starving in the woods for days and that you have been working day and night since you returned. But you're not a bit thinner!"

"Mo*ther*," Babette said in something of her childhood

tones, "I *told* you I'm under a curse and I had to come home before I could effect the horrible cure proposed by that wizard who tried to take over our kingdom."

"Well, if you only had a bit of self-discipline I'm sure you could have—" her mother continued, but her voice trailed off as the King sat up.

"I suppose now you're here and have had a taste of ruling, you with your own sorceress and that hulking bodyguard of yours, you'll be wanting me to abdicate and name you as heir instead of your brother?"

"Hardly," she said, sighing. "I'm exhausted. I was just trying to keep the kingdom together for you until you get well, Daddy. You and Mother and Larry, who is welcome to the crown for all I'm concerned. I don't know what I'll do but I'm not about to hang around here waiting for suitors. Maybe I'll go tend lepers or something instead. I rather liked being needed when I thought Fifi was blind."

But just then Burl rushed in, and fell to one knee before her. "Barbara—I mean, Your Highness, Princess Babette, I know—" confused, he turned to the King and Queen and said earnestly, "I know I ran away before even attempting to take your tests. I was so ashamed I didn't go home, but got lost in the woods and took up woodcutting and adopted Fifi for my mother. But I love Barbara—I love you, Barbara."

"I love you too, Burl," she said. "But we were sort of in the middle of a family discussion."

"That's just it," he said. "I want to be your family—I want you to be MY family."

"You can't be proposing to her!" the Queen said. "Her wedding day will be a disaster. We'll never find enough silk in the world to make her a gown."

Fifi appeared. "That's no problem for a girl with a fairy godmother." Fifi tapped her foot. "*Which* I might add, she

105

can certainly use when her own mother has her priorities so out of order."

"Barbara, a messenger just came to tell me I've inherited my father's throne."

"You're a younger son, Burlingame," the King said. "I distinctly remember that. It's why you were placed at the end of the line of suitors to be tested."

"Well, my elder brother finally decided to run away with another prince he met while *he* was waiting in line for your daughter's hand, Sire," Burl replied. "And I am next in line for succession. So I have to leave. But I want you to come with me, Barbara."

Babette began to cry, with both weariness and happiness, "Oh, Burl, I love you with all my heart and being with you is the happiest place I can think of. Ever so much better than nursing lepers, though if you have any lepers in your kingdom, of course, I'd be happy to run a charity on their behalf. Is Fifi coming too? And Madeline?"

"Anyone you want," he said. "But we must be wed in a hurry."

"You must be mad!" the Queen scoffed. "Surely you want to wait until she's done her cure and had her curse removed!"

"Madame, my Barbara is a Princess fit for any King," Burl—King Burl actually—said formally.

"And in case you hadn't noticed," Fifi said, "the curse has ended."

"Nonsense," said Prince Larry. "Look at Babette! She's still round as a butterball."

He couldn't hurt Babette's feelings now though and she peeked out from under Burl's armpit and winked at her brother.

"But—by my sword, Mother, Father, look at her! The curse *is* lifted! She *is* beautiful!"

Her parents both looked at her and her mother gasped. "But how can that be?"

Fifi shrugged. "It's the same principle as the frog thing. A little genuine affection does a great deal to improve anyone and true love works miracles. So, Your Majesty, have you got a list?"

As it turned out, the wedding was somewhat delayed while King Burl and Princess Babette, chaperoned by Fifi La Fey and Madeline and their retainers, returned to Burl's kingdom for his father's funeral.

Meanwhile, throughout Babette's kingdom, the ladies of fashion who had watched their princess and her fiancé ride away said to each other, "Really, tell me honestly? I'm looking far too thin and pale, aren't I? Did you *see* Her Highness? Did you *see* how he looked at her? She was radiant! Such dimples! Such ample curves. Please pass the chocolates. I've ordered a dress to be made in the style of hers and I simply *must* fill it out in time for the wedding."

Boon Companion

Sassafras was but seven and a half weeks old when her mama finally died. Spring was cold and there were lots of other cats in the barn where Sass was born, which meant very little for a mama cat whose insides were not quite right anymore and an unripe kitten.

"Don't die, Mama. I been watchin' that Sally Cat and I think I can do what she does and hop us a mouse for supper. I will miss you, Mama."

Her mama had shushed her and pinned her down with a paw to wash her face one last time. "Mousin' will come soon enough, baby. But what you got to do is get yourself out of this barn. Barn cattin' ain't a good life for such as us. You know you had six brothers and sisters that perished before you and only you, with that little caul on your face, was born the right way. Did I mention that when I was born I had the same circumstance? And I have come to this barn late in my career, just long enough to deliver my younguns before I die too.

"But you, baby girl, you are a special one just like I was

108

and it's up to you to play fate like a mouse and make it feed you." She licked the long fur of Sassafras's calico face. Sassafras bore red and white patches and a black ear on the blue-eyed side, and black and white patches with a red ear on the green-eyed. The effect was lopsided but fetching, her mama had always said anyway. The other cats hissed her and told her she was ugly.

"Who is fate? Would she really feed me? I heard old Tom Fool say he was gonna kill me soon's you died."

"Don't give him the chance. I want you out of this barn right away. You have to go look for your true callin' and to do that you will need help. Town help. You have a pretty face and winnin' ways and if you're willin' to play the handy mouse-catcher for a time, you can stay alive in the home of some doting town-dweller while you look for your boon companion."

"I got a boon companion, Mama? Other than you?"

"Not yet but you will have one soon or you will likely die. I never have told you how I come to be so low as birthin' my kits in a barn, and I ain't got time to tell you all of it now, but it was through the loss of my own boon companion. One more thing I will say before I gasp my last, little gal, and that is look among the young and healthy for your own first. They tend to hold up better."

Sassafras's mama shushed her with another one of the lullabies she purred to her all the time, but after awhile she broke off and didn't say anything else. Sassafras licked her and tried to nurse but it didn't do any good. All the milk was gone, and so was the warmth, the strength, the protection and the tender care Mama had given the kitten for the whole of her short life.

Presently along came ol' Tom Fool who, seeing the situation for what it was, took a swipe at the orphaned kitten, missed and smacked her poor dead mama on the ear so hard his claws got stuck. That made Sassafras so mad the anger inside her swelled up as big as a house and blazed out of her eyes so it liked to fry Tom Fool.

He knew he was in trouble too, cause he dragged Sass's mama a little ways across the floor trying to loose his claws, and when he did, he ran away, just as Sass growled and pounced.

She nudged her mama back into her sleeping pose, and lay down beside her again, but she knew this was the end of her and the barn. Ol' Tom Fool or some other cat would be after her now that she had no mama to look after her. So when all the other cats were sleepin' in the hay, Sassafras picked herself up and took herself out of the barn and onto the long bumpy dirt road leading off the property to another long road that led to town. It was a far piece and a cold journey for a little bitty kit, but fortunately Sassafras was a longhair, and she would curl up tight in the crook of a tree limb and take her a little nap when she was tired.

One time (because during that period she didn't count by days and nights but by waking and sleeping spells) after she woke up, she heard a lot of noise and felt the sun on the parts of her not shaded by the tree limbs.

Looking down from her perch, she saw she was outside a building and there were a lot of human kittens playing in the yard. These were young and strong, just like her mama had said for her to get, but they could also be mean and cruel, as she knew from Tom Fool's story of how he came to lose his tail to deceitful boys with tin cans and fire crackers.

She watched those children all day long, studying them to see if one of them might be her boon companion.

One little gal sat off by herself reading and Sass was drawn to her. She jumped down from the tree limb and sat in the corner of the schoolroom window, under the branch of a bush growing up against the building. She watched that little girl read. And cough. She coughed over and over, her mouth funneling into her hand, her eyes tearing up. With her common sense as well as her second sight, Sassafras figured that while this child might be young, she was not strong. More than likely she'd be gone before spring came again.

None of the others looked just right. The teacher looked nice but her gown was flecked with many colors of cat fur. Sass reckoned others had a claim on teacher before her.

While the children were in class Sassafras hunted the playground looking for a drop of spilled milk, a little bite of something to tide her body over. Not much was left behind by the hungry youngsters but she did find a dropped bite of chicken sandwich and gobbled it up.

School let out and as the children passed by her bush Sassafras stared hard at each one. This one cared more for dogs, that one was allergic to cats, another one liked cats but except for that didn't have a brain in her poor little head.

Sassafras followed after them at a safe distance. It got darker and colder and pretty soon she was going to have to find another place to nap. But what she really needed the most was some more food. That previous morsel had filled up her little belly good at the time, but it was long gone now.

As she padded along the one rutty windy road, something kept trying to lure her off it, out into the fields again, but she didn't give it any heed. She'd go hunting later on for a mouse small enough she could hop it without too much fear of bodily harm. Right now she needed to make tracks.

When it began to snow, she sat down on her haunches, curled her tail around her, and looked up at the whiteness coming down from the skies. It was pretty. It was cold. She said, "mew," in a complaining kind of way, just to let that fate gal know that she did not like the way this was going so far.

The town was a long way off. Or so she thought, until after awhile when she came to a crossroads. There were no signs and if there had been, she couldn't have read them.

Since it didn't much matter which way she went, she closed her eyes, ran round widdershins following her own tail as fast as she could go and as many times as she could before she got almost too dizzy to stand, then she staggered off in the nearest direction.

She opened her eyes and stared up at the bottom of the grill of a great big old truck about to run right over her. Before she could run, the truck squealed like a rabbit and stopped and a gal in great big galoshes and a heavy coat jumped out.

One hand smelling like soap cupped Sassafras's entire body while another hand slid under her tail and back paws and scooped her up so she was looking straight into freckles and a pair of thick spectacles. "Little kitty, you almost made catsup," the gal said. "What you doin' out here in the middle of the road in the middle of the winter anyway? You got no home, have you? Well, you do now." And with no more ceremony than that, the gal lowered Sassafras into one of the big pockets in the front of the wool coat and they got back in the truck.

As soon as Sass got herself turned around, she crawled up to the top of the pocket and looked around. The landscape whizzed by at a speed faster than she could run and she mewed in dismay at such a thing.

The gal lowered one finger and stroked Sass between the ears. "Hush up, little kitty, Sophy's gonna take care of you now. Nothin' gonna get you with Sophy here. We'll take you home and show you to Mama. She'll be glad to see somethin' as little and pretty as you. She doesn't get to see much these days."

That was because Sophy's mama was not long for the world. She was dying and that was a fact. Had there been any question in anyone's mind at all that Sassafras was coming to stay at the farmhouse with Sophy, Sass put paid to it by making herself indispensable. She took turns comforting Sophy's mama, purring her to sleep, then comforting Sophy while she rested from her labor of running the farm and taking care of her mama.

Sassafras plumb exhausted her own small self just helping out. When the day came that Sophy's mama finally passed and it was time to bury her, Sass guarded the house while Sophy went with the other relatives to the graveyard.

It was a good thing too. The house needed guarding. Before Sophy had returned from her mama's grave, there was a loud-mouthed skinny woman with stiff looking yellow head fur and a thin sour mouth tapping on the door and peering through the windows, then poking around outside. Pretty soon she was joined by a heavyset gal with eyebrows that looked like they'd been drawn on her face with one claw.

Sass just looked at them, then the heavyset one pulled a key out of her purse and unlocked the door and walked in, bold as brass. "I know Melinda kept it around here somewhere," she said. "I always admired it even when we was small and she told me long time ago I could have it when she died. That was way back before she saddled herself with that horse of a girl."

"Well, she took the punch bowl and serving set our Granny meant to leave to me and I mean to have that back too. And Sonny is bringing the truck later for Aunt Thea's sideboard and brass bed." But the woman didn't seem to be looking for the things she was talking about. Sass saw her pawing through the books on the shelves, especially the cookbooks up above the stove. While her back was turned, Sass skittered away down the hall. Behind her she heard the sound of doors and cabinets opening and slamming shut again.

"While he's at it maybe he'll load up that television and home entertainment center Melinda got last year. She barely used it and I offered to buy it from her when she got sick but she said I could just have it later. That girl won't need it when she goes back to the orphanage. No sense in it goin' to waste."

"No indeed. And Melinda borrowed a recipe book from my Aunt Ally before the dear old soul died. I want it back for sentimental reasons."

Sass hid behind Sophy's mama's pillow and closed her eyes tight, trying to make herself invisible as the two horrible women rummaged through the house. In her mind's eye Sass saw them picking up bits and pieces wherever they went, figurines, knickknacks, a set of knives, whatever they could stuff into their pockets and purses.

They were just still poking around when Sophy came home, her eyes all red and her shoulders sagging. Both of them made for the door like they were just going when Sophy came in.

"Hello, Sylvie," one of them said and Sassafras could tell the old gal knew Sophy's real name but was callin' her the wrong one out of contrariness, like she wasn't important enough to take notice of what she was called. "We just came to check the refrigerator to see what you might be needing. I know people will probably be bringing by cakes and casseroles and you can't possibly eat all of that by yourself. We'll be glad to take any of it off your hands so you don't have to get fat or risk offendin' people by lettin' their baked goods spoil," said the woman. Her shoes, in spite of the winter weather, were skinny little sandals on long narrow feet white as plucked chickens with blue veins standing out on them.

"Speakin' of which," said the other one, whose puffy feet spilled out over the tops of new black patent plastic pumps, "your mama borrowed an old recipe book offa me and I want it back. You seen it? It's got a red and white checked oilcloth cover."

Sophy shook her head and, trembling with anger, waited silently while they left, their purses and pockets clanking with things they'd stolen.

Sophy slammed the door behind them and plopped herself down at the kitchen table with her head resting on her clenched fists. Sass jumped up beside her on the table, glad the old biddies hadn't managed to cart it off yet. She inserted herself in the crook of Sophy's elbow and mewed inquiringly.

"Poor little kitty, you probably haven't had a bite to eat or a drop to drink this live long day and for that matter, I haven't either for all their going on about casseroles. If I was to take any casseroles to those two, I'd lace 'em with rat p'ison first."

Once Sophy fixed Sass some supper, the girl looked inclined to sit and cry again. Sass felt it was her bound duty to do something cute and bewitching that would keep her gal from foggin' up her glasses again. So, selflessly taking no heed of her own hunger, the kitten leaped over to the kitchen counter and stretched up to the cup rack where she tapped a tiny paw on Sophy's favorite mug. The one with the cat on it. Then Sassafras walked over to sit beside the tea kettle on the stove-top and wait for Sophy to get the idea. It only took three repeats, but Sass was patient and considerate of her new friend's fragile emotional state. When the girl didn't pay her any mind after the third try, Sass jumped back onto the table and gently, patiently, and considerately sank a single claw into the hand Sophy was using to crumple the Kleenex to her nose.

Sophy screeched, batted half a foot from where Sass had

been, and dabbed at her hand with the end of the Kleenex. Sass, now that she had Sophy's attention, went through her routine again, tapping the mug and sitting by the teapot again.

"Bossy little thing, aren't you?" Sophy asked with a sniff. "I had no idea kittens drank tea." But filled the kettle and put it back on the stove, stuck a teabag that had only been used once before into her cup, and calmed down some.

Sassafras relaxed and sprawled across the kitchen table while Sophy drank. This was no time for her friend to be backsliding just when she had been making so much progress. Already Sass had taught Sophy to produce food, open doors, stroke and groom on request. Not command. Sassafras didn't like being pushed around and she didn't reckon anybody else did either. Besides, Sophy could do all this with just little hints and nudges, unless the poor girl was terribly preoccupied. Then, Sassafras had to allow that it took a little stronger language and a slightly louder voice to produce results. Generally speaking, though, the girl was intelligent and cooperative, mostly biddable, and predisposed to be kind. But those two old hissycats who had come to steal and pry had none of those good qualities. Why, and would drive an orphaned girl and an orphaned kitten from their home and laugh about it afterward.

It was pure and simple up to Sass to help Sophy save their home from those sneak thieves or they'd be out on their ears before the sun set again.

The kitten was studying on the matter when there was a loud commotion at the door, like someone was about to pound it in. Sophy blew her nose and went to see who it was.

A massive sullen puppy of a boy stood in the doorway. His boots were black and muddy and smelled like the blood of slaughtered animals.

"What do you want here, Willie Pewterball?" Sophy asked. Sass could tell by the girl's tone she didn't like him.

"Come for that brass bed and sideboard my mama wants—and the TV and stereo too. You can help me load 'em in the truck."

"I'll do no such thing. Those are mine. My mama left 'em to me."

"That's not what *my* mama says. She sent me to get 'em and I'm gonna get 'em. If you don't want to help, get out of my way," he said, and knocked Sophy aside when she tried to bar his entry. Sass attacked his ankles and he kicked her away.

Sophy, who was half knocked to the linoleum herself, reached down to pet Sass and make sure she was all right.

Sass felt a little jolt, like someone had rubbed her fur the wrong way on a cold dry day and made sparks jump from it. Suddenly she was Sophy and Sophy was her and what they felt and who they were was the same. They were linked. This was the kind of thing Sass's mama had been talking about. What was in Sophy made what was in Sassafras bigger than ever it could have been had the kitten been on her own. And if the kitten had already been in a huge snit, it was nothing compared to the bottled up store of anger and grief that poured into her from Sophy. It was as intense and painful as the fit that came over Sass at Tom Fool when he hurt her poor dead mama's ear. Outrage and anger flooded from the girl into the cat, who had far fewer scruples about directing it back where it belonged. She growled at the boy.

"You keep that damn cat off me or I'll kill it," Willie said, but then he made the mistake of looking down at Sassafras.

He didn't have to look near as far as he thought he would. As it had with old Tom Fool, Sass's rage had made her as big as it was, and bigger, because she had Sophy's anger too.

Sass's back was up, her ears were flat, her fur was all bristly and her tail like a many-barbed whip of righteousness lashing behind her. She hissed, and spat through fangs like the blades of pocket knives and lashed out at him with claws that looked five inches long to Willie.

He turned tail and lit out like his britches were on fire. "You're gonna get it!" He yelled back to Sophy. "You're not allowed to keep wild animals in the house!"

He jumped in his truck and roared away and Sophy, puzzled, looked down at Sass, who sat grooming her neat small self, licking the last few tufts of fur on her white right paw back into place.

"He's on drugs," Sophy said, fists on hips. "Has to be. Nothing else explains it. Somehow or other, even though he kicked you, you scared the pee-waddin' out of him and I say good riddance to bad rubbish." Then the air went out of her and she scooped Sass up and rubbed the kitten's side against her cheek. "But oh, Sassafras, what are we going to do if he comes back with help? Other folks aren't gonna be scart of a little pussycat like that fool. Shoot, he's likely to come back with the sheriff and try to arrest me for keepin' a dangerous animal."

Sass yeowed once and then reflected that both of them carrying on didn't do much good, so she started to purr a little song her mama used to purr to her. She purred the melody into Sophy's ear and beat time with her little tail, which was now a good four inches long, on the back of Sophy's neck.

> *Hush little baby don't you cry*
> *You'll have your own place by and by*
> *Mice in the walls and moles in the lawn*
> *Feed my kit when Mama's gone on*

Sophy sat down and went back to her tea and stared into the cup. Sass kept on purring and pretty soon, Sophy began to run her finger around the top of the cup as she hummed. She wet the end of her finger and her cup made a whirring, chiming noise. Sass didn't like it at first, but it grew on her. It was part of the magic they were going to make between them to take care of their troubles.

They had to make them some protection. "Wards." The word came into her mind and she knew right away that's what they needed. It wasn't like it was just a human kind of idea. Cats did it all the time when they marked their territory. They needed something to mark this house and all the things in it and all the property around it.

Sass jumped down and began racing around rubbing her face at things and wondering why there were no tomcats around when you needed them. They had that handy tail-shaking thing they did that would be just the thing in this situation. Sass stopped rubbing and looked up at Sophy. Sophy looked back at her. Didn't people have anything to ward off intruders? Surely they didn't expect their cats to do everything by themselves.

Sophy screwed up her face and said, "You know, kittycat, you've got a point there. What we need is something to keep people away from our property without knowing why they're doing it. Nothing you or I can say or do is going to make them go away if they know it's us doing it, but if they just DID it. I don't know anything about that stuff, but Old Miss Ally did, and she was a friend of my Mama's. That old biddy niece of hers was awfully keen on havin' her recipe book and I know my Mama got it from Miss Ally before she died but I'm durned if I recall what she did with it."

Sass, who had been wound tighter than a fiddle string, collapsed with relief and began grooming herself. The girl was coming along real well.

Sophy hunted high and low for the book but at last she found it under her mama's mattress, between the ticking and the box springs. The idea came to Sass that if she hadn't been making herself invisible when the awful niece was in the house, the woman would have found the book.

Hugging it to herself, Sophy sat back down at the kitchen table while the kettle boiled again. Sass hopped back up to see what was in there.

"Hmmm," she said. "I was right, Sass. This is no book to make biscuits from. This is Miss Ally's witchin' book."

Sophy said, and stroked her, nose to tail tip, "You know, Miss Ally had her a cat too. She was so worried about her. Asked my Mama not to let her cat nor her recipe book go to that niece of hers. Mama was fixin' to bring the cat over here when Miss Ally died and we couldn't find hide nor hair of that cat. Then Mama got sick before we could look any more.

"Too bad Miss Ally died before Mama or she might have been able to save her. She was wonderful with cures, Miss Ally was. Miss Ally was a witch, of course, but Mama didn't hold with witchin' so she always said Ally was a 'nature doctor.' But she was more what folks here call a white witch because she didn't do any harm. And whatever Mama liked to think, Miss Ally had cures for more than just bodily diseases and injuries.

"She knew how to mend a broken heart or incline love in someone's direction—the girls in school talked about goin' to see her for such things. I reckon all that is in the recipe book."

Sass yawned and put her chin down on her paws. She took a nap while Sophy hunted around the house for things needed for a protection spell.

Sophy was pleased and that pleased Sass. Kittens needed a lot more sleep than she'd been getting lately, and she dozed off again while Sophy chanted happily to herself, "Iron filings—got them and some rusty nails, mountain ash berries from right out in the yard, three times three yards of red thread—why don't they just say nine?" she asked Sass and scratched her behind the ears. Sass yawned and curled her small pink tongue out from between her teeth, then blinked sleepily and rearranged herself into her compact napping posture.

Sophy continued. "Will you listen to this, Miss Sassafras? It says here we need to draw this picture of an eye here on a brown egg shell and break the egg on our doorstep. I reckon that way if someone comes that shouldn't, they'll slip on the egg and fall and break their necks. What do you think?"

Sass thought that sounded a little silly and wondered how it was supposed to do anything. It seemed to her something was missing from all this but she could hardly be expected to figure it out, young as she was, and without her sleep.

After a time during which something tangy and herbal boiled on the stove, Sophy scooped her up again, along with a sugar shaker full of stuff and the egg with the eye drawn on it, and carried her outdoors. It was growing dark later now and Sass realized with surprise that she had been here more of her life than she had been in the barn with Mama. She woke up and wriggled out of Sophy's grasp to climb up on her shoulder and watch what she did. Sophy walked around the house three times sprinkling a sugar shaker full of the herby smelling stuff and broke the egg on the doorstep. She said some words too but they didn't make much sense to Sass.

They both felt vaguely uneasy as Sophy carried her back inside the house, picked up the recipe book and tied it in a plastic bag from the grocery store.

"I thought of the best place to hide this when we're not here, Sass. I'm gonna put it in the bottom of your pan and sprinkle litter over it so don't scratch none too hard, okay? It's got oilcloth on the cover so the top and bottom will be all right."

Sass watched while Sophy did this and then went to her box and dampened the litter to add a little touch of realism to the scheme. Then she jumped up on the bed and stretched out diagonally across the middle of the bed. A few minutes later Sophy picked her up, and laid her back down against the curl of her own body.

A stinging sensation in her nose woke Sass sometime later. She opened her eyes and they began to water. The room was dark and fuzzy looking. Smoke.

Sass mewed and when Sophy didn't wake up that very minute, so she hooked her hard on the hand for the good of them both and jumped down before Sophy's reaction sent a wrathful hand to bat a cat off the bed.

Sophy opened her eyes, sniffed and cried, "Lord have mercy, what now?" She shoved her feet into her fleece lined moccasins and staggered after Sass, who was near the door already.

The old outhouse was in flames. Before Sophy could unroll the garden hose and turn on the outside faucet, the smell was way worse than smoke. Sassafras retreated as far as she could while still keeping an eye on Sophy. She didn't want to return to the house where all the smoke was trapped inside either, so she ran up the road a ways thinking she might hop a mouse while Sophy put out the fire. That's when she saw Luly Pewterball's boy's truck. Good thing she *hadn't* returned to the house. That boy was not kind to small animals.

Still, she thought she had better warn Sophy. She sprinted back down the road to where Sophy was standing away from the soaked and smoldering ruins of the outhouse.

"You suppose somebody'd been smokin' in there,

kittycat?" Sophy asked, and headed back for the house, but Sass meowed and meowed and snatched at her legs and ran away from the house and snatched again. The girl didn't have the sense God gave a goose though and went right in, even though the front door was still standing wide open.

Luly Pewterball and her boy came out of the bedroom as Sophy walked in.

"*You* set that fire!" Sophy said.

"What if we did?" the boy asked belligerently. He paused to cough. The smoke was still thick in the house.

But Luly's mean little eyes narrowed up and she said, "No such thing (*cough, cough*). We saw the smoke and come to see if you were safe."

"You did (*cough*) not!" Sophy exclaimed hotly.

"That's right," the boy said, and moved menacingly toward her. "We (*cough*) did. Cause we figured if you were (*cough*) safe, we'd (*cough*) change that. Now, my mama really wants her (*cough, cough, cough*) inheritance and we can't (*cough*) find it (*cough*) anyway. Where'd you (*cough*) put it?"

"You better not (*cough*) hurt me," Sophy said. "I told people about you (*cough*) comin' here. I could have (*cough*) you charged with assault."

The boy had spotted Sass, and said, still coughing between all his words, "There's no law in this state against killin' feral cats though. That one fooled me once, but I see she ain't so big now. Maybe I should open her up and see how she did that."

"Don't you touch her!" Sophy screamed and tried to catch Sass to put her out the door but only succeeded in blocking the exit. Sass scrabbled on the linoleum for a half a second before rocketing in under the bed, then cursed herself for a fool. Now she was cornered.

Soon she was backed against the wall with a big ugly face

looking down at her on two sides. She heard Sophy's steps and saw her feet edging toward the bedroom window. Bless her, she was going to open it and try to let Sass escape.

A long arm lashed out while Sass was watching Sophy and pulled the kitten's tail. It was a short tail though and the grasp was only a couple of fingers so Sass got it back and huddled closer to the wall. Then the bed started to move.

"Let her alone! We haven't done anything to you. Leave us be!" Sophy hollered, the effort costing her a whole long string of hard hacking coughs.

"Give me my book and we'll go," Luly told her.

Sass could hear Sophy's thoughts. She was about to break and give it to them. But Sass knew that wouldn't do any good. Luly would try to use the book then to get all of the rest that rightly belonged to Sophy, and maybe do them both harm and a good many other folks as well. She was mean. And even if Sophy did give them the book, that boy was even meaner than his mama and he was bound and determined to kill him a pussycat.

Oh, they needed help and they needed it bad. Sass heard a cat crying and realized it was herself, bawling for her mama over and over again. Then she heard her mama's singing again in the back of her mind, the song Mama always sang when she returned to the nest when she heard Sassafras howling from fear and worry.

> *Hush, little kitten, don't you yelp*
> *Mama's come a-runnin' here to help.*
> *Moles in the yard and mice in the barn*
> *Mama's gonna keep her babe from harm*

A pudgy ringed hand side-swiped Sass and then closed around the kitten's leg.

But just then they all became aware that a siren had been blaring outside because suddenly it cut off and there was a banging on the front door, then it slammed open. "Where's the fire?" a masculine voice yelled.

"Here!" Sophy called. "In here!"

Three young men in heavy boots stormed into the room. They started coughing too, as soon as they came in.

Luly let go of Sass's foot and both she and her boy stood up. "We'll just be (*cough*) going now, Sophy, but you give us a call when you find that thing we were discussin'," Luly said, as if the visit had been a friendly one.

"It's nothin', boys," Willie laughed loudly to cover up what Sophy was trying to tell the firemen. "You know how hysterical these old maids get about burnin' outhouses and cats in trees."

The Pewterballs skedaddled out of there quicker than the outhouse had gone up in flames.

Sophy was telling the volunteer firemen, two of whom were father and son, the son being a high school classmate of Sophy's, what had happened.

Sophy began talking excitedly, trying to tell them what the horrible Pewterballs had done, but she was coughing so hard in between her words that the men, who were coughing too hard to be able to listen carefully, didn't pay much attention to her. The excitement was all over, the fire was out, and the house was still full of nasty-smelling smoke. They were in quite a hurry to get out of there. Her classmate's daddy offered to take Sophy over to their house for the night but Sophy said she didn't want to leave her kitten alone and the daddy said that they had a big old dog who would take exception to a cat. So they left, the daddy giving Sophy his telephone number.

Sass crawled out from under the bed.

Sophy sat up the rest of the night in her mama's rocker and Sass curled in her lap and slept a fear-exhausted sleep. The house still stank from the fire but Sass was too played out to care.

Later in the day, when Sophy had cleared the house with electric fans and nice smelling candles as best she could, the girl told Sass, "I should just get rid of that book, kittycat. It doesn't work anyway. I did that protection spell just like it said in there and it didn't do a darn bit of good. And if those firemen were what it brought, all I can say is that it took its time gettin' them here."

Sass jumped down and went to her box to scratch. Sophy laughed, "I know you don't think much of it either but Miss Ally set too much store by it for you to be poopin' on it." She plucked the book from the box and shook the cat litter off it while Sass did her duty.

When Sass returned, Sophy was sitting at the table with the book open, staring at it. "You know, there's something peculiar about this book if it is the spellin' book Miss Ally used for her white witchin'. There's plenty of recipes, like it says, with funny ingredients in them and they all sound magical enough but it doesn't seem right somehow. I thought witchin' had more to it than that. Aren't there spells or somethin' you have to say?"

Sass stepped onto the open book and lay down. Right away she knew the book *was* magic because she could feel all the magical words soaking into her right through her belly, filling her full of spells and sorcery. She felt something else too. She felt something of her own dear mama about this book and it confirmed what she had been reckoning ever since Sophy told her about Miss Ally's cat disappearing. Miss Ally had been mama's boon companion and this was *her* book. And now it was theirs, hers and Sophy's. She stood up and put a paw on Sophy's hunched over shoulder and licked her cheek, backed up, sat down on the book and mewed in a humorous tone. What was missing from the recipes was right under Sophy's nose and right behind Sass's own! It was herself. And as for the spells—her mama loved her and would not have left her all alone in the world without teaching her the magic words she needed to follow her career of controlling world events to suit herself. All those little purred nursery rhymes and lullabies *were* the magic words.

The book was only to give people like Miss Ally and Sophy a list to look at so that they could do the tedious gathering of items a cat couldn't easily describe or tell them where to locate without learning human language.

Excited by her new insight, Sass leaped back and forth from the kitchen counter to the table and batted at the remnants of the ingredients Sophy had used in the useless warding spell of the previous day. *Now* they could make it work.

Sophy looked at her sadly. "You poor little thing. Did all that smoke addle your brains? You act like you belong in the county asylum."

But while Sophy was young and much burdened with cares beyond her years, she was not stupid. She followed Sass's directions and began putting together the same ingredients as the night before. Only this time, there was a difference. Instead of keeping her mama's song to herself, Sassafras sat on Sophy's shoulder as she mixed, grated, pounded, boiled and stewed the fixin's for the ward spell. And while Sophy did all the manual labor requiring the use of thumbs and fingers, Sass purred her the protection spell Mama had taught her, the one that had come into her head when Sophy mixed up the potion before.

Hush little baby don't you cry
You'll have your own place by and by
Mice in the walls and moles in the lawn
Feed my kit when Mama's gone on

But that, Sass remembered as she sang to Sophy, was just the first verse.

The second was:

Hush, little children, don't be afraid
Wait till you see what mama's made
Sprinkle all around like tomcat pee
Keep our house safe as safe can be

But then she remembered a more crucial verse, one that called for an ingredient only she could provide. It came into her head just as Sophy was about to blend all the fixin's together.

Sass hopped down, went over to the doorjamb and stretched herself up as high as she would go, almost a whole entire foot, and scratched her little claws for all they were worth, till some of the casings came away with the wood splinters.

Then she mewed for Sophy to come pick them up.

Sophy had come to know that mew and learn that it meant she needed to pay right smart attention to what was being told her.

She gathered up claws and splinters and all in the dustpan and, with a look at Sass, dumped them into the brew.

Sass sang her the last verse, purring triumphantly.

Hush, my kit, don't flap your jaw
Put you in just a little claw
Gives your ward-juice mighty paws

To smack them breakin' mama's laws

They worked all day long brewing up a huge batch of the magic mixture until Sophy's arms ached and Sass's purrer was worn to a frazzle.

But then it was time to sprinkle it. This time they had enough to circle the house, the drive where Sophy's truck was parked, the hen house and the barn even though it didn't have nary a horse or cow anymore, and the biggest trees. Sophy sprinkled the mixture onto the snow and Sass purred her spells as they circled the property, widdershins, counterclockwise, singing the spell through three times three times seven.

For a long time, they were left in peace and the Pewterballs didn't come near enough for Sophy to know of it or be troubled by it.

Sass grew in length, strength, and beauty and she and Sophy were soon able to talk to each other right clearly with no words passing anybody's lips. She and Sophy practiced lots of the spells, as much as they could by themselves. Sophy carried potion with her whenever she left the house and farmyard and Sass was careful never to hunt outside the charmed circle. One day, Sophy took the recipe book to the town library and used the copy machine to make another book, which she put with her school things.

Then spring came, and as Sass shed much of her heavy long coat, so the farmyard shed the snow, which melted, running away in little rivulets from the charmed circle.

Back came Luly Pewterball and her awful offspring, one sunny day while Sophy was at school.

Sassafras recalled the burping, gasping noise of Willie Pewterball's truck and ran for cover when she heard it.

She hid under the sofa, up inside the frame where she had

pulled loose the stuffing to make herself a cozy nest.

They weren't likely to find her there, she thought.

"Well, I'll be if this ain't our lucky day, Willie!" Luly cried. "There's my very book lyin' open there on the table where that careless girl must have left it! She doesn't deserve such a treasure."

"Then take it and let's go, Mama. This place gives me the creeps."

"It's not like you to be so timid, Willie."

"No ma'am, but let's leave all the same."

When Sophy came home and found the book gone, Sass told her what had happened and she called the sheriff. Of course the Pewterballs lied about it.

But that was all right, because Sophy had her copy and right away between them they whomped up a spell to get the book back.

> *Hush, little children, don't you yearn*
> *Bad folks got them a lot to learn*
> *Their luck will sour and their guts will burn*
> *Till what's yours is safe returned*

That spell was not purred like the others but transmitted in a low, threatening growl. Sassafras enjoyed singing it a lot.

Once it was made, all they had to do was wait. Normally, you had to put a potion or something within range of the people that needed spellin', but in this case the recipe said, the thing that had been stolen provided the contact.

Sass made up her own verse now, which showed she was getting bigger and better at this.

> *Luly and Willie, time to weep*
> *You won't rest and you won't sleep*

You won't drink and you won't eat
While our spell book's in your keep

On the third day after the theft, Sophy found the recipe book in her mailbox with a note from Luly attached.

"Keep it. The damn thing doesn't work anyway."

Sophy giggled as she showed it to Sass but Sass just washed her tail and smiled to herself. Of course the spell book wouldn't work without a cat to sing the words. And as mean as Willy was to animals, he was about as likely to turn into a horny toad as he was to get any cat to do charms for him and his horrible mama.

The Pewterballs picked up and left town after that and nobody heard from them again except the skinny gal who had come with Luly on the first day. She was nicer now and taking her medicine real regular these days. She came by to return what she had stolen from Sophy's house and to tell her that she had received a letter from Willie, wanting cigarette money, since the prison guards wouldn't give him any without him buying them.

Sassafras winked at Sophy and Sophy winked at Sass, but neither one of them let on about what they knew.

Long Time Coming Home

They fought all the way to the Vietnam Memorial, which wasn't surprising since they'd been fighting about one thing and another for the last thirty years. Their fights weren't noisy, they were the low, nasty kind, full of sharp hisses and angry looks like poison darts. It hadn't always been that way. You'd think after all those years and raising three kids everything would have been ironed out by now, smooth and sweet as one of the well blended milkshakes they used to share at the soda fountain before Woody got drafted. Sometimes it was almost like that for them, but always there was a distance, however slight, like the edge of a sock caught in a drawer that kept it from closing. In the Johansons' marriage, the thing between them wasn't a sock. It was a ghost.

Had Woody Johanson never gone to Vietnam, or been in the firefight which killed his buddy, Nick Amato, maybe Woody and his high school sweetheart, Becky would have been happy. But Nam was always there, like the scar Johanson carried as a permanent souvenir from the firefight that got him a three-day R&R at a field hospital. The scar was a tangible reminder, as was Amato's lighter, the deluxe metal Zippo with the 1st Cav insignia, Johanson had borrowed just before all hell broke loose. The lighter had been in his pocket when Amato hit a trip wire at the beginning of the firefight.

The last tactile physical sensation Amato remembered was the intense, searing pain as he was blown to pieces that sank into the monsoon muck of the forest floor without a trace. The pain had lasted only a moment, and then what he supposed he would call his spirit—the core of himself anyway—was free. But he didn't want to be free to wander Vietnam forever. He wanted to stay himself, stay with his friends, and go home to the States. The only thing left of him and his was the lighter Johanson carried. No sooner had the idea of attaching himself to the lighter and to Johanson occurred to him than it was done.

Maybe it had been made easier because Johanson got hit too and was out of it long enough for Amato to join him. Johanson's wound wasn't mortal, but it was bad enough to get him a free helicopter ride to the nearest hospital. It didn't take much from an AK-47. Like the rounds in the M-16's, the bullets tumbled once they hit something, smashing more flesh and destroying more tissue as they went, so there was no such thing as a clean wound.

Johanson's wound gave Amato the weirdest sensation. He was aware that the body he was in hurt, but his friend's pain couldn't touch him.

However, poor old Woody was spouting blood like a fountain and too out of it to do anything about it. Amato knew then that if he couldn't do something to help, he would be out of body a second time—this time with the company of his friend, who from everything he'd told Nick, had a lot to live for.

Unlike Nick, Woody Johanson had a home to return to,

parents who had been together his whole life, a piece of land to inherit, a high school sweetheart waiting for him. He was a calm, stable sort of guy, no drugs, no booze, faithful to his girl from what he said. He even blamed Nick for starting him smoking, and said he should get to keep the flashy lighter Nick had bought himself at the PX for his birthday. Woody said he deserved some compensation for the money he was going to end up spending on smokes because of Nick's bad influence. It was a joke between them. Woody was stubborn as hell and hung onto the lighter until Nick snuck it away from him again, then borrowed it back and the same thing happened all over again. But he was a square in the best sense of the word, a squared away guy who knew who he was and where he was going. Nick, on the other hand, had considered himself something of a free spirit even before he literally became one.

His mother was dead, his dad, a musician, reborn as a melancholy alcoholic who disappeared when Nick turned fourteen, leaving his son on his own. His mom's relatives lived out of state, and his dad's were all dead but Nick didn't want to go into a foster home so he got by, staying with the family of one school friend after another, making up stories and elaborate schemes to cover for his dad's absence while he finished high school. Maybe his friends' folks knew all along that he was lying, but they went along with it. Most of them had big families anyway, and he made himself useful and got part time jobs to help out. He was half Italian, by nature quick to get upset over stuff and just as quick to calm down, and pretty smart, and he went out of his way to fit in, to make nice, to be agreeable. He didn't want them regretting that they helped him. And if every once in awhile one of them patted his cheek or ruffled his hair or called him by a pet name like his folks used to do before his mom died, that made him want to try harder. The last family he lived with was pretty upset with him when he joined the Army. They said he'd get killed and they'd never see him again. But he was old enough to be on his own and he wanted to travel and he wanted to go to college some day too and get to be somebody who knew about the interesting things he saw when he visited museums and galleries, the things he read about in books. He figured all he had to do was make it through Nam alive and he could get a free education. Meanwhile, he'd see what the world was like outside of New York City. He'd meet different people.

And he did. Like Woody. He admired Woody's cool, and Woody was impressed by his edgier, let's-see-what-happens approach to life.

Dying together was not what they had in mind when they became buddies. And dying twice in one day was not the kind of unique experience Amato favored. He reached automatically to staunch the flow of blood from Woody's arm. To Nick's relief and surprise, when *he* reached, *Woody's* arm moved and Woody's hand applied the necessary pressure till the area was secured, the medevac chopper landed, and the medics applied the pressure dressing. That was when Nick realized that by attaching himself to the lighter Woody carried, he could, at least temporarily , take charge of parts of Woody's body.

So Amato stopped the bleeding, but the damned thing still got infected, as they learned once Johanson was bunked down at the hospital, safe except for the swollen red arm and a raging fever.

Nick surfaced in time to see a girl—not a Vietnamese girl but an American with red pigtails and big round hazel eyes— bending over him.

"Geez," he said. "Dying ain't so bad. You're one of the angels right?"

She smiled at him, "Cool it, GI, you are way too hot as it is. Besides, you think I haven't heard that line before?"

"I bet you hear it all the time," he said. He noticed the olive drab fatigues then, and the lieutenant's bars. Her voice was low-pitched and soft when she talked to him. She smelled like perfume—not a lot, maybe some just left over on her skin after a night out and a morning shower. A hint of vanilla and gardenias. Her nametag said "Ryan."

"Shhhhh," she said as she took his blood pressure. He noticed there was a needle in his arm with an IV drip. She had a basin of cool water on the bedside stand and dipped a white washcloth in it and laid it on his—Johanson's—head. He anticipated the touch from the time she lifted it dripping from the basin and wrung it out, until she smoothed it over his forehead, but he didn't feel a thing. He couldn't feel it when she brushed Johanson's hair back from his forehead to make room for the cloth either. Then she moved on to the next patient and a corpsman put ice-filled plastic gloves against Johanson's groin and armpits, to finish bringing the fever down.

As the fever cooled down, he watched her moving around the ward, sitting at the station charting. A tall curvy girl, the kind he'd always been attracted to. He was short and wiry himself and had to try a little harder to impress tall girls, who always wanted someone to look up to. She wasn't taller than he—had been—he guessed, and was quite a lot shorter than Woody.

Johanson kept tossing and turning though, which gave Nick a chance to talk to the nurse again. "Can he—I—have something for pain?"

She came right away with a pill, but took his temperature again first. "Hey, way to go. You're cooling off," she said before she gave him the pill. She had to put it in his mouth. It took more concentration than he seemed to have to move anything but Johanson's mouth and eyes.

"Can I have a smoke?"

It was night time by then and everybody else seemed to be asleep. She cranked the bed up and handed him an ashtray, but he couldn't manage it, so she stood there by him and helped him light the cigarette with her own lighter.

"Want one?"

"No, I don't smoke," she said. "We just carry lighters for the patients."

"There's one in my—was one in my pocket."

She checked the drawer of the stand. "It's still there."

"Good," he said, and he told her it belonged to his friend.

"Did he get med-evaced too?" she asked.

"I don't know. I didn't see him after I got hit," he said, which was sort of true. He changed the subject and told her about the joke he and Woody had with the lighter.

The mortar attack happened the second night they were there, and Lt. Ryan and the corpsman ordered everybody who could move under the bed. Amato couldn't get Johanson's body to move for him. Lt. Ryan—he had heard the other nurses call her Shari, trotted briskly down the ward, her flashlight and the corpsman's the only lights. They covered all the guys who couldn't get out of bed with extra mattresses. When she came to Johanson, she clucked her tongue and said, "Can you get up? You seem to be pretty weak still from your fever. Here, I'll help you." The truth was, Johanson was whacked out on pain meds and weak from the wound infection and fever. The IV he was hooked up to with its hose and pole sort of confused Amato too much to make the kind of basic moves he was able to negotiate with Johanson's body.

Steadying him with a hand on the IV stand pole, Shari Ryan pulled him out of bed, lowered him to the floor, and then, with a kind of a worried frown, lay face down beside him.

A mortar *crumped* so close by, the windows in the Quonset huts rattled. The IV bottle clanged against the metal pole and the lieutenant held onto it so it didn't tip over and break the bottle. He stretched Johanson's uninjured arm protectively toward her and she made a funny sound. It took him a minute to realize it was a giggle. "Don't worry, Johanson," she told him with a reassuring smile that was as excited as it was nervous. "The VC use the hospital too. They're not going to hit us on purpose. They couldn't get treated afterward if they did. Besides, they're lousy shots."

"Not always," he told her.

"I'm sorry. I guess they got you, didn't they?" she asked as another mortar crumped. Her eyes glittered in the dark like a wild animal's but there was something in her attitude of a kid playing hide and seek.

"And my friend," he said.

So then she asked where he was from and he told her—all the standard stuff, about growing up in the City and some of the funny stuff that happened before his mom died. She'd never been to the City and asked him what it was like, about the museums and galleries and all of the places he liked the best. He told her some of the stories behind some of the things he'd seen, some of the artists he'd met, about the band his dad used to play in.

She said, "You are *so* lucky. I would love to see those places."

"Hey, I'll take you there when we get out of here. Really," he said, perfectly sincerely. "So where you from?"

"Colorado," she said, and told him about growing up with horses, cows, dogs and a small army of cats.

"So you're a cowgirl?"

"Not me. My sister was. I'm the throwback. I always made friends with the cats who were better lapsitters than mousers and I'd go find someplace to sit and read."

"Animals are great," he said. "Some of the people I stayed with had cats and dogs and there was the zoo . . ." and he told her a funny story about one of the sea lions that had been in the newspaper when he was a kid.

He wished for the first time since coming to Nam that the enemy would never stop shooting. Lying there in the dark, with the mortars thundering and the rockets whistling, it was very cozy, and he felt very close to her, even though when he did manage to get Johanson's hand to touch her shoulder, he, Amato, couldn't feel anything. He just lay beside her, smelling that sweet scent and listening to her voice, and her muffled giggle when he said something she thought was cute. She told him he was going to get to go home and he asked for her address, which she wrote down on a little piece of paper she took from her pocket and tucked into his hand.

But he still couldn't feel it or really touch her. And when she left after finally getting him back into bed, it started to hit him what had happened to him.

As Johanson regained his senses a little, Amato found he wasn't able to say anything or even get Woody to say something for him. He could only watch while Woody acted baffled when Shari Ryan asked him about some of the things she'd talked about with Nick while they were under the bed. Johanson was flattered by the attention from the pretty nurse, but puzzled by the references to conversations he didn't remember and a little reserved. He said no, he wasn't from New York City, the lieutenant must have him confused with someone else. His friend Amato had been though. Maybe he'd been talking about Amato when he was delirious and the lieutenant misunderstood. Did she know if a Spec 4 Nick

Amato had been admitted? Shari looked hurt, and sounded a little more professional.

But ol' Woody wasn't stupid and he wasn't completely immune to a pretty face. He spent more time in the hospital stateside, and he wrote to Shari a couple of times, even got up the nerve to send her a Christmas present. Amato knew this, but he didn't really instigate it. He felt as if he and Woody were together inside a long tunnel and Woody was at the mouth of it, where he could talk to everybody and see the sun and move around, while Amato was trapped in the back in a dark narrow part, trying to come to terms with the fact that he was dead. He didn't notice a lot of what Johanson did and if he influenced his friend's behavior at all, he wasn't aware of it or much of anything else.

He started reviving when Johanson got a note back from Shari, a really sweet thank you note saying how touched she was by his gift and that she hoped he was doing well and she wouldn't mind hearing from him again. So he—Johanson, that is—sent her a Valentine—the biggest, fanciest velvet heart full of Russell Stover's chocolates he could find, and a funny card, which Amato got him to pick out instead of the mushy one Woody reached for first. If Nick was going to have a second-hand life, he wanted the guy representing him to show a little class, at least.

Woody covered his bets by sending his Becky the mushy card and a box of chocolates too but he could have saved his money on the second box—the first one came back, the package unopened. She must have rotated out—gone home maybe. But she'd told them that she still had time left to serve after she left Nam—funny they hadn't forwarded the package to her new duty station.

Johanson didn't pursue it then because he was on his way home, and the lighter and Amato with him. Becky was waiting.

At first, Amato was simply glad they had somewhere to go. He was starting to reconcile himself to his situation as part of Johanson's life. Johanson's parents had moved from the farm to Florida while he was gone, but he went back to Ohio first and found Becky at the bank where she worked. The folks came back up from Florida briefly when the Johansons got married a couple of weeks later.

Amato watched Johanson's dad, who never touched his son, barely tolerated Becky's brush on the cheek, and his mother, who fluttered and talked a little too much as if to make up for the father's silence. Nick was glad when they left. He had idolized his own dad when he was a kid, learned to play guitar like him, remembered all of his stories, all of his expressions of speech and face, learned from him how to get around the City. He thought having his own father half his life was maybe better than what Woody had after all.

Woody deserved better than that. With all this good stuff around him, his new wife, his folks, the nice house and land he inherited from them, Woody was still worried about what had happened to Nick. He'd light up, using the Zippo, and stare at it. He made a few phone calls, and got quietly, stolidly pissed off when nobody seemed to know anything or be very interested. Most of the other guys in their unit were dead or still in Nam now. Everybody had been real busy keeping alive when Amato got hit and none of them saw what happened to him. Amato knew this, from the eyeblink between the time he died and the time he joined Johanson. Not one other guy had any idea that he was gone. Amato wished he could tell Woody what the deal was but somehow or other, it didn't seem to work that way.

The only time Amato was able to come out was when Woody slept, or got drunk, or sick. Then it was easier to sort of take control. The first time Becky and Johanson made love,

Woody checked out, mentally, for a short time and Amato moaned Shari's name, wondering what it might have been like with her. He knew in that moment that the love making which seemed to Johanson too trivial to talk about in view of all the death he'd seen was about the most important thing a person could do. It would be worth dying all over again if he could feel this, do it with someone he cared for.

The profundity of the moment was interrupted by Becky smacking poor old Woody silly and rolling out from under him. She'd heard the moan, of course, since it had been made with her husband's vocal equipment. She left him for a couple of weeks, but then she found out she was pregnant and returned.

Amato knew he was causing trouble for his buddy but he couldn't seem to help it.

After that, whenever Woody tried to talk to Becky about Nick, which wasn't all that often, she shut him down.

"Yeah, sure. You say it's your old buddy but it's really that nurse you met, isn't it? You fell for her and now you want her and you're sorry you married me. We promised each other before you left that we'd be faithful—I kept my promise, Woody. Did you?"

And Johanson swore he did, of course, and felt annoyed with Becky for dwelling on some imaginary love thing when he was trying to tell her about life and death. He couldn't talk to her about the important stuff. Not back then. So he didn't talk to her very much.

He started to drink heavily after his first kid was born.

Instead of letting him lapse into one of his brooding silences, Amato came out during a blackout and made Becky listen to what he had to say about the last firefight and about himself. He made her believe him too. He was a better talker than Woody, even when he was pretending to be him, and

Becky wasn't used to that, so she listened, if grudgingly.

Maybe interfering wasn't the best thing to do, but if he was going to still be part of life, even by proxy, he didn't want to spend it on the streets someplace when "he" had a wife and a kid and a home. He didn't want Woody's kid to go through what he'd gone through. Maybe if he had felt everything Woody felt and had the chance to enjoy the drinking, it would have been different. Maybe he wouldn't have cared about the consequences if he could have just got drunk too. But Woody's life was all he had and while he wasn't mad that he was dead and Woody was alive, it seemed like *Woody* was. There were times over the next thirty years when Amato had to wonder who was haunting whom.

Becky was as stubborn as Woody and stuck it out. Both of them were hard workers and the kids turned out okay, though all of them moved away from home. Amato didn't blame them. His own parents used to argue, before his mom died, but they did it out loud, got over it, kissed and made up. Woody and Becky didn't say much when they fought but the house filled with tension way more tangible than Amato could ever hope to be again.

After a long time, Amato realized that in spite of all the fighting, and all of her bitching, Becky actually loved Woody, actually saw him as something more than a paycheck, even if the marriage seemed more like a battlefield sometimes than anything in Nam. Becky wasn't trying to be a pain in the butt. She was a desperate woman who had been using every weapon in her arsenal over all those years to try to get Woody back.

Finally, she bought them both tickets to D.C.

"I'm not going there," Woody protested. "Nothing there but damn politicians. Why do you want to go there now? We could take the grandkids to Disneyland cheaper."

"Why would the grandkids want you spoiling Disneyland for them?" Becky asked, not sounding mad, though she was. "Come on, Woody, you're not in the rice paddies any more. I want you to go see the Wall. That's where they put the guys who died there. Look. If your name is on there, I'll leave you alone. If it isn't, you come back and come home with me. You got to put this behind you sometime."

"That's easy for you to say." He brandished the lighter and held it in front of him like she was a vampire and it was a cross.

"What are you hanging on to that thing for? You stopped smoking ten years ago."

"Amato gave it to me," he mumbled. That was a lie. Amato had loaned it to him and the cheap SOB still hadn't given it back when they were hit. Woody crammed the lighter deep in his pants pocket, like Becky would try to take it away from him.

"Come on," she said, "Maybe you'll find his name on the Wall. You can give that damn thing back to him."

So he got on the plane. They *all* got on the plane in Columbus and got off in D.C.

And here they were. And there it was, like a giant tombstone or the half-buried wing of some black marble airplane, sticking up out of the ground. There was a hill behind it so you could only see most of it from the front side.

Becky herded Woody down the hill toward it. The sun had set an hour ago but the place was lit up with floodlights and there was a guard on duty.

"Twenty-four-hour service, huh?" Woody said.

Becky ignored the cynicism in his question and said, "They say a lot of the men who most need to see this won't come during the day, with tourists here. They wait until it's dark. Nobody will bother you. Come on."

Woody strolled up to it nonchalantly, pretending disinterest as he read a few names. Amato was struck by how many people were here, even at night. Everybody but them seemed to be guys, most of them in jungle fatigues. A reunion maybe? It was nearly Veteran's Day. There was one other couple in civvies, just leaving, and a guy in a dress uniform standing by a book. Becky walked up to him and he explained to her how to find names. While he was talking, Woody walked up and asked, "I got a buddy who went MIA at the same time I got hit. Where would he be?"

"MIAs aren't on here, sir," the guy told him. Young guy. Maybe twenty. Still, he looked older than all the guys in the jungle fatigues. Now that Amato looked at some of them more closely, he decided they were way too young to be vets having a reunion. Maybe they were one of those historical re-enactment groups. Or maybe there were some guys on active duty who were training to go some place like Nam, God help them.

"Why not?" Woody asked belligerently.

"Because the memorial is for those killed in Vietnam, sir. Missing personnel are not classified as killed."

Woody glared and fidgeted, as if he were ready to leave. Becky was examining the panels, name by name.

Amato took in the scene, before Woody could haul them both away. He wanted to remember this. Remember people remembering, if not him by name, then at least remembering people who went through the same thing he did. He found himself tuning in to the conversations going on around him.

"Damn, these guys look *old,* don't they?" one jungle-fatigued kid was saying to another.

"Yeah, well, man, time has passed out there in the world," the other replied.

"No shit," yet another said. "And it just goes to show you

long life ain't all it's cracked up to be. Look at that bald dude and know that there but for the grace of Charley go all of us— gray hairs, gravity, hemorrhoids, heart problems and all."

Woody moved toward them, and they parted. Becky was kneeling, still scanning names.

Amato looked at his friend and his wife with Woody's eyes, but without his viewpoint. Other than being dead, Amato felt just as he ever had. Woody on the other hand did have all of the afflictions the girl had mentioned, including high blood pressure, high cholesterol, reflux that woke him up at night feeling like he was going to puke, and a bad back and knees. Arthritis, the doctor said. He also lost most of his hair.

Becky was no spring chicken either. Her fair skin, after fifty-two years, was wrinkled around the mouth and eyes and her chin sagged a little, as did other parts, and she'd packed on a little weight, hard as she tried to watch it. She was still a pretty woman but no spring chicken.

"Woody?" Becky said suddenly.

"Yeah?"

"She's here. Oh, Woody, I'm sorry. I know I've been jealous of her because of the way you used to talk about her when you were drunk or asleep. You didn't tell me she'd been killed."

"Killed? Who got killed?" Woody asked, but he knelt beside his wife and looked where she pointed.

The engraved letters were silvery shadows in the black. "Sharyl P. Ryan," it said.

"Shari?" Amato and Woody said in one voice. Woody said, "Well, I'll be damned. Guess that's why she never wrote again. I just figured she rotated or got married or something. That's too bad."

"Too bad?" Becky demanded indignantly. "Is that all you

have to say? I thought you were in love with this girl! I thought all these years you were still wishing you were with her instead of me, which is why I never seem to be able to get your full attention, no matter what. And you find out she's dead and you say 'too bad'? What the hell is the matter with you, Woody? Did you get replaced with some sort of pod person when you went to Vietnam?"

Woody scratched the back of his head and then tucked his hands under the opposite armpits, standing with his legs straddled. This was his serious thinking posture. For once he wasn't clamming up and turning away. "It *has* felt like that sometimes," he said slowly. "But whatever you think, it had nothing to do with Shari."

It seemed to Amato that the people in uniform had all stopped talking to listen, though their backs were still turned to Woody and Becky.

The Wall curved around them all like the ironically sheltering wing of an overfed carrion crow.

"It didn't?" Becky for a change seemed ready to believe Woody instead of just believe *in* him. She stood up. "Is it *really* more because of the firefight? The one where your friend died? I mean disappeared?"

"Yeah, I guess so." He took the lighter out of his pocket and Amato watched, fascinated, as Woody rolled it over and over in his hand as he had done a hundred times, until the insignia was almost entirely worn level with the rest of the metal surface. "But you were right the first time, hon. I just didn't want to admit it. He probably got hit when I did and they never found him."

Before Amato knew exactly what was happening, Woody knelt and propped the lighter up against the section of wall under Shari Ryan's name, then stood and took Becky's hand.

"Honey, are you sure?" Becky asked.

"It's time," Woody said, and they strolled back up the hill again . . .

Which was all very well for them but there was Amato, alone for the first time in thirty years, his disembodied ass sitting by the big black wall that didn't have his name on it. Abandoned. Soon to be forgotten for good. After all they'd been to each other—the three of them.

"Hey, bro," a voice said, and Amato looked up to see one of the fatigue-clad guys standing over him, extending a hand. "Welcome home, buddy. What kept you?"

"Can you believe that? I've given those people the best thirty years of my—well, thirty years. I kept him from becoming a drunk and her from divorcing him. I—I—" The guy nodded slowly, grinning. "I guess I got too good and now they don't need me any more."

"Guess so. That's okay. You gotta be tired of all that hitchhikin' anyway."

Amato reached out a hand that was not Woody's hand, but a younger hand, more deeply tanned and slimmer in shape—his own hand, and grabbed the one extended to him. He rose to feet that wore jungle boots, like the ones the other guys wore. He was wearing fatigues too. He almost didn't recognize his own—well, not body, exactly, but his appearance. It had been a long time since he'd been just himself. "You can see me?"

"Sure I can. You can see me, can't you?"

"Yeah."

"Same difference. Look, Amato, you've had a long detour on the way home but you're okay now."

"Who *are* you guys?" Amato asked as the two of them walked over to the group. "Are you all haunting this place or what?"

"You could say that."

"I bet all of you have your names there though, right?" Amato said, jerking a thumb—his thumb—back toward the Wall.

"Most of us, yeah. But look, man, if they knew you were dead, you'd be here too. Don't make no nevermind to us. We don't stand on formality."

"So isn't there a heaven or a hell after all?" Amato asked. He hadn't thought about any of that since the split second before he attached himself to his lighter, but now found the subject vitally interesting.

"Oh yeah, sure, but you're not stuck there, you know. You can come and go. Most of us were ready for a war when we died. Eternal peace is a little hard to take when you're jazzed for action. So we hang out here a lot, look at the presents, read the poems, wait and see if any of our folks or our old buddies are visiting."

"So you can go on leave from heaven? That's a new one."

"Yeah, and some of the brothers have been to hell and back too."

"Sounds complicated."

"That's why we're here. We're sort of the pathfinders for any new recruits. We've lost a lot of guys *since* Nam too because of it. Died from wounds, physical or otherwise, or got cancer from agent orange and died that way. Not too many of you dudes who were missing show up like this though. We're glad you're here. Even if you're not so sure."

"Oh, I am. I mean, I thought that I had to stay with Woody to stay—well, me. But—" he looked back toward the lighter, feeling a little insecure without it. Kind of like a genie without his bottle might feel, he guessed.

Someone was there, reaching for the lighter.

Amato freaked. " 'Scuse me," he said to his guide, and headed back to the intruder, "Hey, my buddy left that for a friend of ours. It's very special to us and—"

The intruder looked up, the boonie hat falling back to reveal wild red curls corralled into pigtails, and wide round golden brown eyes. "Sorry," she said. "But I think it was left for me. I had a patient once who carried a lighter like this. It belonged to his friend who disappeared during a firefight."

"Shari?"

She stood up. The boonie hat was the only piece of military attire she wore now. Otherwise she was in sandals and one of those Mexican dresses in bright turquoise embroidered around the neck and hem with flowers in hot pink, purple, red, lime green and bright blue.

"Do I know you?"

"Well, we didn't meet while I was alive exactly but I'm Woody's friend—Johanson's friend. I died in the same firefight where he got wounded. That was my lighter. And uh—my ride home and my connection with life for the last thirty years."

"I can see why you might be a little possessive of it," she said. "I wasn't going to take it anywhere. I just wanted to see it, kind of as a reminder . . ."

"Oh, hey, no, that's okay. I haven't smoked in years—I mean, Woody hasn't. He left it with you. I guess he left *me* with you. Only—what's a nice girl like you doing in a place like this?"

"I was on my way to a party with some other nurses and the chopper was shot down," she said, after all these years still looking as bewildered and hurt beyond death as he had felt himself. Life had dumped her out so early.

He reached out, awed and exhilarated by how easy it was this time, and gathered her into a hug. "Oh, baby, I'm so sorry. I didn't know. Woody didn't know."

She returned the hug for a moment, but then backed off a

little way. She still didn't really know him.

So he used the charm that had got him through his teens and said, "Well, a party huh? That explains the dress. Very nice, by the way."

"Thanks."

"You weren't here when I got here," he said, when she remained silent.

"No. I stayed here for awhile right after they put my name up. At first I met a lot of my former patients who crossed over after Nam in one way or another—and a couple of other nurses I served with. But, I don't know. I just feel like something didn't go right in life, you know? That something was interrupted, or left undone."

She looked back at the lighter and sighed, her golden eyes bright and teary.

"I really liked your friend," she said. "He was a little strange and had a pretty short memory, but—did you know he sent me a Christmas present?"

"Yeah, I knew. We sent you a Valentine too . . ."

The dress was sleeveless, her crossed arms bare. She shrugged, as if she was suddenly cold. "I wish he'd left that here too," she said in a small voice. "My folks didn't want me to join the service. They put a stone with my name on it in the veterans' cemetery." She smiled up at him but her smile was a little quivery.

He quickly began telling her about life with the Johansons, the irritating funny stuff he knew she'd appreciate.

But instead of laughing, as he hoped she'd do, she said wistfully, "It must have been great living with Woody all these years, being close to people."

He thought about it for a minute then dropped the act and said seriously, "Better than staying in Nam, I guess. But I was sort of eavesdropping on *their* lives. It was okay when Woody was younger, back when we first got home from Nam. But he should have got rid of the lighter—rid of me—sooner."

"But you helped him and his wife."

"Maybe if I hadn't been in the way, he wouldn't have needed so much help. The only time I was really glad I was there—all the way glad, was that night we were in your hospital and taking cover with you under the bed."

"*You* remember that?" she asked. "Your friend didn't. He promised he'd take me to see New York when we got out, then he said he didn't remember anything about it."

Amato said, "Of course he didn't. He was out of it. But I wasn't going to let him waste time being delirious when we could be talking to you. When *I* could be talking to you. And that was *me* by the way."

"All that time I was talking to a ghost and I didn't even know it?" she asked. "You sure fooled me."

"I didn't mean to. I didn't—well, I didn't feel like a ghost."

"No, you didn't. You felt more like a person than your friend did, to tell you the truth." She bit her lower lip and those big golden eyes searched his face. At last she grinned.

"Sounds like you remember an awful lot about it after all these years."

"I do."

"Me too. I've never forgotten your face."

She laughed and moved closer to him. "You're way ahead of me. I never saw yours before now. But it's very familiar—you're very familiar."

"I ought to be," he said. "I was living through Woody and Becky and you know what? Becky is a terrific woman, and Woody is so damned lucky to have her. But I was really disappointed when we didn't hear back from you at Valentine's Day and he just turned around and married her. I always wished he'd married you, because I wanted to."

She reached up and touched his face, and he was thrilled all over again that now he could feel her fingers, light and strong and cool as he had imagined they had been touching Woody back in Nam.

"I doubt I ever stood a chance with him," she said. "I was surprised to get that bracelet for Christmas. I just knew that in spite of the feelings that I thought were between us, he'd forget all about me."

Amato looked down at her left wrist and saw that just above the big sturdy nurse's watch she wore, there was an MIA bracelet, a simple thin silver-colored cuff. He suddenly felt a lightness that had nothing to do with being disembodied.

She followed his glance and held up her hand. He took it in his own, supporting her wrist with his fingers as he read the name engraved on the bracelet.

"Sp 4th Class Nicholas Xavier Amato, " it said.

"Of course he wanted to forget about you," Nick said, slipping his arm around her. "He knew, somehow or other, that you're my girl."

"Yeah?" she asked, and snuggled against him a little. He could even feel warmth, just as if they were still alive.

"Yeah. That's *my* name you're wearing, lady."

"No kidding," she said. She hooked the wrist with the bracelet around his neck and said, "Well, then. I guess I can date enlisted men if I want to now."

"Damn right," he said, eyeing the group of guys still laughing and talking at the far end of the Wall. "But this place is a little crowded with people who can eavesdrop on our private conversation."

"We don't have to stay here," she said. "We can go anywhere we want."

"So I hear. Okay, that being the case, tell you what. You want to see the City. I know a nice little Italian place in my old neighborhood. We won't be able to taste the food but the atmosphere is great."

Author's Note: This story is dedicated for those still missing in action, whose names have not been inscribed with those of their comrades on the Wall.

Although I actually did the writing on the story, I asked my friend Rick for an idea for a story he would like to see written. As he often can do, he told me a story with a plot line and a complete first scene, which I used pretty much as he narrated it, though I added a few details. I checked with him to make sure my changes jibed with his concept. His original idea would have been pretty much a guy kind of story—all of the characters being buddies who served together. He liked the idea I had come up with in an earlier draft of the spirits who hang out at the Wall being Pathfinders for their comrades who come later, as an elite group in Nam had been Pathfinders in a different sense, so that concept remained.

Because I am a female vet and I was writing it, I felt like there needed to be a strong feminine component in it too and the nurse was a natural under the circumstances. Finally, as I turned Rick's ideas and my own over and over in my mind, I realized that this was a love story, and the MIA was the soulmate of the nurse, whose name was on the Wall. One symptom of PTSD is a failure in the ability to bond and have a lasting relationship—especially with the opposite sex. Woody Johanson is obviously having that kind of problem with his marriage. My own romantic fantasy about those of us vets who do not find someone to share our lives with is that for us, our personal Mr. or Ms. Right died in country before we met them. It's nice to think everything could still work out in the afterlife.

Mu Mao and the Court Oracle

Mu Mao became Aware as he was reborn yet again. That is to say, once more he became embodied, for his rebirth occurred not at the body's physical emergence from the mother's womb, but from the time Mu Mao realized, "Here I am again. Here I go again. What now?" The current body gained Awareness as it was dumped unceremoniously into a cage with three siblings, all as hungry as Mu Mao, reincarnate, suddenly was.

Just once it would be nice if rebirth took place in a lovely home, somewhere warm, with soft blankets laid down for the arrival of the sweet little much-adored and wanted kittens. Instead, Mu Mao the Magnificent found himself in an animal shelter, among many other cats and kittens.

He knew it at once by the smell—it was clean, which was a blessing. And at least there would be some food. Often he was born into the wild, or into some great colony of wild cats. Being a *bodhisattva* and helping others work out their destiny and achieve Enlightenment was no easy task when one had to skitter up trees to avoid being eaten by larger predators. Worse was having to avoid being eaten by other larger and

156

more feral cats. Mu Mao was now born into perhaps his thousandth lifetime, the first several hundred of which had been devoted to evolving into the wise person, shaman, healer, priest, lama, hermit, monk, and counselor he had ultimately become, the latter thirty devoted to his reward—being born into the highest possible lifeform, that of a cat. He found it particularly upsetting when others of his exalted species aimed their teeth at his own helpless little kitten tail. True, even some cats had to evolve, but he found their process unnerving.

Did *no one* in charge of fate think it necessary for Mu Mao to help his fellow lifeforms from the standpoint of being a companion animal to some doting two-legged being with opposable thumbs?

When he had slaked his hunger and thirst, he researched his current situation by examining closely the papers covering the floor of his erstwhile home. They looked fresh and current and he could still smell the ink so he knew they must be no more than a day old at the most. It was the Year of the Cat, according to Asian astrologers, and from the date, within the sign called Leo in Western astrology. The sign of the cat. Very catty. Reeking with cattiness. Very clearly, Mu Mao's current mission would be concerned with events unfolding in the realm of his fellow felines.

"Ahem," his Mother of the Moment said. "What do you think you are doing? Tear up that paper at once! Cats can't read!"

"I beg your pardon, gentle mother," he said politely, "But I can. In several languages actually. Which I also speak, though only after judicious consideration for the sensibilities and circumstances surrounding me. However, other than the information I have already gleaned, the reading matter lining our cage tells me nothing of value concerning our current situation. Perhaps you can enlighten me. Is there some great event in the making within the realm of cat-kind?"

His mother, a calico of undistinguished markings, reached out a hard paw and swatted him across the cage. "Don't get saucy with me, young kit! While you drink my milk you go by my rules. Cats don't read and cats of our clan don't meddle in the affairs of the realm. What business have we with royalty? Did royalty step in a prevent my farmer's land from being sold, the barn which has been the personal domain of generations of my ancestors from being torn down to make a parking lot for a shopping mall? Did it keep my elders from being put down and you and your brothers and sisters and me from being put in here where no doubt we'll be gassed as soon as the kits take the kennel cough? Don't speak to me of matters of the realm!"

"I beg your pardon," he said with what sounded like a small pitiful mew as he washed his face very quickly to try to wash away the pain of the blow. It didn't take much to hurt when you were five and a half inches long from nose to tail tip.

However, a small thing like personal discomfort could not obstruct his duty and so he sought other sources of information. The cage beside theirs was filled with what looked like a vast black and gray striped fur pillow. Mu Mao reached out a paw and touched the pillow. "I beg your pardon, sir or madame as the case may be," he said to the pillow. There was no reply. It might have actually been a pillow—it might have been dead, except that there was some warmth emanating from beneath the fur and the coat twitched ever so slightly as Mu Mao touched it.

"Hey, little fella, don't bother the poor old guy," a man said. Mu Mao turned. The man was looking sadly toward the cage containing the inert animal. Mu Mao, sensing that there was something for him here, rubbed himself against the front bars of the cage and gave a small, cute mew. Manipulative and disgusting perhaps, but effective.

The man undid the latch of Mu Mao's new home and lifted him out, holding him in one hand and stroking his head with a finger. It felt very good. Most nice things that happened to Mu Mao felt very good. Feeling very good when at all possible seemed to be one of the benefits of possessing the qualities of Catness.

"Would that older cat have hurt that little baby kitten?" a woman's voice cooed from somewhere to the left and slightly behind the man.

"I doubt it. But the poor old guy has enough problems without being harassed by a little punk like this guy," the man told her. He wore a nametag. It said "Andy."

"Oh?" the woman asked without much interest, and sneaked a finger around Andy so that she could tickle Mu Mao's chin.

"Yeah, poor old cat is a sad case. He's lived with the same guy for almost twenty years and now his master is dying. The guy thought maybe if the cat came here, he'd have time to find a new home before his master died. But the old cat ain't havin' any. He sits like that with his face to the back of the cage."

"Maybe he needs more attention," the woman said. Her voice carried no reproach that Mu Mao could hear but Andy reopened Mu Mao's cage and returned him to his siblings, then opened the adjoining cage and extracted the other cat.

The other cat lay like a lump in Andy's arms, unresisting, but also indifferent and stiff, a deeply resentful look in his narrowed eyes.

He did not respond to Andy's voice or touch or to the woman's. He just sat there and glowered and pretty soon

Andy put him back into his cage.

Mu Mao's heart went out to him, but when he tried to speak to the old cat again, his siblings pounced on him and rolled him around the cage and his mother began to wash him with more energy than was strictly required.

After that, he needed a nap. When he woke up, the people had gone home. The first time he lived in a shelter, he thought that when the people went home, all of the animals would go to sleep. He was wrong. This was when the cats gossiped through the bars and wires of their cages.

"Did you hear?" asked a bobtailed black tom two levels down. "The King of the Cats is dead and nobody knows who the new king is or where he might be."

"That's silly," said a fluffy neutered calico spinster. "How can anyone mislay a king?"

The tom tried to lash his bobbed tail and thumped it against the bars. "It's more a case of the king mislaying his mistresses—and potential heirs. Tom Gamble was a very busy cat. The ladies always liked him and he hated to disappoint them."

"Perish the thought," Mu Mao's mother said, yawning and settling her chin on her paws. "The world never has seen such a lot of scruffy longhaired tawny striped kits as His Majesty sired. And which of them is the crown prince, well, that's anyone's guess."

"His Majesty wasn't much to worry about details," sniffed a gray tabby. "He never did appoint a court oracle."

"You don't *appoint* one of those," a white almost-a-Persian said loftily. "They are born, not made. Not even by kings."

"Well, whoever was made didn't get recognized anyway. So now here we've got Bast-knows-how-many potential heirs and nobody to sort them out. There'll be fur flying for sure, bloody civil war because of it I tell you." The black bobtail was warming to his subject.

Mu Mao peered carefully down through the screen of his cage. He wondered if black bobtail tom had any idea what a war was like. By now, many generations of cats had come and gone since the end of the world. The warlords had made way for governments which were, if no less rapacious, at least more peaceable about it. These governments were extremely polite to each other. For now. A cat civil war wouldn't involve nuclear devices, probably, but it could still be an ugly and horrible thing. As the many times great grandsire of almost all of the cats in existence today, Mu Mao mourned any carnage among them.

A frightening thought occurred to him then and he checked his own body. Whew! He had a little sooty black tail and a white chest and paws, black back with a white spot, white belly with a black spot. His face would either be black or have a mask he supposed. It didn't matter. He was not a ginger cat as Tom Gamble and his likely heir were. So the heir was not him. Nor did he feel especially oracular. Therefore, he was free to pursue whatever business seemed to call for him to put a paw in.

As soon as the others settled down for the night, he began.

The first thing to do was get from his cage into the adjoining one, to confront the terribly depressed cat.

This presented only a small difficulty for Mu Mao, who as the most esteemed of lamas had excelled in the Tibetan psychic sports, which naturally included breath, and even molecular, control. He simply exhaled all of the air in his body. His mother was not watching. Perhaps if she had been, she would have been alarmed for when he exhaled, he exhaled the air between his very atoms, becoming so small as to be virtually invisible. Thus he could easily slip through to the next cage, after which he inhaled mightily and regained his former kitten size, perhaps even adding an additional ounce or two of air.

Then he padded forward to confront the bitter old cat.

The old one was not sleeping, but brooding with both green eyes slitted resentfully.

"My dear sir, you simply cannot continue like this," Mu Mao told him. "You frighten away those who would save you by your unfriendly demeanor. I have it on good authority that it is nearly impossible for an adult cat to find a home from one of these places as it is."

Mu Mao thought for a moment the old cat would swat him but the poor fellow seemed to lack the energy, and instead sighed, letting much of the air out of himself, though not to the degree that Mu Mao had done.

"Don't speak to me of homes. A home is nothing but an illusion based on the whim of a fickle and callous race. I should know. From the time I was smaller than you, all through kittenhood, I was with him, his true companion, loving him when others rejected him, bringing him mice and birds when he was hungry, licking his wounds. I even submitted to the veterinarian's knife so that my natural urges to mate and sire children would not interfere with my closeness to him. And now, after all these years, he has betrayed me. Dumped me like so much feline garbage, given me into the hands of these people who cage me here, without my pillow or dish, without my weekly treats or my toy, without the drug that gave me the feeling of being wild and free—and without that cruel unworthy man I have loved for so long. He doesn't want me any more. I don't care. I hate him now. I hate all humans and I don't want to live with them. If I must live with another one in order to live, then I prefer to die."

"Oh, you will die if you keep this up," Mu Mao said. "But

then you will be with your friend if you do, I suppose."

"What do you mean?"

"You heard Andy. Your friend is dying. That is why he had you sent here to find another home."

"You understand what they say? It means something?"

"You mean you don't? You lived all those years with one man and didn't understand what he said?"

"Well—no. Not really. It didn't matter. I didn't actually need to. He would say things in a kind voice and I knew I could do as I wished, and if he sounded stern and pointed at something I knew I shouldn't go back to it until his back was turned. Otherwise, he fed and petted me and babbled to his heart's content and I sat on his lap and purred for him and meowed when I wished him to do something in particular. I must say, he spoke better cat than I did human. But then he stopped speaking to me, would not lift his hand to pet me, and finally turned away from me and allowed others to take me from our bed and put me into a vile case and bring me to this place where you see me now. Perhaps he was bored with me, do you think? I have heard others here speak of how their people became bored with them when they no longer performed kittenish antics such as someone like yourself might do. When that happens, I understand it is not uncommon for the people to simply dispose of one, as has happened to me, and get a newer edition."

"No," Mu Mao said firmly. "That is not what happened at all. Andy explained it to the woman. Your friend was dying. He wanted to see you in a good home before he had to leave, to make sure you would be cared for. Even as he dies, he cares for you and worries for your welfare."

The old cat stared at Mu Mao and a large tear ran down the short fur along the side of his nose. Mu Mao noticed that he had black circular stripes that joined on the bridge of his nose, like spectacles. "He will be all alone and he sent me away to spare me. But I don't want to be spared. I want to be with him. I want to go to him. If I die too, I don't mind. But I can't bear to be locked up in here when he needs me." The old cat stretched briefly then rose to his feet and began pacing in a manner that was extremely tiger-like. "If I thought he would live until morning I would raise such a ruckus that the man—Andy—would unlock my cage to see what was wrong and then I would give him a great scratch and make him release me and I would run out the door very fast and home again."

"Oh, good! You could find it again?" Mu Mao asked hopefully, for he was sure now he knew what his first mission in this young life must be.

"Well, it must be around here somewhere!" the old one snapped. "I know I would find it only—only, now that you tell me what is happening, I have a feeling."

"A feeling?"

"Yes, I think—I think he is still here but I don't think he will be here tomorrow. I think he needs me now. Of course, it is all his own doing that I am here but you and I both know this isn't working. I need *out*." The "now" and the "out" were drawn out and agonized, and meant the same thing in cat as they did in English.

"Calm yourself," Mu Mao said. "I am here to help you. First, we must release you from your cage."

"Yes, but how?"

"Patience," Mu Mao said. He thought about it. He could make himself small again and slip through the front of the cage, but that would not release the old cat. If he were full grown, and the cage on the lowest level, he could easily undo the latch with his teeth and paws and the cunning of thirty remembered feline lifetimes and prior lives as a holy man. But this was not the case. "Hmmm," he said to himself and then, "Hm?" That was it. A simple mantra, a chant—a purr, done with great concentration and deep vibration.

He leaned against the lock and purred with all his might and all his energy and all of the depth of his tiny being. The lock never stood a chance. It shuddered open within moments, and Mu Mao and the old cat leaped to the floor.

Instantly all of the other cats were awake and scratching at their cages. Mu Mao's new mother was particularly vociferous. "Ungrateful spawn of a lecherous tomcat, why are you liberating that washed up old alley cat and not your own family?"

"Mother—friends, at least here you will have a warm place to sleep and food. Outside you will have nothing."

"Except our freedom," said the bobtail black. "And a certainty that nobody will pluck us helpless from our cages to take us to a gas chamber. I've heard about what they do in these places. Where do you think I was before I came here if not out there?"

The old cat was pawing and mewing at the door and Mu Mao turned from him to the others and back again while the old fellow went frantic trying to get out.

"Very well. There's no time to argue." He went to the door and jumped up on the handle and said to all of the other cats, "Repeat after me:" and began the purring Mantra of Liberation once more.

Moments later two dozen cats and kittens were straggling at various speeds behind the tail of Mu Mao, who was struggling to keep up with the old cat, his face never getting further forward on the old one's body than the butterfly spirals of black stripes in the gray of his sides.

Mu Mao's mother continually lost ground as she shifted kittens and at last Mu Mao in his tiny voice told three of the other adult cats that if they wished to go in the same direction he was, they should help carry the young. Much to his surprise, they agreed. But even more surprising, the old cat turned for the only time since their escape, and scooped up Mu Mao by the nape of the neck. After that, their caravan went much more quickly.

The old cat was not lost, nor was he confused. He unerringly homed in on his former home. A strong chill wind blew them along, but it was not yet raining or snowing and the night was clear, with many stars Mu Mao could not properly appreciate from his berth under the chin of the old cat.

The cortege of cats passed over and under a series of back fences, alleys and yards until they came to a small house with high grass. A light was on in a back window. The old cat dropped Mu Mao, hopped up to the sill and scratched, mewing.

Mu Mao jumped up beside him. The others started to do the same but the old cat hissed warningly at them and then modulated his tone to another plaintive meow.

Inside the room was a bed full of tumbled covers and a small, frail person. The person turned toward the window, as Mu Mao looked on. He seemed to have no attendant or helper however, and had barely the strength to raise his hand. Someone had brought him water and tidied the place recently, from the look of it however. Perhaps he had help come in during the day, or perhaps they slept elsewhere in the house, though it scarcely looked large enough for two people.

"Let me in, Fred! Let me in!" the old cat cried over and over and Fred seemed aware of him but unable to move. Finally the old fellow jumped down, narrowly missing Mu Mao's mother and two of his brothers.

"If he won't open the window, then I will take a run and break through it," the old cat declared.

"Oh, that will be a grand surprise for your friend. A concussed unconscious if not dead cat lying cut to ribbons and bleeding all over his floor. I believe there is a better way," Mu Mao said. "A moment please." He began his chant of levitation, aiming at the window. It was a tricky business. Once he himself rose into the air and he had to start all over again. Another time he saw something move from the corner of his eye and looked around to see all of the other cats lifting from the ground, and once more started over. Fred lifted once, briefly too, but then Mu Mao at last chanted with the correct intonation and the window creaked, jerked, and flew open. The old cat flew through it as if he had wings, landing on the bed beside his friend and purring madly, rubbing himself so hard against the fragile body in the bed he threatened to crush it.

"Gently, old one," Mu Mao cautioned. "His fires burn low. You wouldn't want to extinguish them entirely before you had a proper reunion."

Just then, however, Mu Mao heard paws on the sill and turned back to the other cats. "It's a private moment," he told them but bobtail black tom sauntered saucily forward, and had to bounce unceremoniously back to the ground to avoid losing his nose as the window flew shut again.

Mu Mao saw with surprise that the communication between the two did indeed consist only of cat noises on the one side and human murmurings on the other. It seemed to suit them fine, however, and he decided not to offer his services as a translator.

Fred was immediately enlivened by the presence of his feline friend, and gave the cat weak strokes and spoke to him while the cat purred and rubbed. Mu Mao found such extravagant affection almost distasteful, as he himself had learned to practice detachment in all things. However, in his heart he knew that love was not merely a great catalyst to many important changes and events, but the only catalyst if such things were to have Merit.

Slightly bored, nonetheless, Mu Mao looked about him while man and cat reunited. He noticed many framed photographs on the dresser. They were all of Fred and the old cat, who in some of them was a young cat, and Fred a younger man. In one of them the old fellow was a mere fluffball of a kitten and Fred himself barely dry behind the ears. Most of the photos said, "Me and Delf" although one, a portrait of Delf as a kitten, said "Delfy, seventh son of Alison Gray." Delfy himself was very gray in that picture. The dark stripes would have come in later life.

Photographs also covered the walls but they were too high for someone of Mu Mao's diminutive stature to see. Photograph albums were piled on the table beside the bed, as if Fred had been looking at them before his caretaker tidied up. Mu Mao jumped up on the table to see if any of them were open, but none was and they were too heavy for a small kitten to manipulate. He didn't want to knock one off the table and disturb the reunion.

However, from his fresh vantage point, he saw a computer sitting on a table in one corner of the room. This was something even a kit with the right know-how could use. After all, it involved only the pushing of a few buttons and something called a mouse.

It was a small computer, and its power button responded readily to the touch of a tiny paw. Fred was not a secretive man. No password was required to see what concerns he filed on his machine. One choice said "Delfy" and Mu Mao pounced on the mouse. A number of things happened inside the computer with the result that soon there was a chronicle of Delfy's life from the time he was born until Fred became too ill to be Delfy's biographer any longer.

Man and cat had been intertwined throughout their lives to the extent that it was amazing to Mu Mao that Delfy had never learned more of Fred's language or had mistaken Fred's intention when the man sent his cat companion to find a new home. Actually, according to the sad note in Delfy's chronicle, Fred had given Delfy to a friend who promised to find him a home. Apparently the friend had simply dumped the cat at the shelter.

But from the time Delfy was born, a Gemini in the year of the Dragon, when Fred had helped Alison Gray deliver her kittens and had wiped the caul from little Delfy's face, they had been together. There were snapshots of the house Fred and Delfy lived in before and after the earthquake. Fred wrote that before the earthquake, Delfy had leapt from his arms and flown back and forth to the frame of the door, hooking his claws into Fred's pants and insisting that Fred follow him. Fred credited Delfy's instinct for survival with saving his life. There were the women friends that Delfy didn't like who eventually broke Fred's heart and the man friend that Delfy hated, who turned out to be a crook.

Fred even spoke sadly of when he first began to feel ill and Delfy began shredding a magazine that had an article about bladder cancer in it. Had he paid attention at the time Delfy did this, Fred believed the doctors could have treated it.

A Gemini in the Year of the Dragon. Well. Yes. Auspicious? Certainly.

Mu Mao gave the mouse a final, rather unenlightened bat, and jumped down from the table.

Fred's initial joyous greetings had dwindled to incomprehensible murmurings. His pets grew feebler as the joy that had flooded him with adrenaline could not sustain his strength, and his hand faltered, and lay still.

169

Delfy stopped in mid-purr and looked into Fred's face. His eyes, so fond and happy moments before, were now glazed and empty, though his lips still curled in a slight smile.

Delfy gave a mew that was half a whine and nosed at Fred's limp hand.

Mu Mao jumped up on the bed and with his tiny tongue began grooming the old cat's head. "We were just in time," the kitten with the old soul said. "And you did a good thing for Fred. He was very glad to see you and had missed you very much, as you saw for yourself. I have read his words concerning you and it is true that he only sent you away to save you. But you didn't want to be saved, so now what?"

"You who can open doors with your purrs, make yourself invisible and levitate windows ask *me* what's next?" Delfy asked in a dispirited voice.

"I do," Mu Mao said. "We are all wild again. The others seem to wish to stay together for the time being. How about you?"

The old cat sunk his chin into his paws. He remained snuggled next to Fred's body. Mu Mao licked and licked, projecting calming and healing thoughts as he did so.

"I don't care."

"You cannot stay here, friend. I know the ways of people. Soon they will come and take Fred away and someone new will live here. Probably you will not be welcome and will find yourself back in the place where we were. I think you and I both know you have a life with and a duty to your own kind now."

Delfy turned away to lick Fred's ear, and tried to groom his hair.

A horrible wild yowl sounded from without and Mu Mao jumped upon the window sill in time to watch a gang of strange cats descend upon the refugees from the shelter,

170

tearing into them with ferocity meant to kill. The fur flew; screams and spits, hisses and the sound of ripping flesh met him. For just a moment, the small feline he was in this life thought it best to stay put, but he saw a grizzled calico with one ear leap upon his mother and try to get at one of his litter mates. He levitated the window with such force that the pane rattled in its frame.

The Bobtail black tom flew into the grizzled calico and tore her from Mu Mao's mother's back. Mu Mao was levitating his small siblings to the relative safety of the windowsill when Delfy sprang up beside him.

The striped cat's fur bristled until he was enormous, ten times the size of Mu Mao and his brothers and sisters. With a roar like a lion's, a roar so unlike his mewlings and purrings to his former companion that Mu Mao could hardly believe this was the same cat (a true Gemini, he reflected with satisfaction), he stilled the furor of battle. "HEAR ME AND BE WARNED!" he snarled. His eyes were rolled back in his face, and the black spectacles around them became a spiraling infinity knot that hypnotized the cats below and quite surprised and pleased Mu Mao with the definitiveness of its declaration of Delfy's unique status.

"The King is Dead. You anarchists who would rend the kingdom apart for lack of leadership, beware. The new king is among us now. Long live Bobtail Black Tom, the only legitimate and non-neutered heir to His Former Majesty, Tom Gamble!"

The strange cats slunk away from those they were mauling, just far enough to roll onto their backs, as did the other refugee cats one by one, while Bobtail Black Tom strolled among them licking their faces or giving their bellies a warning tap with his paw. Mu Mao's mother, having made her obeisance, brought her youngsters from the sill one by one, the last being Mu Mao, who jumped down unaided.

Beside him, Delfy landed but neither of them showed their bellies to the bobtailed black king. Nonetheless, the king graciously sauntered forward, quite full of himself now, Mu Mao noticed, though he doubted the black cat had had any idea of his own royalty prior to Delfy's announcement. With great ceremony he licked Mu Mao's forehead and then lowered his own head for Delfy to lick his ears, which Delfy did in the feline equivalent of a coronation.

"Great Oracle," the king asked when this was done, "You took your own sweet time about announcing yourself. What kept you?"

Just then Fred's caretaker, who apparently had been asleep in another room in the house and been aroused by the racket, came to the window. "I never saw so many damned cats in my life. Shut up, you lot! There's been a death in this house and—why, Delfy! You came back. Come on back inside, kitty, and we'll find you a good home. Fred wouldn't want you to be a stray."

But Delfy, a true Gemini now joined with his second path, turned his tail to her and nosed the king, who led his court back into the dark backyards and over the back fences and across the shadowed alleys that were his new realm. Mu Mao, his small body weary from his exertions, begged his mother for a ride.

Don't Go Out in Holy Underwear or Victoria's Secret or Space Panties!!!

Victoria Fredericks, Space Cadet, was just your average titian-haired, emerald-eyed temptress of a time and space traveler, nothing out of the ordinary really. Except that Victoria had a secret. She had an underwear fetish. Long ago, back on earth, even before she began the cadet training program, she had fancied lacy silk underthings in shades to match her eyes and clash with her hair, as well as scanties in purple or black or aquamarine, in tiger stripes or leopard spots or little pink and red hearts. She liked knowing that under her standard issue uniform, she had on something fine, something she wouldn't be ashamed to show in any emergency room.

Her mother had impressed the importance of underwear on her at an early age. "Vicky, baby," she had told her. "I don't want to catch you goin' out to play with holes in your underpants. What if, God Forbid, you should fall off your air board or get hit by a low-flying shuttle and have to go to the emergency room? What would the doctors and nurses think to see your holy underwears?"

That was Mom all over. Not well-educated herself, she

slaved for hours in a spacer bar saving the money so that young Victoria could have a better education, a broader horizon, than she herself enjoyed. And better underwear too. Mom's job in the spacer bar was such that she particularly appreciated a well-placed piece of lace. In good condition, always. Victoria was brought up to do the same.

However, once Victoria shipped out, she found that her secret satisfaction became her secret sorrow. Her lovely undies wore out, set by set, first the black, which was so basic she wore it for all occasions, followed by the white with the little pink rosettes and bows accenting the lace, then the emerald which went so well with her eyes, followed by all of the other colors until she was in desperate danger of having to wear—ugh—standard Space Cadet issue underwear. And that was just on her first mission! She sent an urgent dispatch earthside with a supply ship, begging her mother to send something suitable from her favorite boutique.

The time thing had entirely slipped her mind. If it seemed like forever until another supply ship brought her special package; it must have seemed longer than that to her mother, who wrote in a shaky hand.

"Vicky, baby, forgive that I don't write so good but for God's sake I'm nearly ninety, so I think I'm doing pretty good, don't you? I hate to tell you, baby, but the port has gone to hell since you left and your favorite boutique closed up. I don't get around so good, but I got my Elderaid to go shopping for me and asked her to buy you something nice. This is what she came back with. It was in a closeout sale at the souvenir shop at the spaceport. Sorry, it was the best I could do. Just remember to change often and don't go out on any missions with holes in your scanties, okay? Take care of yourself. Love, Mom."

Victoria sniffled, ashamed to realize she'd been thinking only of herself in asking her mother to sacrifice precious time, energy and money for her wish, but the Space Corps stuff really rubbed her the wrong way after all those years of silk. So she bravely wiped her eyes and with fingers trembling with anticipation, opened the package to pull out—plain cotton briefs. Her heart sank. They were perfectly respectable, and would surely be more comfortable than the Space Corps ones, but they were so ordinary! And then, examining them closer, she saw that they weren't ordinary at all. The package said "Space Panties," but at first they just seemed to be the sort of typical days-of-the-week panties girls had once worn in school. "Monday, Tuesday, Wednesday, Thursday, Friday," Victoria counted to herself, "Saturday, Sunday . . ." but that was only the first seven. There were thirty eight more pairs to go, one for every day in a spacer's week! "Sheperdsday, Glennsday, Gurguriansday, Kristasday . . ." she named them in order, all of the spacer days named for the early astronauts. There was a fresh pair of briefs for each. If she was careful, washing by hand and mending when necessary, she need never be without a special pair! Or so she thought, tears of gratitude, relief and homesickness dampening the white cotton and industrial strength elastic.

As her time of service lengthened and her data bases became engorged with knowledge as she grew in wisdom, experience, and, of course, beauty, her elastic began to give out and her fabric to fray.

A few pairs of her precious undies had become ripped in the line of duty—a couple more, before she came to value them so highly, in the line of other, more pleasurable pursuits. And so the space panties were carefully stowed in her locker to be worn only for good luck on special missions.

Like saving whole entire planets. Such as the one she was saving now, while wearing the Glennsday pair. Not only were they her most especially lucky pair, they were also the only ones left that had no holes, not even the tiniest. She'd cried when she opened her locker to find her entire stack of treasured unmentionables full of bitty little holes. Nobody had told her about space moths or she would have brought along space mothballs.

Only the Glennsday pair had escaped with the tiniest of punctures. Barely noticeable, really, but it worried Victoria, as she set forth to save the simple, quaint, low-tech inhabitants of the earthlike planet known in space jargon as Hotel Whiskey.

"But, Commander," she had protested to her gruff, stern-but-fair commander, when given the assignment. "Why don't the Hotel Whiskonians simply zap the silly Hasslebads into the next dimension?"

"Because," Commander Helen Highwater replied, "they have chosen a simple, quaint, spiritual life and aren't good at fighting. Unfortunately, the Hasslebads are much more sophisticated technologically and are *very* good at fighting. So your mission, Space Cadet Victoria Fredericks, is to defend the planet from utter destruction and the domination of the forces of evil and so forth. Okay?"

"Sure, yeah, okay, fine," Victoria said, with a snappy salute.

"Here are the keys to the top secret battle-shuttle, the Rikki Tikki Tavi. If, and when, you return with your mission successfully completed, you will have passed your final test and will no longer be a Space Cadet but a full, entire, completely commissioned and graduated officer of the Space Corps, and in a really swell ceremony will receive your insignia as *Ensign* Victoria Fredericks of the Space Corps."

"Just for defending one little planet and destroying the forces of evil that threaten it? Gee, Commander Highwater, piece of cake. Send me in there, Commander."

With only a brief stop, so to speak, to don her special lucky lingerie and her space suit, she had gone to the shuttle bay and inserted the keys into the ignition of the battle shuttle Rikki Tikki Tavi and, prudently waiting for the bay door to iris, had blasted off into space.

What a rush!

It was the first time the commander had let her take a shuttle out on her own, though of course she had practiced flying in simulators and under the supervision of seasoned Space Corps veterans such as Captains Flash Morgan and Chuck Rogers. But this was her premier solo flight *and* fight.

She continued being really thrilled right up until, as she approached the tasteful emerald and purple sphere that was Hotel Whiskey, she saw her enemy sneaking up on her from the far side of one of the planet's pretty lavender moons. She knew it had to be the enemy ship because it was this really ugly, mean looking black thing with a nose-cone flanked by what looked like twin spikes, or fangs, but which were really space-to-dirt missiles. No doubt meant to blow the peaceful, gentle, quaint Hotel Whiskonians to smithereens! The rest of the Hasslebad ship rose like a hood behind the slitted dual view ports on either side of the nose-cone.

Mere badly conceived exterior design wasn't about to intimidate Victoria, however. She got right on her com set and opened the pre-programmed Hasslebad hailing frequency and said, "Hey there, you in the cobra ship! Come in. This is Victoria Fredericks, Space Cadet in the Space Corps battle shuttle Rikki Tikki Tavi and if you don't stop picking on that poor little planet beneath us *this very instant,* I will open fire and you will be really, really sorry."

"Ha, brave and beautiful but sadly doomed and deluded earth woman, we defy you and your dainty little space shuttle to keep us from enslaving the puny world beneath our jets!

177

Surrender now and you can have a ringside seat as the consort of our emperor while watching us make that world go away."

"Absolutely out of the question!" Victoria replied spunkily. "Your sort are evil, odious, wicked and mean and wish only to dominate others *and* you have a very ugly spaceship. I would never feel comfortable as the consort of an emperor who employs such tacky designers."

"Impudent earthling vixen, we will blow you out of the cosmos for that! The emperor himself designed this vessel. Prepare to die!"

"Oh, grow up!" Victoria retorted, and opened fire just in time to intercept their volley, which rocked her sideways. Fortunately, since the days when prescient science fiction had predicted ships of her sort, appropriate seat belts had been designed so she was only slightly stirred, not shaken loose from her command console.

But their next volley knocked out her auto controls, her life support systems, her computer, and the communications system. All she had was her viewport, her manual controls, and her wits. She was flying by the seat of her panties!

Fortunately, she also had her laser rockets and they could be fired by manual control.

She sent another volley right into their guts and, since she was a dead shot, with or without computer control, she watched with satisfaction as the ship exploded into many many . . .

Her satisfaction evaporated as a particularly large chunk came flying, despite the lack of atmosphere, toward her viewport, smashing into it.

The last thing she remembered was the jar of the impact, the hiss and sizzle of the control console as it tore apart in sparks, and the feeling of thousands of tiny pricks of fire burning through the cloth of her suit.

Then all she saw was stars and darkness as she descended down, down, ever downward.

To awaken, bruised, burned, in terrible pain, but still apparently intact, in drastically compressed darkness, lit only by the still flickering mini-fires of the Rikki's electrical bits.

Fortunately, the impact of landing had jarred open the shuttle's hatch. Victoria wriggled toward it. Her leg hung at a peculiar angle and she couldn't feel her toes, but she scooted on the bottom of her shredded space suit across the rubble strewn deck and out the hatch.

What a mess! The shuttle crash had produced a crater many feet deep, with sides so steep she could barely squirm between her vessel and the grave encompassing it.

The ground was also still very hot, though the outside of the shuttle, made of special heat-repelling space ship stuff, was still cool. Her leg was killing her. She ought to have splinted it, but long pieces of anything weren't part of space shuttle design. If only she could climb on top of her shuttle, she might be able to hoist her well-conditioned though still curvy feminine form out of the pit with her strong but shapely arms. She had aced Space Cadet basic training and worked out daily in the ship's gym.

Her leg hurt so badly that she nearly passed out from the effort. She planted her hands on the roof of the shuttle and pushed—and to her surprise boosted herself three feet above the shuttle before coming back down on its roof, rather lightly, and with ample time to protect her injured limb.

That was easy, she thought, and bounced again, with a slight change of direction that landed her beside the crater.

About that time, the press arrived.

That is, a press of robed, girded, masked, painted spear carrying folk Victoria could only assume were indigenous

179

Hotel Whiskonians arrived.

They didn't look quaint and charming. They looked— well, dangerous.

But of course, Victoria Fredericks. Space Cadet, laughed in the face of danger, or at least giggled nervously. "Hi," she said, twitching her fingers up and down in a little wave she hoped did not have a radically different meaning in their cultural milieu. "I guess you've come to welcome me as a conquering hero, on account of I just saved your planet and all."

One of them nudged her with a shard of pointed crystal borne on the end of his spear and she yelped. "Please don't do that. My leg is broken, I think. I don't suppose you could call my ship, could you? My communications unit was destroyed in the crash when I was nearly killed defending *your* home world," she paused for a moment with significant glances into each set of masked or painted eyes she could make contact with. Her mother had taught her a thing or two about responsibility, not to mention guilt, a weapon that, like primitive magic, was very effective on those who believed in it. It probably wasn't fair to use psychological warfare on these simple people, but it was nicer than skewering them, as they seemed willing to do to her. She intensified her gaze, mentally projecting the words, "Naughty, naughty. This is a nice way to treat a person who gets herself crashed to save you?"

Gradually, first spears and then eyes dropped groundward and toes began describing semicircles in the lush violet petals blanketing the ground.

Two or three of the Whiskonians edged toward the lip of the crater and, looking in, pointed and began speaking in gibberish. They consulted, jabbering among themselves in their simple native tongue. Then suddenly they surrounded her and two of them grabbed her leg. A bolt of agony shot through her and the last thing she thought as they attacked her leg was that if she lived through this, she could never wear her Glennsday panties again.

Sometime later she awakened, still suffering but not so acutely, to find herself floating along atop the shoulders of her erstwhile attackers, who were singing a charming native folk song of surprisingly complex melody and interlaced harmonies.

Overhead the orchid-hued fronds and leaves of the forest frothed above her, fanning her as the breeze passed through them. At eye level were trees with familiar looking leaves shaped like two tiny bat wings stuck together at the tops with the wings fanning out on either side. Lovely little red berries festooned the trees giving them a cheery look.

And then suddenly they were passing beneath a stone archway, and the warriors, as she thought of them, were transferring her to other, gentler hands. She was deposited upon a table of some sort and carried deeper into the building. Her bearers were not masked but veiled in violet that matched the ground cover she had seen near the crash site. They seemed to be both male and female and spoke in murmurs.

She was carried into a room containing many stone slabs, like altars, with other people on tables laying atop them, their bodies clothed in tattered and bloodied robes and draperies.

Some of the bodies lay very still.

Some were screaming.

And two of her attendants pulled out long wicked looking knives and plunged them toward her space suit. From the corner of her eye she saw the splints and bandages, and realized that they were only removing her clothing to examine her wounds.

Or were they?

As the equipment was being arranged, the nurses, as she now thought of them, pushed her back down onto the table and the doctor, as she now thought of *him,* began touching her inappropriately in the area more or less covered by her ruined Glennsday panties. "What's he doing?" she asked them but no one answered. "I'm sure Space Corps insurance will NOT cover this procedure, whatever it is!" she threatened, but to no avail. These were aliens, after all, despite their humanoid appearance and behavior.

The doctor looked up suddenly and jerked his thumb in the air and before Victoria could do so much as scream they held her aloft, high over their heads. At least they were good enough to support her injured leg as they did so but she could feel the physician's prying fingers lightly tickling her behind through the fabric and holes of her ruined undies. Then suddenly, he let forth a cry that sounded like "Tonda Roga!"

And the others all responded, "Tonda Roga? Tonda Roga!"

And all of them began genuflecting and moaning the same name at the top of their lungs.

"No, no," she said, pointing to herself as they lowered her gently to the table. "Victoria. Victoria Fredericks."

But they failed to heed her words, though they stopped genuflecting finally and bustled about with a gleeful energy that seemed misplaced in a hospital. They busily splinted her leg, gave her a soothing drink that eased the pain, and draped her in first a violet veil then in many other layers of rich apparel that she privately considered a little overdone.

"Thank you too much, I'm sure, but if you could just send up a smoke signal or something to hail my ship, that would be plenty of gratitude," she said modestly, adding, " I really have no need for all of these things. They'll catch on the equipment back at the ship."

But no one was paying any attention. The ones who weren't backing away from her slab, still genuflecting, had moved on to the next patients. Puzzled, she watched while the medical staff first disrobed the patients and fingered and muttered over their underwear, which was at least as disreputable as hers had become. Only then did anybody treat anybody.

"Is this whole hospital staffed with perverts or what?" she asked, the pain making her impatient and not too prone to consider the reasonableness of what appeared to be local folkways. "My stars, the malpractice suits around here must be astronomical."

To her surprise, one of the masked figures, she thought it was the same one who had tickled her—fancy—while examining her undies—turned to her and said, "Not at all, Tonda Roga."

Victoria gasped. "You speak English!"

"Naturally. Oxford Space Academy actually."

"But—but—"

"You are surprised I speak your language? You see, the priestly class is the aristocracy on our world. Healing and prophecy go together—"

Victoria observed where his fingers were walking across the groin of his current patient, a groin clad in a tattered garment that resembled a pair of shorts. "But not exactly hand in hand?" she asked with a brave, knowing little smile.

"Please, none of your earthling prudery, my dear. I am both Chief Physician and High Priest on my world. Allow me to introduce myself. My name is %^&**(+@#."

"That's a toughie," she said. "Okay if I just call you Doc or maybe Reverend?"

He regarded her girlish confusion with less dignity than he had previously displayed. "Of course, Tonda Roga. My name, being the highest on the planet, is naturally of the old tongue, virtually unpronounceable to all but the priesthood. In time, I hope you may even come to call me—but never mind." He readjusted his visage into a stern expression once more. "You are the Tonda Roga. You may be an off-worlder, but you must not look askance at our perfectly normal diagnostic function I am performing."

"What diagnostic function?" she asked, returning determinedly to the subject after being lost, for a time, contemplating the invitation in his eyes to call him—what? Sweetheart?

He returned her to reality. "Why, reading the holes in this patient's unga gao roga of course. It is our chief form of divination and diagnosis."

"Excuse me?"

"The sacred undergarments. Not so sacred as your own, of course, but nonetheless very holy indeed."

"You mean my undies aren't just full of holes, they're holy too here? I don't want to be ethnocentric or anything, doctor, but that sounds like something you'd hear at Callahan's Saloon."

"Not at all. On our world, we believe that the knowledge of character, the future, health, everything, can be read from the condition of that garment which covers the seat of passion, the outlets of the innermost being, the very foundation upon which one balances oneself throughout much of life."

"Is that so?" she asked petulantly, for she was very groggy from the pain medicine.

"It is. How else would we know you were the Tonda Roga?"

"That just shows you how silly it is. I'm not Tonda anybody. I'm Victoria Fredericks, Space Cadet, serial number 00111001."

"Not to us. To us you are the Tonda Roga, the chosen one. It's all right there on your knickers. You can read for yourself if you don't believe me."

"So what's this Tonda Roga chosen to do anyway?" she asked. She decided to pass on the knickers-reading part. She thought it was dumb and besides, he had already done it and he was the expert, wasn't he?

"Save the world as we know it, of course."

"Well, you're safe there then, aren't you, since I already did that."

The eyes over the top of the mask—kind of cute eyes, really, she'd never seen that shade of reddish brown in an eye color before and it was a little like being looked at through infrared—looked momentarily confused. "I beg your pardon."

"I said I'm way ahead of you. I saved your world this morning, I guess it was, just before I came here. Didn't your warriors tell you? They found me at the crash site."

"They mentioned something about how you fell from the sky but—"

"I blew up the Hasslebad ship that was threatening your planet, only I got knocked dirtside by the debris."

"I had no idea."

"I told the warriors. They seemed to understand."

He shook his head. "They understand emotional messages but of everyone on the planet, I'm the only one who understands your language, I'm afraid. That's why I hope I can explain to you the meaning of it all."

"What all?"

"What you must do to save us, beautiful one."

"I told you I—"

"Okay, save us again then. It is foretold that the Tonda Roga will come and we shall know her by her *unga rao roga* and she alone will possess the skill to brave the underworld and the dragons thereof and repair the World Wide Warning Web."

"Bet you can't say that fast," she said, giggling from the pain soothing drink.

"There'll be a great feast tonight and we'll have a procession leading you to the entrance to the underworld."

"But I can't walk on this leg!"

"I thought a Space Cadet never says can't," he scolded, shaking a finger at her.

"How do you know what a Space Cadet does and doesn't do?"

"I attended the Academy as a student, before the web was broken. My family is wealthy and aristocratic and I am considered a very good catch—" he added with eyebrows raised to indicate he was waiting for a response from her that indicated she cared about such unprofessional things. To her surprise, portions of her that had recently been a party to the reading of her *unga rao roga* indicated that she did indeed care. She hoped he wasn't really gross when he took his veil off. "But my mother insisted I get an education first. I came home just as the web was breaking."

"What is this web thing?" she asked, determinedly all business.

"It is the mandala grid that protects the planet from the attentions of those who would harm us, such as the Hasslebads. It conceals us in the invisible protection that kept us safe all through time."

"But now it doesn't?"

"Correct."

"Well, then, I don't want to sound critical, but if it's so important, and you're such a leader here, why didn't you fix it yourself?"

"Because only a Tonda Roga can do so." He replied,

sounding mildly shocked.

He wasn't the only one. "*A* Tonda Roga?" she asked. "I thought it was *the* Tonda Roga and I, Victoria Fredericks, Space Cadet, am she. The one you've been waiting on."

"Sort of," he replied.

"Sort of what?" she demanded with some of the pique those of her hair color are known for.

"We couldn't wait *quite* that long, you see. Long enough for you to maybe show up some day, maybe not. So there've—er—been others."

"And they couldn't do it?"

"Evidently not," he said, shrugging.

She didn't like that shrug. "What do you mean by that? Don't you know?"

"Not exactly. They *never returned.*"

She took a deep breath. "Oh, it's one of those is it? A Class 3 situation." She remembered that from her manual as something very grave indeed, though she couldn't recall the exact text at the moment. No doubt because of the pain medication. "In that case, I'll require a few things from my vessel. Can someone please take me back there now?"

"That won't be necessary," he said, and motioned for another attendant. They carried her between them to another large stone clad hall, and she saw her ship sitting in the middle of it, very much the worse for wear.

She did hope her little bag was still untouched. She described it to the doctor and he said to one of the warriors, "The Tonda Roga requires her magic bag. Enter her steed and fetch it forth."

Trembling, the warrior did as he was told and after a few false tries, during which he emerged with the broken communicator, a spare space helmet, and a half dozen replicated bowls of Jello, he brought her bag. She drew from it a carving knife and then said, "I need a branch from those trees with the funny leaves and the red berries."

"You mean the holly trees?" the doctor asked. "They're a mutation on the same tree you have on earth."

"We didn't have any trees around the Space Port," she said sadly.

"How deprived you were!" he said.

"Yes, but though we had no natural surroundings, we had the glory of Space Port in our very air and of course, we had love. My Mom used to buy me the most beautiful underwear. You'd have loved it."

"Ah, yes," he said dreamily. "I feel quite sure of that."

The holly boughs were duly fetched and, using her Space Corps Knife with the five thousand attachments, she cleverly fashioned a sturdy cane to help her walk into the danger she must face.

Then about three hundred scantily clad handmaidens paraded into the hall and carried her *and* her cane away on their shoulders. She was taken to a chamber where she was tenderly washed, oiled, buffed and polished, groomed and perfumed before being reclad in some rather beautiful lace and more gossamer soft veiling that flowed into a diaphanous garment revealing more than it concealed.

Dreamily, she fingered the material. "This is lovely. Where is it from?" she asked, but the girls didn't speak English and her universal translator had been broken in the crash. Fortunately, despite the filmy nature of her outfit, it did have a handy pocket for her Space Corps knife.

She heard the drums just as the polish on her toenails dried. Pulsing, primal rhythms throbbed through the sultry night carrying the heady scent of nocturnal blossoms.

The maidens bore her from the hall out into a huge garden-courtyard ablaze with torches. The smoke from them wrapped everything in cinnamon scented gauze, giving it an otherworldly feeling, which was not surprising, Victoria thought, considering she *was* on another world.

The night-blooming flowers were draped over everything, swags and garlands of them, all purest white, all smelling like a really exclusive perfume shop back on earth.

A double line of simple, quaint natives, all drumming, dancing and singing their charming indigenous songs, opened before the procession. At the end of the human corridor, flowers and fire arched dramatically over a solitary figure. Toward this man the maidens bore Victoria Fredericks, whose heart was now beating with danger, excitement and another, less familiar feeling, one she couldn't remember having in all the years since she had finally gotten to know all too well every single guy aboard her spacecraft.

Finally, the maidens set her down at the feet of the man. She languished there for a moment, staring up at him through the cinnamony smoke. He was the best looking thing she'd ever seen, and looked absolutely human, without funny nose wrinkles or strange ears or bald head or anything. Well, his hair *was* sort of a pale lavender, but that could have been the lighting and besides, it was one of her favorite colors.

He held out a strongly muscled arm to her. He wore only a loincloth and a few posies around his neck and she could see that all of him was as strongly muscled as the arm. His voice was familiar, tender and warm as he said, "Come, my Tonda Roga. The time has come for you to save the world as we know it. By the way, you look stunning in your ceremonial robes."

"Thanks," she said, rising to her feet—or rather, her foot and cane, with the help of his strength. "It's not very practical but—"

"Tonda Rogas usually also wear eight-inch spiked sandals

for running through the tunnels but, in view of your injury, we relaxed the dress code," he told her.

"It's nice to be special," she smiled up at him, feeling woozy from the pain potion or the smoke, or maybe just the moons and stars, she didn't know. But she thought she would drown in his eyes.

"You are special. I have come to love you, titian-haired earth girl. I pray to our benign native gods that you do not perish on your mission of mercy."

"Me too," she murmured, her lips so close to his she could flick out her tongue and taste them.

"But now," he said, stepping aside so quickly she nearly fell over, "it is time for you to brave all. Farewell, my brave beauty!"

"Bye!" she said, and, taking the proffered torch, stepped through the arch and into a long, long tunnel whose floor descended rapidly.

It also twisted and turned as it descended and branched off many times. Victoria had covered that eventuality in the Cadet Academy however and began unraveling the hem of the diaphanous garment so she could find her way back.

But though her training and her spirit were equal to any task, her body was not doing so hot. Her leg hurt and she stopped to rest just where the tunnel forked and twisted again. After a few minutes, when she'd caught her breath and the pain subsided to a slightly duller ache, she leaned forward, holding her torch in front of her, to peer into one of the passages. An orthodontist's nightmare of stalagmites and stalactites over- and under-bit each other into an impassable mass through one passage.

She pulled the torch back and stuck it into the other branch of the tunnel. She could see nothing so she scooted forward on her bottom and thrust the torch around the corner.

The torch guttered and flared, guttered and flared, and in its fitful light, she could see nothing but grayness. She inched forward a bit more and stretched her hand forward to balance herself. She touched something hard and brittle and looked down. It was a bone! A bone sheathed in white diaphanous material. Like what she was wearing. Oh dear. Next to it was a grinning skull.

She looked away, up into the light of the smoking torch, and made out other bones poking through the grayness. She got only a glimpse, but it looked to her as if the gray matter was composed of zillions of fine threads. Then a portion of the thread extruded and gobbled her torch.

For just a moment before the light went out, she saw through the grayness, far back beyond it, to what seemed to be long sinuous moving shapes that seemed to be waving at her. And still shapes that looked like pairs of wings, trapped in the incredibly tangled web. And of course, more slender young girlish bones.

Then with a singeing smell and a slurping sound, her torch was extinguished and she was alone in the darkness.

She backed away, trying to rise to her good leg, but as she rose, something slithered forward, touching her bare toe, and sucked at the tip of her cane. Holding onto the cave wall, she backed further away and ever further.

What was she doing? A Space Cadet never retreats!

Pulling forth her Space Corps knife, she cut through the slithery material and severed a sample. It did not seem to be alive actually, but lay still in her hand, soft and fine as Asian silk.

"Aha!" she said pluckily to herself, an idea dawning as she recognized certain pieces of this situation as a monstrous blowup of something she was already intimately familiar with.

For though the web threads weren't silk as she knew it, it was certainly some sort of silky fiber. And though the previous Tonda Rogas had been engulfed by it, Victoria in her more sophisticated wisdom doubted that it was a hostile life form. After all, the people of this planet believed there was a web down here and the stuff she held in her hands was what webs were made of.

It seemed to her that what was necessary was a little ingenuity and good old fashioned Space Corps knowhow. And, of course, the right tools.

When the next surge of gray stuff popped out at her she slipped to the side and shook her finger at it before hobbling into the adjoining cave. Groping with her slender fingers, she found the tip of a stalagmite. With the Sawzall blade of her knife, she cut off the tip at a point where it was about five diameters wide. Then she cut about a half inch below the first cut, and lifted off a fairly regular disc-shaped piece of the stone. Using the laser-punchall beam, she bored a hole in the center to slip her cane through. It was a perfect fit, of course, and stopped a few inches from the bottom.

There was also a small flashlight beam on her knife and with this, she saw that beyond the shallow shelter of the stalagmite cave, the gray matter had gotten really pushy and extruded several more feet into the main tunnel. Instantly, the sensitive Cadet realized why. When she had seen the "dragons" they had seen her and were wiggling in anticipation of her saving them! Poor things! That was what had happened before and they'd ended up killing the very Tonda Rogas who had come to help them. But of course, those had just been simple village girls, not Academy trained and space-seasoned Corps Cadets!

She reached out and grabbed a handful of the gray web and gave it a saucy twist around her cane just above the rock whorl. Then, when it was secure, she dropped it and began spinning.

The gray matter spun and spun and every time her make-shift spindle was full, she cut off the thread and attached another hunk to spin more. Soon she had cleared a large enough path for herself to escape, retreating back the way she had come.

The party was still going on and seemed to be a wake in her honor.

Indignation overcame her as she saw the natives dancing and wailing over her supposed fate instead of showing some initiative.

Standing in the archway she cried, "Hear the Tonda Roga! I have returned and I have divined the nature of your problem!"

The crowd, as one person, albeit not a very brave one, shrank back and looked at her as if she was a ghost, which, considering the ensemble they'd given her to wear, she no doubt appeared to be.

The doctor however, looked toward her with his mouth agape and his tear-reddened eyes filled with wonder and hope. "But—but how?" he asked.

She shrugged and tossed her flaming locks, her green eyes flashing. "I'm a professional. Those other girls simply shouldn't have tried being a Tonda Roga on their own. You sent me to be a human sacrifice, didn't you?"

"No, I swear. It is simply written that the Tonda Roga will be a woman and ye shall know her by the holes in her *unga rao roga,* just as I told you. I personally couldn't be more delighted to see you. But—"

"No, I have not yet saved your planet from destruction from within. No one person can do that, however valiant. It will take all of you to do that. This party is traditional too, isn't it?"

"It is written that we shall watch for the Tonda Roga for five days and five nights after she enters the underworld."

"Good. Now I know why you were all called here. I want everyone to go into the woods and start collecting branches and rocks."

"But whatever for?"

"We have a yarn to spin," she told him in her perky, mischievous way, deliberately being mysterious. "I'll reveal all in my own time." She gave him a wink. He blushed.

It took plenty of hard work, encouragement and grit but she had the problem completely under control two weeks later when a landing party from her ship appeared in the courtyard.

"You're out of uniform, Cadet Fredericks," Captain Flash Morgan said with a low appreciative whistle.

"Like it?" she asked, twirling to show off the slight tulip skirt of her slithery saffron silk slip, which she had just been modeling for the doctor.

"Very much, but what's going on here?" he asked, taking in the long line of people stretching from the cave, through the courtyard and out the doors of the hospital into the woods, where spindles, looms, tatting shuttles, crochet hooks and dyepots were busy transforming the gray fibers into colorful, slinky material and strips of lace.

"Just saving the planet, sir," she said with a snappy salute. "As ordered."

"Isn't she wonderful?" the doctor asked from a kneeling position. He had been about to kiss the hem of her garment when the crew showed up. Darn it, Victoria thought mutinously, if momentarily.

"And can you tell me, Cadet Fredericks, just how you're doing that?"

"Because she's the Tonda Roga," the doctor said.

"I asked her," Captain Morgan told him.

"No need to be rude, sir," Victoria reminded her superior officer of his diplomatic obligations. "The doctor, I'll have you know, is the high priest of this planet and by doing a—er—reading, he discovered I was supposed to save it. Of course, I'd already saved it from the Hasslebads but the reason it NEEDED saving was because the internal net, this sort of organic technical thingy inside the planet, had broken down. Only a Tonda Roga could fix it, but since it was sacred here, none of the other girls had a clue what to do and ended up getting enveloped."

"So you slew the monster with your laser gun?"

"No, sir. My laser gun was broken, sir. In the crash when I was injured destroying the Hasslebad ship, sir. But I didn't need a laser gun. See, nothing malevolent was at work, actually."

"It wasn't? But it enveloped all those girls?"

"An avalanche isn't malevolent, sir, but it still kills people. This was more like a flood—of all these little silky things, wiggling out and tickling me all over. I had a torch with me and before my torch went out I saw that there were these long wormlike creatures way back in the tunnel. When I felt the gray stuff trying to roll over me, I realized it was similar to silk. It's the stuff the web is made of and the wormthings—"

"The dragons," the doctor corrected.

"The dragons, are like giant silk worms. Only problem is, over the years, being sacred and all, they've multiplied too often and have spun so much silk that they can't escape to become giant moths. The silk was blocking all the tunnels and exits and there was so much of it there was no longer any room for anything else except for the worms, who pushed it out into the tunnels a little farther with every movement.

That's how come it enveloped the other Tonda Rogas."

"She diagnosed our planet's ailment. Its arteries were clogged," the doctor told Captain Morgan. "The gods told her that we must accept the bounty not needed for the web and make of it useful items. Always before cloth woven from the web was sacred—it is from it that our *unga rao roga* come, and our other ceremonial garments. But it was very scarce, emerging from the ground only at certain holy places. Now, however, all are to wear sacred garments both inner and outer, giving the dragons space to weave, room to grow and time to fly."

"The giant moths are the early warning system," Victoria said. "They sense spacecraft within a certain distance and communicate this to their children, the dragons, who cause the web to send off certain biochemical signals that make the planet sort of er—disappear. Kind of like a chameleon."

"Good work, Fredericks," Captain Morgan said. "But what I don't get is how you figured all this out?"

"Well, sir, fine fabric has always held a certain—fascination for my family. And I knew how to repair cloth from an early age. My mother was extremely particular about the condition of my—er—*unga rao roga* and didn't want me ever to go out with holes in my underwear. Naturally when the spinning, weaving, and dyeing portions of primitive culture survival came up in Space Cadet Academy Survival Skills 101, I paid close attention to these portions as vital to good grooming and wardrobe maintenance. It came in handy, as did my handy Space Corps knife. I owe my training and equipment—and my mother—my life."

"And we owe the lives of our people and that of our planet to this lovely young lady, our Tonda Roga . . ." the doctor said, taking her hand with a sigh.

"Well, sir," Captain Morgan said, checking his chronometer, "It's always a pleasure for the Corps to be of service. We're glad to have had one of our people instrumental in saving you folks here on Hotel Whiskey. But now Cadet Fredericks must return to the ship and receive her commission as Ensign Fredericks of the Space Corps."

The doctor and High Priest snapped his fingers and the three hundred handmaidens sprang forth, each bearing a full set of lingerie made to Victoria's measurements and in every color of the rainbow. They piled the garments around Victoria's feet while she squealed with glee at each new arrangement of lace, each naughty or nice detail, each glowing color.

Then, taking Victoria's hands in his, the doctor looked deeply into her eyes and said, his voice trembling with suppressed passion, "My sweet titian-haired earthling Tonda Roga, you must take these *unga rao roga* back with you as a token of our thanks and esteem. In place of your holey undergarments, we give you holy undergarments to wear and remember our reverence for your beauty and bravery. It will warm my—uh—heart, to imagine part of us so close to certain parts of you." Then he turned so that he stood beside her, facing her superior officer and now his voice with its quaint charming accent was full of primitive dignity and nobility, "As for you, sir, were you sleeping at the Academy when they taught that diplomacy requires you to learn the name of a world as it is called by its own inhabitants? Our world is not called Hotel Whiskey, but is named for the lovely trees that grace its surface and provided the wood for the first sacred spindle. As for this gorgeous and valiant creature, she may be to you Cadet Fredericks or even Ensign Fredericks, but to us she will always be our own Tonda Roga, Fredericks of Holly Wood."

And with that, Victoria and her precious new undies returned to the ship. She wore the tatted lace bra and panties in

Space Corps dress blue for her commissioning and as her new rank was pinned upon her secretly lace-encased chest, her heart swelled with pride and tears came to her eyes recalling how much she owed to her dear mother's advice, and how surprised mom would be if only she knew the impact her words had had upon her daughter's adventures.

The Invisible Woman's Clever Disguise

The invisible woman opened the envelope with a thrill of anticipation. There was no question of it being a bill, or a fake check
made out to her if only she would change her long distance service. It was oversized for one thing, and bright turquoise for another. It might have been an offbeat wedding invitation, though
it was too big and not pastel enough for a birth announcement.
Some time after she had become invisible to the world at large,
she continued to hear from distant relatives and friends who had
not seen or spoken to her in years but who now had children,
even grandchildren of marriageable age. It had occurred to her
to notify these people of her new status by sending them checks
written in invisible ink.

However, this could not be from any of those people, because now not even they knew where she was. The turquoise
object had been slipped under the door of the deluxe hotel
suite she currently occupied. The suite was far too expensive
for most people and now, at Mardi Gras, was probably the
only room in New Orleans still unrented. She did not have to
rent it of course. The maid service left much to be desired

since nobody knew she was here, but the price was quite affordable for an invisible woman.

She had not become invisible all at once, of course. It was more of a gradual fading that happened over the years. She had been married once, because it was time to be married. She was invisible most of the time then to her husband, who worked at a traveling sort of job and eventually found someone who suited him better. They did not have children.

Her parents died, and as she had only one sister who lived very far away and with whom she had never been very close, her past faded into oblivion with no one to remind her of what she had been like as a child.

She had to work very hard after the divorce to maintain herself, to pay bills she had foolishly run up, and as she never made time to see her few friends, she was soon invisible to them too.

As slowly but surely as a stalking mummy, age crept upon her and she was no longer twenty-something, thirty-something, and soon would not be forty-something either. Much more quickly, her absorption in her desk work and her rapid consumption of empty calories to fuel herself during both work and lonely hours caused her to become invisible to men.

She first realized this when men she met socially did not seem to hear what she said and looked over her head or right through her to some younger and more attractive woman or another man. It was not that she was particularly boring. They had never found her so before at least. But somehow, she truly became invisible. At last she was even invisible at work to the men and then, finally, she showed up one day to find someone else—a younger, better-educated woman—at her desk. The woman looked right through her too and at that point, the invisible woman bolted for the bathroom mirror and found that except for a somewhat shapeless and rather tasteless pants and top set, bulging more than she liked to think she bulged, there was nothing of who she was, who she had been, reflected. She was glad the chic young thing who had her job had not seemed to see the clothing any more than she had seen the invisible woman.

That day, she took off her clothes and went home to her apartment.

At first, finding that she was totally invisible depressed her terribly, but gradually it occurred to her that there was a sort of freedom about it that appealed to her sense of humor.

She could go where she liked and do what she wanted. It wasn't as if she could walk through walls or anything like that, of course. She wasn't a ghost, merely invisible. But she could slip through doors unnoticed along with other people. She could snatch food when they were not looking at it, snatch money if she liked, but she didn't like to do that most of the time. She wasn't a dishonest person at heart. But there was so much in the world, for an invisible person with her eyes open, that there was no need really to take too much.

She could snatch a book and leave everyone scratching their heads when alarms sounded as she left the store. She would read it and return it in very nice condition as soon as she was able. She couldn't get served in restaurants of course, but she could take bites from other peoples' plates or help herself in the kitchen. After seeing the condition of some of those kitchens however, she thought of applying for a job as a health inspector—by mail, of course—and informing the public health officials that they could have protected public health much more efficiently had they employed invisible people all along.

At first she spent a great deal of time playing with clothing and jewels—she had enjoyed looking at them so much when she was younger and more visible, though she never could afford what she liked. Now she could have anything at all that she desired, but somehow it wasn't much fun to see her body's over-ample contours in chic designer clothing without a face above them, no face to be set off by a collar, no wrist or arms to be flattered by a certain sleeve length, no feet to enjoy the priciest shoes. Boots were nice. They gave the illusion of feet and legs at least.

But she could hardly wear them in public unless she swathed herself in bandages, which rather defeated the purpose. Once or twice she went out wearing a lot of makeup with the clothes, but she always worried that people would notice she was wearing something she hadn't paid for. After awhile, she gave up and returned most of the clothes and jewels and shoes.

At least, as an invisible woman, she could go out and hear interesting conversations people didn't want her to hear, and that gave her something to think about and for awhile relieved her isolation and loneliness. She quickly decided that if she was going to revel in invisibility she needed to move from Portland to a warmer climate. Running around nude in the rain made her want to steal nothing more than indoor warmth and a cup of coffee.

Thus, here she was in New Orleans, home of the Mardi Gras, voodoo, and of the Anne Rice books she had always enjoyed. She was feeling greater and greater kinship with the main characters all the time—although she, unlike many of them, did not need the cover of darkness to do her business. She found that she liked to go out after dark, nevertheless. The town was more interesting after dark. The smells were sharper, not such a jumble, and the noises clearer. She even fancied that from time to time she had seen some of Rice's eldritch friends lurking elegantly near the shadows. Besides, for most of her life she had been afraid to go out alone in a city on foot after dark. Then she realized that while she might need to be extra careful crossing streets, muggers didn't target invisible people.

Besides, she didn't carry a purse. Mostly what she took could fit into her hands. Otherwise she had to be fairly stealthy about moving it around. Disembodied floating objects might possibly attract unwanted attention. In darkness, at least, she could filch dark colored objects without too much bother.

Even before Carnival began, she enjoyed prowling the darkness. There was violence at times, and all of the things one normally read about in the morning paper. But she could pass by unnoticed and, after awhile, there was very little she feared.

Now that the season and the parades had begun, it was rather wonderful to pass through the crowds unnoticed.

She had always thought of Mardi Gras as one big parade, but actually there were two weeks' worth of parades put on by, this year, fifty-three different organizations right there in New Orleans. Surrounding areas had their own parades.

She had made the mistake of attending a parade while *totally* invisible only once. Her feet were so bruised and bleeding from being trod on by the time she extracted herself from the surging crowds that she was sure she had left bloody tracks. She had finally taken to wearing running shoes. The crowds were so thick that nobody noticed an extra pair of shoes milling with the shoes that had legs attached. It was too hard on her feet to do all that walking without arch support. To protect the rest of her hide against such intrusions from elbows and other painful and damaging objects, she walked down the street with the revelers, beyond the barrier separating the parades from the spectators.

It was fun! She could dance with the music, a blend of jazz, Caribbean mambo, blues, heavy with piano, ethnic drums of indeterminate origin, trombones and saxophones and other instruments she associated with jazz or big band music. There was a sort of jingling percussion instrument too that contributed heavily to the wild feel of the music.

She loved catching the "throws" or trinkets thrown by the people on the floats. The items were mostly cheap and gaudy long strings of plastic beads, cups, doubloons (fake coins with the names of the clubs or krewes that put on the parades), even lace panties and gilt or sequined tiaras. Some of the stuff had collector value but most of it was right up there with what you might give for favors at a New Year's or children's party. Most of them she gave to people she spotted at the back of the crowd, looking disappointed, children sometimes but even other adults—including other lone middle-aged women she thought were beginning to look a bit see-through themselves.

A few of the trinkets she took back to the hotel to drape over the lamps and spread out on the bed and television. To take full advantage of her invisibility, she had to travel light. She had pretty much abandoned her own things when she left home. Even the trinkets she hid behind the furniture or under the mattress when she left the room, in case the maid came in or the room was rented while she was away.

She was still lonely a lot, but sometimes now she enjoyed herself. Like last night. There was a wonderful night parade along the river. Some of the maskers danced in feathers and sequins and very little else on the shore; some were aboard boats decorated to look like sea serpents and Atlantis, complete with a whole squad of long-tailed mermaids. The music had been darker and more mysterious than usual—the same festive beat but with a lot of the Indian undertones some of it had, and more drums and jingles.

Unlike most of the parades, this one was entirely lit with torches or flambeaux. Even the street lamps had been turned off for the parade, and a whole phalanx of robed figures, whom she had at first feared might be some branch of the Ku Klux Klan that wore only black, formed a torchlit barrier between the crowd and the floats, boats, and maskers. Hell for the fire marshals, she thought, wincing a little. She was surprised they permitted it. Most of the parades she had seen featured the torches only as fiery atmospheric touches provided by a few of the parade participants—not as a primary source of lighting. In the firelight the shadows were long and grotesque and seemed to caper demonically independent of the fantastic creatures who cast them.

The throws were rather wonderful too—heavy crystal beads that sparkled in the torchlight instead of plastic ones, and bracelets and necklaces of marcasite and garnets, hard to see in the dark, but really quite beautiful. Something she would have been proud to wear back when she had a self to wear it on. The doubloons they threw made heavy clanking sounds as they hit the street too. She picked up two, though she could not make out inscriptions in the feeble torchlight. She held onto the coins, but had passed the jewelry on to some of the women in the back of the crowd who looked like they needed some luck.

The parade wound past the French quarter where some of the women, not all of them young and firm either, flashed their breasts from the balconies. Well, so did some of the women in the crowd. This mildly shocked the invisible woman until she realized that she was at least marginally barer than even the most scantily clad of them. Only nobody could see her. Or so she thought.

When she read her name on the envelope, she felt herself blush. Deeply. Apparently someone *had* seen her. All of her. And they knew who she was. She felt a distinct chill, although the temperature was already, in early March, in the mid-seventies with humidity of about the same percent.

"Mlle Vanessa Lightfoot" was elegantly calligraphed on the envelope. No one knew her name here. No one. How had they found out?

From the envelope she pulled an elegantly die-cut, embossed and gilt edged card, a fan shape with a shell design containing a mermaid with an elongated tail in a symphony of purple, green, and gold, the Mardi Gras colors.

She knew what this was, she thought. She had seen similar things in the Mardi Gras guides and magazines. And she had seen the mermaid design last night. It depicted the same character as the costume worn by the maskers on the Atlantis float.

Yes. Written in gold ink across the green sea in which the mermaid swam was the invitation: *"Krewe of Melusine 2000 commands your presence at her Melusineranade on the evening of Mardi Gras the seventh day of March, year of two thousand from seven of the clock until two-thirty."* Added to the bottom in an elegant hand, this time in green ink on a golden shell, "Come as a character from your favorite folk or fairy tale."

It further listed an address in the French Quarter.

She was already hearing some of the Mardi Gras terms on local television. The Krewe of Melusine, the krewe responsible for last night's wonderful parade, was oddly absent from the television stories that had been running steadily since Carnival began.

She stepped back out long enough to go to the hotel lobby newsstand and grab a copy of the ubiquitous Mardi Gras Guide.

Through the big glass windows, festooned with gilt banners and plastic beads, she saw the glitter and heard the music of a parade two blocks away.

She returned with the Guide to her suite. It showed the parade route of the Krewe of Melusine, the parade she had followed last night, but there was little else about them in there, except that their organization had entered into the festivities for the first time this year. Well, perhaps that explained why they were recruiting new blood, if not why they could see her. Perhaps, she thought, they were simply more observant than most people. Wouldn't that be nice? Maybe there were people out there who were interested in whatever particular group of characteristics made her unique and saw her because of them. A bit daunting that she would be stark naked when they did. However, in the course of Carnival so far, she had already seen a great many people wearing very little more than she did. Perhaps down here nudity was viewed somewhat different. Maybe Krewe Melusine was made up of middle-aged nudists for all she knew.

But they expected her to show up in costume for their ball so she would have to get busy. She smiled as she considered that she quite literally hadn't a thing to wear.

Who would she go as? She was a bit long in the tooth for the heroines, but then again, nobody could see her so she could get the appropriate disguise and be Rapunzel with yards of blonde hair if she wished! She felt like a cross between Cinderella and the fly invited into the spider's web.

Costume shops were all over the city but she couldn't find a costume she liked, that fitted, anywhere. With the season so well underway, the selection was well picked over and she was not the petite size that most designers fondly imagined their customers would be. For two days she hunted the racks and the temperature rose into the eighties. Even though she risked wearing her running shoes in the daytime, she was growing footsore. Her invisible skin prickled with heat rash and was rubbed raw from chafing. Unused to even mild heat during this season, she was so terribly hot and dripping with perspiration she was surprised people did not try to elude the moving vertical lake she felt she had become. And her search was fruitless. Except for kiddy Halloween costumes, little remained in the city.

Why on earth hadn't the people throwing the party issued their invitations a bit earlier? Probably because they had only spotted her, maybe even recognized her from someplace else, at their parade the night before the invitation arrived. Whoever they were, whatever their reason for inviting her, she desperately wanted to discover.

Perhaps she should just go as she was after all, drape a length of cloth over her arm and be the emperor wearing his new clothes if anyone DID see her and asked. But the emperor (or empress, as anyone who could see her would be quite aware), though naked while wearing "invisible" new clothes, was not himself invisible.

For a fancy masked ball you really needed to wear something unlike yourself. For her, that would be someone visible.

Someone normal. Or almost. Character from a favorite fairy tale?

She found a mask in one of the shops that reminded her of something, something she had a hard time remembering for a time. The mask was covered with holographic film that bounced reflections from its surface. It was trimmed with gilt and sequins. The main part of the mask covered the upper part of the face, but it also featured a cascading veil of crystal and gold beads to cover the lower face. She also found a gold gilt wig with carefully arranged curls such as the white ones a judge might have worn in the old days. Both of these items appealed to her and she took them without quite knowing what she was going to do with them.

She saw the black robe crumpled in a box of discarded costumes in the back of one of the shops. It had a hood. Probably featured a skull mask and a scythe too, but it had black spangles on it so that it would sparkle. She took it too.

Still, she didn't know which fairy tale character she had in mind with that odd assortment until she returned to the hotel room and saw the ornately framed and gilded dressing table mirror. One more foray to a hardware shop and a sporting goods store and she began assembling her costume.

She dithered a little about whether to arrive early or be fashionably late, but she didn't really know the protocol. Finally, because she couldn't stand the wait, because it had been so long since her presence or absence made a difference to anyone, and because she didn't want to miss anything, she arrived at the address on the invitation just after "seven of the clock."

Completely covered in her hooded black robe, gloved and booted in black and her face and hair made visible by the golden wig and holographic mask, glittering and sparkling with every step, she was, in the crowd of elaborately garbed and/or half-naked maskers, more invisible than she had ever been before. She was sweltering by the time she arrived at the address on her invitation, the mirror concealed in a portfolio-sized black bag she carried close to her robe.

The address belonged to a three-story building with the vast numbers of tall windows and the two wrought-iron balconies that were a trademark of French Quarter architecture.

A doorman, dressed in a gray suit with a rat's mask and tail, ushered her inside. The rest of the staff of what seemed to be a rather exclusive historic hotel were also masked and garbed. She wondered if most of the hotels hosting the costume balls did this. The staff in her hotel remained stolidly in the day-to-day uniform of modernity and conformity.

Even more amazing, in this twilight hour, the entire lobby was lit only by candlelight from the wall sconces, candelabrum and some quite impressive candle-bearing chandeliers. The air carried some flowery perfume—gardenia, maybe?

Another rat looked at her invitation and ushered her into a ballroom.

She *had* been expecting the usual Holiday Inn sort of ballroom—a large room with a folding fiberglass curtain that could be pulled across the center to make two smaller meeting rooms. An area of parquet floor for dancing, the rest of the floor covered with utilitarian carpet and furnished with rather institutional tables and chairs perhaps covered with white cloths. Sometimes they had one of those prismatic balls above the dance floor, the kind you used to see in roller rinks, and later, discos.

But if the room she entered had ever looked like that, the decorations committee of the Krewe of Melusine was to be commended on the transformation.

This truly looked like the ballroom from Cinderella as it never had been done but should have. The lighting was supplied by candles, just as it was in the lobby. Crystal and silver chandeliers reflected the light from the flames flickering within them. The light and shadow played across a floor that seemed to be a solid sheet of lavender-veined white marble. A patterned carpet that looked as if with only a little help it could be airborne, padded the steps under her dancing boots.

Beyond the marble dance floor, tall doors opened onto a courtyard where concealed colored lights played on the waters of a splashing fountain with a mermaid at its center. What looked like ancient cypress trees and weeping willows and a couple of palms were lit with what the invisible woman rather hoped were not thousands of tiny candles—Christmas tree lights, more likely, in purple, green, and gold.

The room was edged, not with the conventional round tables and hotel chairs, but with great groaning sideboards filled with all sorts of things to eat and drink. The centerpiece of each table was an ice sculpture, the largest of which was a replica of the Melusine themed float-boat with the mermaids.

She took all this in while peeking past the herald, closed the door softly and repaired to the ladies' room to finish her costume. It felt odd to actually have to go into a separate room for privacy after having, for such a long time, more privacy than she had ever needed or wanted.

When she returned, the herald glanced at her, blew a real trumpet, and announced, "The Magic Mirror from Snow White has arrived."

The ballroom was considerably more crowded than it had been when she ducked into the bathroom. On each step was at least one masker—sometimes a couple, sometimes more, filing down to a reception line that was now in place. She would have to run the gauntlet. Oh dear. Somehow she thought these things were much less formal than this.

The band began playing in the background, heavy drums and jingles, saxophone slithering through with a melody. Perhaps out of deference to the reception line, no singer had as yet taken the stage.

She descended behind Rapunzel and the Prince, who was covered with a thorny vine. On his other side walked a woman wearing a tiara, a brief sheer set of baby doll pajamas the invisible woman thought she had seen in a Frederick's of Hollywood ad, and carrying a spinning wheel. Rapunzel, the Prince, Sleeping Beauty. A threesome? That didn't bother her somehow. Not nearly as much as trying to see through her mask and over the mirror so that she did not tread on or trip over the long yellow braid that formed a train to Rapunzel's costume. As the trio turned to face the reception line, she saw that Sleeping Beauty was a man. She wasn't sure about the other two.

Fortunately, nobody could see from her invisible and masked face if she was surprised or not. The Guide had warned that cross-dressing for males particularly was a Mardi Gras institution.

First in the reception line was Snow White. Next to her—him actually—were seven very little men—children rather than dwarves, from the look of them, though their eyes looked very old, and some of them, she was fairly sure, were girls. One of them spoke up, laying a proprietary hand on Snow White's pale arm. "Oh, darlin' look," the little man said in a high overly sweetened feminine drawl. "If it isn't the magic mirror! You must check and see if you're the fairest of them all!"

Snow White flashed teeth—fangs—at the child and said, "How very droll you are this evenin', Dopey, isn't it?"

The invisible woman was still taking in the fangs when the Snow White smile was flashed at her. "Thanks, mirror. That's real cute but I'm gonna have to pass. You understand, don't you?"

"Maybe she doesn't, darlin'," said the next tall person in line. This was interesting. A woman dressed as a man in drag. Overly made up and coifed but the décolletage in the gown was deep and genuine. "Never mind that little bitch, honey, you just come over here and tell Queenie who is the fairest of them all. My, that's a cute costume! Made it yourself?"

The invisible woman, unsure if she could make herself heard, nodded.

"Oh, you are soooo mysterious! I just love it. And you're new too—not that I can see you, but I can just feel that you are. I know you're going to have so much fun with us. You just run along now. Red Ridin' Hood, honey, would you get Ms. Mirror here some punch? I don't think she can manage with her—uh—reflectin' side in front of her like that."

Little Red Riding Hood turned a red-hooded head to her—and revealed a human face in the process of growing a snout and extra hair. "Never mind," the invisible woman squeaked aloud for the first time in years. "I can manage!"

"Oh lookee there!" squealed the first of the seven dwarves. "Look at all those gorgeous gals!"

Descending the steps in plumed tiaras and a variety of dancing costumes—everything from ballroom and tango through Irish step dancing—came twelve pseudo maidens, at least half of whom were male. Behind them came a fellow in a Confederate officer's uniform with a cloak draped over his arm.

Little Red Riding—wolf? said, "Well, if it isn't the twelve Dancin' Princesses!" He had a nice deep voice.

While he was looking at the princesses, the invisible woman looked more closely at his increasingly wolfish face. If it was makeup, it was the best makeup job she had ever seen. You couldn't even simulate that with a computer. Looking at the princesses, he licked his chops, running a long pink tongue over a long mouth full of long teeth and—what big ears he had!

A werewolf. And the fangs on Snow White. They could be dental appliances of course. The dwarves, grinning up at the princesses, had fangs too. Oh dear. And she had thought Anne Rice was writing fiction! But here they were, all around her, the creatures of the night Rice referred to. The fangs weren't part of their costumes. The fangs were the real deal.

That was how they'd seen her.

She turned to head to the ladies' room again and take off her costume and run away. Except—what good would that do? They had *seen* her. At the parade, where she was as invisible as usual. Some one among them at least *had* seen her and somehow found out her name. Well, sure. The Krewe of Melusine looked like it was largely composed of vampires and werewolves, that sort of creature. They had their ways of finding out stuff, according to Rice and Bram Stoker and bad movies from the forties. Maybe, as creatures of the night, they did as much eavesdropping as invisible people.

Slowly, she made her way toward the punch table. She was very hot and very dry in this outfit, in spite of the ballroom air conditioning that was also wasting energy by trying to cool the courtyard. She took a glass of punch and drained it, took another, and sipped.

A hand touched her sleeve and she jumped, sloshing wine onto the marble floor. "Would you care to dance?" a masculine voice inquired.

It was the Confederate officer. Now that he was closer, she saw that around the domino mask from which showed deep brown eyes, his face was rather badly scarred—seamed, as if he had been cut up at some point and clumsily stitched back together. He was very tall. And his smile didn't have any fangs in it.

"Yes," she said. "But I'll have to shift my costume."

"You have a lovely voice," he said. "It matches your costume. Silvery and rippling."

She was completely taken aback. If this was southern charm, it worked. Especially since this was about the first positive thing, not to mention being a very graceful compliment, she had been paid since she was young and slender and visible.

"Thank you," she said, shifting her mirror to her back and hoping he was so tall he would not see that her neck was invisible in the shadows of the black robe. "I don't quite under-

214

stand your costume, though. It doesn't look like a fairytale character to me. Who are you supposed to be?"

"Why, honey, I'm the old soldier who returns from the war and answers the king's challenge to find out where his twelve daughters go every night to wear out their shoes."

"Oh," she said. "Of course. I just never thought of him as being a Civil War veteran."

"My own little interpretation," he said with a smile. "Now then, this is your first Mardi Gras, I take it?"

"Oh yes. And it was very kind of the Krewe of Melusine to invite me."

"Nonsense," he said gallantly. "Having you here is our pleasure entirely."

"New blood?" she couldn't help asking. Would all those fangs sink into her at some point during the night? Or maybe somebody would offer her immortality and a cozy coffin. And here she was without a smidge of her native earth!

"Now, then, no need to talk like that," he said.

"I didn't mean to be gauche," she apologized. Miss Manners didn't cover these situations, nor Emily Post. How was she supposed to know what to say? She felt giddy and rather girlish. Maybe it was the punch.

Probably her situation was dangerous. Here she was, on her own, unknown in a strange city, having fallen in with vampires, werewolves and—whatever her dancing partner was. Why had they invited her to fall in with them, she wondered? Were they all going to fall on her and bite her neck at midnight or was she going to get offered immortality or what? Well—those choices were ones she would expect of the vampires.

She decided to fish a little, and really, now that she had found her voice, and the "old soldier" seemed to like it, she found it a pleasure to talk and be heard. "Have you known these people long?" she asked. "The rest of the Krewe of Melusine, I mean?"

"Oh, for ages and ages," he said, with a smile that was appealingly bashful if a bit grotesque. "They're a fine bunch of characters."

"Ummm," she said. She decided not to press but go about sussing out the situation more indirectly. "Is the mermaid symbol the Melusine you are the Krewe of?"

"She's not exactly a mermaid," he said. "In fact, a lot of the French nobility—and some of the folks here, claim descent from her. She was supposed to be half fairy and half human. Her father was what the social workers these days would call an abuser and Melusine managed to lock him up in a cave. Her mama punished her by makin' her a serpent from the waist down for part of every day. This didn't keep the girl from marryin' the Count of Poitiers and they were real happy and had a mess of kids until he broke his promise to her and peeked at her while she was takin' a bath. Our own Count De-Base', that's Snow White to you, darlin', claims descent from her through his mother's line, and Louis Garou, Red Ridin' Hood, is related to her from the wrong side of the blanket. She's sort of the patron ancestress for all of the—well, if you were bein' politically correct, you'd probably say differently gifted, breathing challenged, in touch with their inner beast, folks on the Krewe."

She looked back at the emblem of the Krewe of Melusine and saw that the long mermaid's tail was indeed serpentine, and had no fishy fork at the end. She nodded and turned her mask back to her partner.

"And what's your story?" she asked.

"Me, I don't normally come to this kinda thing but the Count is bound and determined to improve our civic image. He even sent a couple of the boys over to get interviewed by a lady writer. Then he and Louie got this notion that we would become the Krewe of Melusine and enter into the festivities this year. Raise our profile. Only none of them, after all the years they've lived, has learned come'ere from sick'em about practical matters. Me, I've got a carpenter's hands and I'm good at buildin' things, so I decided, even though I thought I'd feel silly in fancy dress, to go along with it, help 'em build the float and such."

He did have carpenter's hands—rough and callused, though he had evidently tried to soften them with lotion, and there were more scars at the wrists. Was he maybe a bipolar personality and had become so depressed at one time that he had attempted suicide? She hoped not! His eyes were wonderful, soft and deep and humorous at the same time. They seemed wise. Plus he was tall and he liked her voice and for such a big fellow, he danced divinely. No doubt it was idiotic, but she felt safe in his long arms. She asked quickly, "And are you glad?"

"It's the smartest thing I've ever done," he said. "I knew that the minute I saw you standin' in the front of the crowd, catchin' throws like a little girl." His arms tightened, drawing her to him. "Nobody else was lookin' so I knew they either had to be blind or you were invisible. I followed you—I'm sorry, I know stalkin's got a bad name these days, but I didn't mean any harm. I just wanted to know who you were so I could get you invited here, meet you, get to know you so maybe you'd be—less alarmed, seein' us lookin' so ridiculous in our masks and costumes."

Her breath left in a rush of belief. "Then it wasn't the vamp—the Count and the others who wanted me to come?"

"Not at first, darlin', no. They're kinda self-absorbed, if you know what I mean. But I bet when they're gonna be as impressed as I am once they take notice. I just love your gumption. Not many ladies when they turn invisible start havin' fun the way you do. And I can just tell you're not narrow minded or anything. You're still here, after all." His close embrace graphically demonstrated just how interested he was. When she was twenty, this might have seemed coarse or gross and annoyed her. But maybe not from someone she liked. And she liked this big fellow, even if he was a little on the seamy side.

"And you can see me?" she asked. "Even without the costume?"

He gave her a cheerful leer. "You bet I can, sugar."

"Well," she said, more boldly than she had ever dared even at the pinnacle of her youth and beauty, since in those days the men had to make all the moves. "I am so glad you invited me. It's nice to be a part of things, when I'm such a stranger here—everywhere, actually. It was very sweet of you to take such pains to impress me. I admit, at one point, this would have all been a little too—unconventional for me. But I'm unconventional now myself."

He gave her another little reassuring hug.

"The only thing is, I've had too much of crowds already and I'm not used to being stared at." For she had begun to notice that all over the room, people were staring at them.

"That's not you, honey. It's just that everybody who isn't one of the Count's kind is admirin' their costumes in your costume." Another leer. "You could just sorta slip out of it and into somethin' more comfortable and we could get outta here if you like."

She laughed and put on a Miss Scarlett voice. "Why, Sir, what makes you think I'm that kinda girl?"

He put his finger to his lips, his eyes twinkling, and helped adjust her mirror so that it was once more in the front of her costume. Then, taking a step back from her, he plucked up the cloak he had been carrying over his arm and swung it over his shoulders, adjusting the hood. In the mirror, one moment he was there, the next moment he was gone.

"Now how did you do *that?*" she asked.

"Don't you remember your fairy tales, darlin'? When the old soldier took on the case of the disappearin' princesses, he first got him a cloak of invisibility so he could tail 'em without bein' spotted. I do a little detective work myself, so I find this comes in real handy. It is also how I know what kinda girl you are."

"Oops," she said, then, again in the Miss Scarlett voice. "But that is so unfair. You have the advantage of me! I don't even know your name."

"Names are not all that important among kindred spirits, darlin' Ms. Vanessa," he said, still smiling visibly—to her. "But you can call me Lamont."

She gasped appreciatively. "Lamont *Cranston,* the Shadow who used invisibility to fight crime?"

"Oh, no, darlin', he'd be way too old for you by now. My given name is actually Montmorte but close enough. And I—acquired—many of the original Shadow's traits after he disappeared last time. Includin' bein' able to make myself invisible with the help of this cape, which I got for savin' a poor old bag lady from a street gang, and a taste for crime fightin'. Say now, you bein' invisible yourself and all, I don't suppose *you* would want to try your hand at crime fightin' too?" His big earnest scarred face looked down at her hopefully.

She thought of all of the violence she had fled from in the dark, glad that she could not be seen but feeling guilty for not helping the victims. "Could be. It's crossed my mind to tell you the truth, though so far all I've managed to do is keep out of trouble. Speaking of trouble, for an alleged good guy, don't you keep sort of questionable company?"

He smiled. "These folks took me in when I was barely a few days old, darlin,' when even the folks who gave me life didn't want me. The Count and Louie and their friends may not be real conventional but less like friends and more like family to me. And surely you've read Carl Jung, darlin'? Even us shadows got ourselves a dark side."

"Just how dark is that?" she asked, intrigued in spite of herself. Her heart was pounding. This was the kind of man she had longed for—powerful, intelligent, charming, complex, articulate—and a man of many parts.

He led her to one of the tall floor-standing candelabras and helped her take off the mirror, mask and wig. All around them the masked dancers swirled. He pulled up the folds of the voluminous cloak and gazed into her eyes. It was so nice that he was even gazing at the right place. "Let me put it this way, Vanessa, honey, while I am on the other side of the crime-fightin' fence from the Count or Louie, I *do* have my little—kinks. You and me, I knew it the first time I saw you, we're two of a kind. And I just happen to know that out there under that big old cypress, right near that cool splashing fountain, there is a little patch of soft grass just big enough."

It was an outrageous idea, something she would never have considered before, ever, even with football heroes or movie stars, had she ever known any. On the other hand, she was glad it wasn't just another career opportunity. The night was warm and perfumed, and the courtyard was cool and not *quite* as public as the ballroom. The music had begun in earnest, with a throbbing, primitive beat. And now, well, she was invisible. And he was too. No one would see, or know, but him. It was a uniquely intimate situation. And intensely erotic. Stealth, danger, romance. She felt as if she were seventeen again. Very much in the mood for some serious sexual harassment as a prelude to her new line of work, she played with the buttons on his uniform shirt. "We-ell," she said in the Miss Scarlett drawl, "I suppose if I'm going to help you fight crime, it's high time I reacquainted myself with the evil that lurks in the hearts of men."

He wrapped her in the cloak and kissed her, saying "And women, dearheart. This shadow *knows*."

A Rare Breed

I met my first unicorn, appropriately enough, when I stepped into an enchanting forest glade. It was enchanting for a couple of reasons.

The first reason was that it was out of shouting and phone distance from my place, where an unexpected visitor snoring in my bed reminded me never to wish for anything too much lest it come not only to pass but to remain for an indefinite stay.

The other reason was that I normally don't venture out in the morning too far from the house because I take blood pressure medicine. This medicine displaces the pressure on your heart by creating pressure on another bodily system. That morning, however, I had to go out or go nuts, so even though I did think of it before I left home, I had a certain personal function to perform. The strategically placed trees surrounding the glade provided cover from the road as well as from the hiking trail.

It requires a little extra agility for a female wearing sweatpants to assume the position in semi-bondage without falling over, of course, but I'd had considerable practice while living in the woods in Alaska. With sufficient privacy, such a moment can be ideal for achieving a calm, earthy oneness with nature. However, the occasion is not, as I discovered, the ideal moment for a close encounter with a unicorn.

Up until recently, unicorns were never a problem. No one I knew had seen one except in the movies or in books. Then all at once, people started seeing unicorns. This was my first one. I wasn't crazy about its timing.

It lowered its head, its little goatee quivering and its long spiral horn aimed right at me. Before I could—er—point out to the beast that it was supposed to be mythical, extinct, or at the very least an endangered species and therefore should have better things to do than menace me, it charged. Fortunately it was a good few yards away—the enchanting forest glade was a largish one.

I stood, hastily rearranging my attire for maximum mobility, and did a bullfighter twist to one side at the last minute as the damned thing galloped past me.

Undeterred, it turned, gave me an annoyed look, and lowered its head to charge again.

Clasping my garments to my loins, not from modesty but practicality, since they weren't properly fastened and would hinder movement otherwise, I recalled my meager store of woods lore and pondered my strategy.

With a mountain lion, you're supposed to make yourself big like an angry cat and back, not run, slowly away. This will make the lion think you're too big to swallow in one handy bite-sized chunk. With a bear, you make a lot of noise and hope it really is as scared of you as you are of it (though it couldn't possibly be). If it's a mother bear, you don't interfere with cubs. If you're camping, you hide your food in a sack in a tree well away from where you sleep, praying the bear eats your food and ignores you, mummied in your sleeping bag. But what in the hell you were supposed to do in the event of a unicorn attack had never been covered in any literature I'd ever read.

The unicorn galloped forward again, an ornery look in its green eye. "Hey, you," I said to it, side-stepping awkwardly. "You just cut that out. I didn't do a damned thing to you that you should go harassing me. Go find a virgin to impress!"

Shaking its head and emitting a snort that sent a cloud of steam rising from its nostrils, it turned to charge again. I ducked behind a tree long enough to fasten my pants, and prepared to duck again, but by this time the unicorn was pawing—or rather hoofing—at the place where I'd formerly positioned myself. It was covering my—er—scent, the way a cat would cover its scat.

"Prissy damn critter!" I muttered, and used its preoccupation to scoot away back to the road. I was not followed.

I definitely needed human company then and a latte. My guest would no doubt follow his lifelong custom and sleep till noon, so I headed down to Bagels and Begonias Bakery. It was Wednesday, and on winter Wednesdays particularly, when the tourists were all back at work in their own towns, groups of friends met to gossip and pore over the *Port Chetzemoka Listener*, our town's weekly newspaper.

I grabbed my latte and a plain bagel and joined a table. Conversation was already in full swing but I broke in, which was okay etiquette for Wednesdays at the bakery. "You'll never guess what happened to me!" I said to the two people nearest me while Ramona Silver continued to regale everyone with the problems her friend Cindy had been having since her fifty-something boyfriend had gone back to drinking. The AA group in Port Chet has a much larger and more prestigious membership than any of the lodges with animal names.

Ramona stopped in mid-sentence and turned to me. "What?" she asked.

"I got attacked by a unicorn."

"Where at?"

"Walking up the Peace Mile at Fort Gordon. It just came out of the woods and tried to gore me." I didn't mention the circumstances. It didn't seem important then.

"Oh, well. The paper's full of that this morning," Inez Sunderson said and directed me to the front page.

Local authorities, the *Listener* said, attributed the recent proliferation of unicorns in urban areas to the effects of deforestation and development.

"It's said that a unicorn won't even step on a living thing," Atlanta, the real-estate saleslady turned psychic reader, told us.

I snorted. "If that were true, they'd only walk on concrete. The one I saw walked on grass and was getting ready to walk all over me—after it shish-ka-bobbed me, that is. I think the only thing that kept me from panicking was that I couldn't believe it was real. I've been writing about unicorns for a long time now and I always thought they were make-believe."

"Oh no," Randy Williams said. "The Raven people have several legends in which the unicorn is an important transformative figure. Of course, they refer to unicorns as the One-Horned Dog."

"Surely they're not *indigenous?*"

He shrugged. "The legends are pretty old. Of course, they might have been prophetic instead of historic, I guess. I don't speak the Raven tongue very well."

"You mean the Indian legends maybe foretold that the unicorns would be here?" asked Ramona, a jeweler and artist who like every other artist in town works four minimum-wage jobs to sustain herself. She twiddled the silk flower she always

225

wore in her hair, an orange one today. She always twiddled when she was thinking particularly hard. Her "Wow" was so reverent I understood it to actually mean, "Far out."

Lance LaGuerre, our former Rainbow Warrior and present head of the Port Chetzemoka Environmental Council, said, "That doesn't necessarily mean the unicorns are indigenous or even a naturally occurring species. Some Indian legends also foretell such events as space travel and nuclear disasters, isn't that true, Randy?"

Randy just gave him a look. He doesn't like Lance very much. Lance is the kind of guy who would probably have grown up to be a religious-right-wing industrialist if his father, whom he detested, hadn't been one first. So he brought all of his genetic judgmental Calvinistic uptightness over to the other side. Thus he was a liberal, except that he wasn't awfully liberal when it came to being empathetic or compassionate or even reasonable with anyone who didn't agree with all of his opinions. And he had an awful lot of opinions.

"I mean, now the Forest Service is acting as if they knew about the unicorns all along but up until now, who ever heard of them? I'll bet they're the result of a secret genetic engineering program the government's been conducting . . ."

"Yeah," Ramona said, "or maybe mutants from toxic waste like the Ninja Turtles."

Lance nodded encouragingly, if a bit patronizingly. I doubt the patronizing had anything to do with the Ninja Turtles. I don't think he knew who they were.

"Well, whatever they are," said Inez Sunderson, "they've been stripping the bark from our trees, digging up my spring bulbs, and terrorizing the dogs and I mean to plug the next one I catch in our yard."

The men gently, supportively encouraged her to do so.

Inez, you have to understand, gets that kind of response to everything she says. I think the reason is that she is one of those incredibly ethereally beautiful Scandinavian blondes who look really good in navy blue to match their eyes. She used to be a model, I know, and was almost as old as me, but she looked about twenty-five. She is also intelligent and well-read in the classics and has a good knowledge of music and only watches PBS when she deigns to watch TV and never sets foot in a mall. All that is fine but sometimes her practical, stoic Norski side makes her sound like Eeyore.

I didn't say much more. I was still bemused—and amused, because by now the incident seemed funny to me—by my first meeting with a unicorn. I wasn't quite ready to go home and face my other problem though, so I hung out till everyone left, though Randy was over at another table talking with some of his other friends. He's lived in Port Chet for years and has all these close personal ties with the other folks who worked for the Sister Cities group, were with him in South America with Amnesty International, or used to live in school buses at the same time he did.

My alma mater is a little different from that of most of my friends. I wasn't living in school buses and going to peace marches. I was nursing in Vietnam. So was Doc Holiday, whose real name is Jim, but since he was a medic in Nam, and has sort of a Sam-Elliot-gunfighter presence, everyone calls him Doc. It's appropriate. He's the local Vietnam vet counselor, Amvet coordinator, *and* how-to-avoid-the-draft-should-it-come-back-into-fashion resource person. He's a Virgo, which Atlanta has explained means he's very service oriented.

He walked right past me and sat down at a table by himself.

I figured he didn't see me and I wanted to tell him about

the unicorn, so I got up and walked over to his table and said, "Hey, Doc. How ya doin'?"

"Hey, Sue," he said, shaking his head slowly. I could tell right then that he'd sat down where he was because he figured he was best off alone. He gets these depressions sometimes, but then, so does Randy. They belong to the half of the town that isn't already on Prozac. "Not so good, lady. I lost another one."

"I'm sorry, Doc." He was referring to clients. He told me once that more than twice as many Vietnam vets had died from suicide since the war as died in battle during. He still lost several more the same way every year.

"Can't win 'em all, I guess," he said with a deep sigh.

Randy wandered back our way just then. "Doc, hi. Sorry. I heard about Tremain."

Doc shrugged. "Yeah, I'm sorry about your buddy too."

I hadn't heard about that one. "Flynn?" I asked. They both nodded. "God. AIDS is so awful," I said completely unnecessarily. But then, most things you say about how someone dies are unnecessary.

Randy's mouth quirked. "Well, hey, we never thought we'd live to thirty anyhow and look at us—old farts now. I guess it's just the time when your friends start dropping. But we never thought it would be us."

"Too cool to die," I said. "Old Boomers Never Die They Just—finish that sentence and win a free all-expense-paid trip to Disney World."

They nodded. We all understood. The three of us were graying lone wolves. Armchair analysts would say we had each failed to bond due to post-traumatic stress disorder— Doc's and mine from the war, Randy's from a number of things including the wars he observed with Amnesty. Actually, I think I'm in the club under false pretenses—I bond only too well and stay bonded, whether it's a good idea or not. Doc and Randy didn't care, as long as I didn't try bonding with them in any significant way, but it was good having a woman in the group since they both felt they had a lot of shit to work out about women. So, okay, it's tokenism, but nobody ever asked me to make the coffee so I didn't care.

"Doc, you know what happened to me this morning? I got charged by a unicorn."

He gave me a slow grin. Twenty, thirty years ago it would have made my heart flip flop. Fifteen years ago it would have sounded fire alarms that my feminist integrity was about to be breached. But now I just waited politely as he asked, "Oh, yeah? What was the offense? Did you get his badge number?"

"Very funny. I see my first unicorn after all these years of writing about them and all I get is cop jokes."

Doc's known me for, what? Seven or eight years now, but he still takes my joking kvetching seriously.

"Sorry, Sue. I'd be more impressed except that our facility down by Port Padlock is about overrun with the critters. They're all over the place, and they fight constantly. It's sort of hard to teach people to be at peace with themselves when there's all these unicorns going at it cloven hoof and horn out in the back forty. Makes me want to get out my huntin' rifle again, but I swore off."

"I think I'll go for a walk. See if I can spot any," Randy said, and left. I followed reluctantly. I didn't want to go home.

Jess Shaw, my houseguest, was on his first cup of instant coffee when I returned. He had the remote control to my TV in his hand and was clicking restlessly between channels. The MUTE sign was on the screen. None of the cats were in sight. I think the smell drove them off. They're not used to people who reek of cigarette smoke and whiskey fumes, half-masked by men's cologne. There was a time I couldn't get enough of that scent. Now I wanted to open a window, even though it had started to rain and the wind was whipping up the valley from the Strait. It wasn't that I didn't care about him any more, it was just that ever since my first youthful infatuation more than twenty-five years ago, the emotion I felt toward this man was something like unconditional ambivalence. It was requited.

After not bothering to pick up the telephone for the last couple of years, the man had just driven two thousand miles to see me. In the years I'd known him, he'd gone through several live-ins and marriages. Since my own divorce, I'd done a lot of thinking about who and what I was and who and what the man I'd married and the men I chose tended to be, with the result that I'd pretty much retreated into my own private nunnery. So I just said, "Is your own remote at home broken? Is that why you came to see me?"

"Mornin', darlin'," he said, his voice as soft and growly as ever. The darlin' was nothing personal, however. To him everything that can be remotely construed as being of the female gender is darlin'. He sighed deeply and kept flipping channels.

"You'll never guess what I saw on my walk this morning," I said.

He obviously didn't give a rat's ass.

"A unicorn," I said.

"That's nice," he said.

"It almost killed me," I said.

"Huh," he said.

But two cups of coffee later he was up pacing a dented place in my splintery softwood floors and talking a mile a minute. He wanted to get his gun out of his van and go looking for the critter.

"Not a good idea," I said. "In this wind, a tree could fall on you."

"Well, bring the sonuvabitch on then," he said in that bitter tone he gets when he's both grieved and pissed about something. "It's not like I'm gonna live that long anyway."

"You've made it farther than I thought you would," I told him, a little tartly. He's like a quadruple Pisces and prone to throwing pity parties, so I wanted to head him off at the pass.

He stopped pacing and sipping coffee long enough to look over at me and grin. "Yeah, me too," he said. Then he shrugged, "But I pushed the edge of the envelope, babe, and now the doc says I've ruptured the sonuvabitch."

"What do you mean?"

"The big C, darlin'."

"You've got cancer?" I asked. "Where?"

"Liver," he said. "Just like you always told me."

I used to warn him about cirrhosis but after all the ups and downs he'd been through, I figured he was probably made from good old pioneer protoplasm and would end up grossing out the staff of a nursing home some day. I also figured I might hear about it from one of the mutual friends I was still in contact with. Funny that I hadn't. Now I didn't know what to say. Finally, I resorted to being clinical. "Did you get a second opinion?"

He lifted and dropped a shoulder. "Yeah. No good. They wanted me to go through chemo and all that crap but I figured, hey, I'd rather keep what hair I got and go finish up a few things while I feel like it."

I swallowed. "You know, doctors are wrong about a lot of stuff. And I have several friends who were supposed to have cancer and just got over it. How about alternative therapies? Have you tried that?"

He just shook, kind of like a dog, kind of like someone was

231

walking over his grave. Now I noticed that his color under his tan was terrible. He'd always been thin but now he looked like he was made of matchsticks. He took a long shuddering breath and said, "It hurts, Sue."

"I'm real sorry," I said. Another friend I would have offered a hug but though he always talked like he could barely wait to jump any woman in his vicinity, he was weird about hugs when he was upset. So I put my hand in the middle of the kitchen table and waited to see if he'd take it. It seems to me that we had always taken turns being White Fang. He being wild and needing to trust, and me being, at least in some ways, blindly loyal.

He took my hand and gripped it hard for a moment, then got up to pace again. By that time the wind had died down a little and the rain was just a drizzle. "Look," I said, "Do you want to walk someplace instead of just around the room? That way you can smoke and I'll show you where I saw the unicorn."

"It's still raining," he said.

"We'll be in the trees. Are you up to it?"

"I ain't dead yet," he said.

His breath was even shorter than mine but he enjoyed the walk and picked up the unicorn's tracks right away. We followed them back into the woods but then it started pouring rain again and I felt bad because I'd encouraged him to come out and he was shivering, despite his Marlboro man hat and sheepskin jacket, by the time we got back to the house.

I felt worse (and so did he) when the chill didn't go away, in spite of a shower and being tucked back in bed. The cats showed up again and curled up next to him. He seemed to appreciate the warmth. I asked him for the name of his doctor but he wouldn't give it to me, said he was going to "ride it out." Well, I respected that, but by the second day, when he still hadn't improved, I called my own doctor as well as the mutual friends to find out if any of them had any ideas. He had no kin left, I knew, except for a couple of ex-wives. Finally Brodie Kilgallen told me that Jess had walked out of the hospital, telling the doctors what they could do with their tests and treatments, and that was the last anyone had seen of him down there. Brodie knew the name of the hospital, so if everything went well, I could have my doctor call and get his records from there if need be.

He slept all through the day while the wind drove the rain against the windows, made the trees do the hula and the wind chimes ring. I tried to write but finally, after the storm outside caused two brownouts and one brief power failure, I gave it up for fear my computer would be ruined. The TV's old, though, so after dinner I settled into my nest of pillows on the end of the couch and with cats, remote, hard-wired phone and a bag of pretzels, flipped on the evening news. The wind was booming now, window-rattling, and house-shaking, a thug growing bolder in the dark.

According to the news, the storm was raging throughout the Puget Sound area. Trees were across the roads, across power lines everywhere. One motorist had been killed already. Highway 101 was closed along the Hood Canal, and both the Hood Canal Bridge and the Narrows Bridge, which joined the Olympic and Kitsap Peninsulas with the mainland, were closed. They often were, especially the Hood Canal Bridge, during high winds. Right after the bridge was built, the first big storm blew it away and people had to drive around or take a ferry for a couple of years until it was repaired. With 101 closed, you couldn't even drive around now.

Pretty soon Jess padded into the room, wearing only his jeans. He walked into the kitchen and put the kettle on for his first transfusion of the day, then, for a wonder, came and sat

233

down on the couch next to me.

"I didn't know y'all got hurricanes up this far north," he said, and we sat in one of the only companionable silences I can remember in our association, just touching, watching the tube. He didn't drink or pace or smoke or anything but watch the tube, making a brief remark occasionally or responding to one of mine without rancor at me for interrupting the sacred broadcast.

Then the kettle went off and he got up to fix his coffee, even inquiring if I wanted any.

Just as he returned with the coffee, the TV winked off, along with the lights and the fan on the propane stove, and we were left staring at a ghostly blue screen.

I found a flashlight, lit a couple of candles, and called the power company. The line was busy, of course.

Jess started telling me about hurricanes he had lived through along the Gulf of Mexico and continued into a rambling story about his boyhood. I'd heard it before, many times. He always revises it in the retelling. I opened the blinds to try to see how far the power loss extended. The whole neighborhood was dark, as was the hill above us and the streets all the way into town, as far as I could see.

"Jess?"

"Yeah, babe?"

"Play me something, will you? I haven't heard you play since you've been here. You up to it?"

"Hell, yes," he said, and got out his guitar and began playing a song about the death of the Nez Perce Appaloosas. He kept on singing one after the other, songs he had learned since I'd last seen him, songs he used to play constantly, new songs he admired but had only learned bits of. I heard a sort of tapping sound and looked toward the window.

Four whiskery mouths were pressed against the glass,

above them the tips of four horns. I touched Jess on the shoulder and turned him, still singing, to look. He caught his breath and gave me the same "Oh, my God," look he'd worn when we saw the Marfa Lights together. But he kept singing, segueing from "Blowin' in the Wind" to the Shel Silverstein unicorn song. At this the critters gave a collective snort and turned tail for the woods between my house and my northern-most neighbor's.

"I never cared for that one myself, actually," he said, shaking his head. "Damn, Susie-Q, what the hell do you folks do around here when this happens?"

"I was thinking we might go see my friend Doc and see if he's up to a visit," I told him. "He's a vet counselor who lives out in Port Padlock at old Fort Chetzemoka, which is a pretty interesting historical site. I think you'd like him and find the area interesting."

"Okay with me. You think he's got a beer?"

"Could be," I lied. Doc's been dry for fifteen years, six months and he'd have to tell you the rest. "We should take some candles though."

Soft light glowed from Doc's windows when we drove into the park grounds. Several pale four-legged shapes lurked at the edge of the woods, down by the water, and behind the house and the caretaker's buildings at the park. Randy's truck was in the driveway beside Doc's.

I felt immensely relieved. Randy and Doc would know how best to help Jess. I could get him medical help, of course, but Jess has been in the habit most of his life of turning over the unattractive practical details of daily existence to some woman until she had control over all of his associations, jobs, and where he'd be and who he'd be with at any given time. Then he'd rebel and sabotage her, chewing his own foot off to escape from the trap he'd laid for himself. I was too old for that game and he was too sick. I wasn't going to turn my back on him, and I didn't want to do a whole co-dependent number either. What was left of his life was his to do with as he wished, and if he was going to drink it away, I was going to need backup to deal with it.

"Hi, Doc," I said, sticking my head in the door. Doc likes to adapt Indian ways when he's off duty and it's rude to knock. Usually you try to make a lot of noise outside the door but there was no way we'd be heard over the storm and I wasn't going to expose Jess to another chill.

Doc and Randy sat in the recycled easy chairs Doc keeps by the fireplace. A candle burned in the window and on the table between them.

"Don't you have sense enough to come in out of the rain, young lady? Getcher buns in here," Doc said.

I walked in, half pulling Jess behind me, and as we shook the water from our ponchos I introduced him.

Randy said, "I was just warning Doc to start filling up water containers, Sue. I heard on the scanner that the flood water's reached the point where it's within an inch or two of compromising the reservoir."

"Holy shit," I said. "That'll shut down the town *and* the mill."

"You betcha," Doc said. "I got some extra jerry cans though. I could let you have a couple."

"I wouldn't want to run you short," I said, "But I'd appreciate it."

Jess was standing at the window, staring out at the rain and the pale shapes dancing in it. Randy looked over his shoulder. "Wonder where they all come from."

"I don't know, but they're getting bolder," I told him. "Jess was singing me some songs and they came right up out of the woods and crossed the yard to listen."

"No kiddin'? They're music lovers?"

"Good to know they like something besides destroying trees and flower bulbs," Doc said. "You folks want some coffee?"

"Sure," Jess said, his hand going to the jacket pocket with his flask.

"I'll hold a flashlight for you while you find stuff, Doc," I told him, catching his eye with a meaningful look that he met with a puzzled one. But he nodded me toward the kitchen and we left Randy and Jess to stare at each other.

"So, you're going to tell me who this guy is, right? Long lost love?"

"Close enough," I said. "He's lost anyway." I filled Doc in while he made loud noises crashing around the shelves of the white tin cupboard he packs both dishes and non-perishables in. The coffee was instant, not that big a deal.

Randy was regaling Jess with some of his better stories about Central America. Like Jess, Randy can be so quiet you can't get a word out of him or so garrulous you can't get a word in edgewise.

Jess seemed content to just sit and listen. Doc handed him his coffee and, after giving his a splash from his flask, he offered it to the others. He didn't have any takers.

By the time the coffee was gone, Jess, Doc and Randy were swapping stories. Jess felt compelled to keep his hand proprietarily on my knee, though I knew from long experience he had no interest in that knee at all—it was a territorial thing, about as romantic as your cat pissing on your shoe. But aside from that, everyone was getting along famously. Both Doc and Randy liked music and at one point someone said something that reminded Jess of a song with a yodel in it and he started singing again, but this time he winked and half-turned to the window. Sure enough, there was a whole herd of unicorns out there, their faces blurred impressionistically by the rain.

"That's the damndest thing I've ever seen," Doc said. He peered more closely at the creatures in the window. "You know, I haven't looked at these guys this close up before. There's something a little funny about them."

"Funny how?" Randy asked.

"Funny familiar," he said. "I'm getting one of those psychic things I used to get in Nam—"

"Maybe we ought to call Atlanta," I said facetiously. "We could have a storm party."

Doc turned away, chewing his lip. Without another word, he pulled on a slicker and went out in the yard. I watched through the window while Randy and Jess pretended not to notice he'd done anything out of the ordinary.

The unicorns scattered at first, then Doc hunkered down beside a mud puddle and waited. I thought, oboy, he's going to look like a sieve by the time they finish with him. A couple of them did feint towards him and I saw his mouth moving, his hands making gentling gestures.

After a bit Randy asked, "What's he doing?"

"Talking to the unicorns."

"What about?"

"Your guess is as good as mine." So then he had to go out too and Jess put on his coat again to join them. I wanted to say, don't go out there and stand around in the rain like the other damn fools, you'll catch a chill and die this time and then I guessed he probably knew that. I used Doc's phonebook, found Atlanta's number, and called.

"Sue! How nice of you to call. Do you have power at your place yet?" she asked.

"Not that I know of. Actually, I'm out at Doc Holiday's in Port Padlock."

"He caretakes the grounds at Old Fort Chet doesn't he? Is he okay? No trees down on the house or anything?"

"No. Nothing like that. But he said something about thinking he was having a psychic experience with the unicorns."

"Really? I haven't gotten close enough myself to pick up anything specific but there's definitely *something* about them. I'm not the only one who's noticed it, either."

"No," I said, looking out the window at the three men sitting on their haunches in the rain, a loose circle of unicorns surrounding them. "Do you think you could come out here?"

"In this?"

"Yeah, I know. And it might be for nothing. But it could be interesting too."

"Okay."

I put on my own coat and went out in the yard to join the boys. Two unicorns danced skittishly sideways to let me inside the circle. They were learning manners since my first encounter, maybe? I was as skittish as they were. I didn't hunker down either. My knees aren't that good. The rain was letting up at least and the wind quieting a little.

None of the men said a word. They stared at the critters. The critters stared at them. Then the lights came back on and the unicorns, startled, scattered to the edges of the woods surrounding the house. About that time, Atlanta arrived.

Doc seemed to have a hard time snapping out of his trance but he did give her a little wave and say, "I was just thinking about you."

"So Sue said," she said, not smiling but looking sympathetic and receptive. "Where are the unicorns?"

He nodded toward the woods. Some of them were creeping back out, watching. A couple were brawling up in the north corner of the property.

"Will they let me touch them?"

"I think so, maybe. I'll come with you."

The two of them headed for the nearest of the beasts while the rest of us stayed behind for fear of spooking the one Doc and Atlanta were stalking.

"Well, so much for the virgin thing," I said, surprised to hear myself sound so disgusted. "They're not real unicorns."

"Of course they are," Randy said. "Just because they don't do what you were led to expect they would doesn't mean they're not real."

I felt let down and excited at the same time. On the one hand, they weren't turning out to be what I thought they should. On the other hand, it promised to be a kick seeing what they did turn out to be, other than a nuisance.

Doc approached the unicorn first, and it let him lay his hand on its neck in a friendly way. With his other hand, he took Atlanta's forearm and guided her hand toward the beast's nose.

The unicorn tolerated that closeness for a second or two before it bolted. Doc and Atlanta rejoined us.

When we went back inside the house, the phone was ringing and Doc's TV, set on our local news bulletin board, was saying that the recent rains had caused the flooding to overflow the reservoir and we should all used bottled water for drinking until further notice.

Doc apologized for not getting out his jerry cans sooner. I introduced Atlanta to Jess and he gave her the best of what charm he still had to call on, to which she responded with girlish confusion. I fought off a pang of jealousy and asked, "What did you think of the unicorn?"

"I think Doc's right," she said.

"Right about what?" Randy asked.

Jess just sank back onto the dilapidated couch and closed

his eyes. His mouth and nose had that strained look about them I've seen so often on people who were suffering but afraid to ask for pain meds. After a moment, he drew out his flask but from the way he shook it, I could tell it was empty.

Doc cleared his throat. "I know this sounds a little crazy, but the unicorns remind me of some of my clients. I'm pretty sure the one I was trying to talk to at first out there in the yard was Tremain.

"It would explain why you have so many of them around here, anyway," Doc said.

And these were the guys I turned to for practical help for Jess! "You think that's what they are too, Atlanta?" I asked her.

She did a Yoga inhale-exhale number then said, "They're frightened. Disoriented. And—I don't know how to say this. They aren't quite real."

"What do you mean, not real?" Doc asked.

"They're all adult males for one thing, and none of them seem to have been unicorns very long. They're not sure what to do, where to go, how to act. They're like souls in limbo."

"So you think they're reincarnations of the vets?" I asked. "Then why did one try to attack me while I was taking a leak in the park the other day?"

"Maybe that one was the reincarnation of LaGuerre's old buddy Jenkins? Remember? The guy who took potshots at the sewage plant when they started building over by the lagoon?"

"Yeah," Randy said. "He didn't want you polluting the pristine parkland, I bet."

"I still don't get it," I said. "Why should they come back as something that was just mythical before? I mean, even taking reincarnation as a given, why not come back as another person, or a worm if you've behaved in a pretty unevolved fashion or one of my cats if you deserve to be spoiled?"

Atlanta shrugged. "I don't know. But it seems to me like maybe, well, because there's too many of them dying at once? Maybe there isn't really an established place for them?"

"Yeah," Doc said. "And a lot of these guys weren't bad or good, just confused. Maybe Great Spirit didn't know what to do with them either. Take Tremain. He was well educated; for awhile after Nam he was a mercenary, then he switched and became an agent for the Feed the Children Foundation, meanwhile going through three families before he tried settling down and working as an electrician. Then he kills himself. Who'd know what to do with a guy like that?"

Atlanta nodded soberly. "There's a lot of people that way now. Too many maybe. Well educated, semi-enlightened, lots of potential but just never could quite find a place among so many others—even after, I guess . . ." Her voice trailed off as she looked out the window toward the woods again.

"So all our contemporaries who are dying are coming back as horny old goats?" Randy asked, chuckling. "I like that. That's real interesting, folks. I think I'll wander over by Flynn's place and see if he's around. Maybe he'd like a game of ring-toss."

These were the people I was counting on for practical help with Jess? They were nuttier than I was. I just wrote about this stuff. They believed it.

"So what do you think of all that?" Jess asked in the car on the way back to my place.

"I hate to say it but I think the sixties were way too good to some of my friends," I said.

"Maybe that's why they're comin' back as unicorns," Jess laughed. "They're all hallucinations."

"Or something," I said.

"If I come back as one, I promise not to gore you when you try to pee, darlin'."

"Gee, thanks."

Just as we were pulling into the drive he said, "Susie?"

"Yeah?"

"Say your buddies are right about the unicorns. Why are they only around here?"

He was serious now. And it occurred to me that questions about the afterlife, however ludicrous they might sound to me, were probably of urgent interest to him right now. So I said, "I dunno. Maybe because there's such a high concentration of guys kicking off around here, but it's a small place. Maybe it's like some sort of cosmic test area or something."

He nodded, very soberly for him.

While he slept in the next morning I spoke with my doctor, with a friend in Hospice work, trying to figure out what to do if Jess chose, as he seemed to be doing, to die at my house. I half wished they'd tell me it was against the law. It had taken me a lot of years and miles to find a place to work and be peaceful while I got over him. I didn't much want it polluted with his death. On the other hand, I wouldn't be able to live with myself if I sent him away. Ordinarily, I'd figure whatever ulterior motive brought him to me would take him on his way soon enough but now he was dying and I knew about that. The bullshit stopped here.

Ramona called me about two that afternoon. "Sue, it's awful. They're going to start shooting the unicorns."

"Who?" I asked.

"The public works guys from the city. They're trying to get in to fix the reservoir and the unicorns won't let them."

"I don't think they can do that legally, Ramona," I said as soothingly as possible.

"They don't f-ing care! They're going to just do it and take

243

the consequences afterward. I'm calling everybody to get their butts up there and stop it."

"Okay, okay. When?"

"Now!"

"What's to stop them from doing something after we leave?"

"I'm not leaving," she said but she was a little over-wrought. In her hippie days she could have chained herself to a tree. Now she's got a son to think of and an elderly mother to care for.

I was just debating whether to wake Jess or to go by myself and leave him a note when Doc and Randy drove up.

"Jess still here?" Doc asked, without even greeting me.

"Yeah," I said. "But he ought to be up soon. You can stay and wait for him if you want. Ramona just called and said the city workers are planning to kill the unicorns blocking work on the reservoir and they're organizing a protest."

"I know," Randy said. "I called Ramona."

About that time there was the sound of bare feet hitting the floor in the bedroom and Jess padded out and peered be-nignly but blearily around the corner before disappearing into the bathroom. A few noisy minutes later he was back out. In the light of day he looked worse than he had before, his skin stretched tight and dry over his cheekbones, his eyes fe-verishly bright. The smile he greeted us with was more like a grimace and he walked stooped a little, his hand pressed to his side.

I didn't want him to go, but for once he didn't insist on six cups of coffee. He took one with him. He threw it up on the ground outside when we got to the reservoir.

Armed men in uniforms squared off with Ramona, yellow silk flower quivering with indignation, and a small crowd of people, only some of whom I recognized from the bakery.

Lance LaGuerre for one, Eamon the Irish illegal, Mamie who used to run the gallery downtown, lots of others. A rerun of the sixties, except for the unicorns stomping, splashing, bleating, fighting, kicking, biting, and diving in and around the reservoir and the flooded river overrunning it.

Doc strode over to talk to the city workers. Some of them were clients of his, others Amvet buddies. Gun hands relaxed a little. Randy hauled Jess's guitar out of the back of the truck.

He nodded at Jess, Jess nodded at him and spent a minute or two tuning.

"Shit, oh dear, they're gonna sing Kumbaya at us," one of the city guys said.

Instead, Jess swung himself and his guitar into the back end of the truck while Randy started the engine. I joined the protesters, as Jess began to sing in a voice that never did really need a sound system.

The unicorns that were in the reservoir climbed out and dried off and followed the others, who were already trotting down the road after the truck while the pied piper of Port Chet sang the National Anthem. Doc saluted and the city workers put their hands over their hearts while the unicorns, brown, black, white, spotted, dappled, gray and reddish, their horns uniformly shining white, passed by. Jess kept singing the National Anthem until they were well down the hill and into the trees (and out of rifle range). Then I heard him launch into Hamish Henderson's "Freedom Come All Ye" in lowland Scots with a fake Irish accent.

"Wow," Ramona said. "Some guy. How'd he do that?"

I shrugged. "He's been doing it all his life."

"For unicorns? He got some special thing with them?"

"I don't know. I expect a ghetto blaster with loud rock'n'-roll will work as well for some of them, or maybe the Super

Bowl on a portable TV, but we already knew they were attracted to Jess's music so this'll get them out of harm's way while everybody cools off. Maybe someone would like to call a lawyer for the unicorns and get a restraining order against the city? Before Jess runs out of breath and the critters return?"

But that wasn't necessary. Five o'clock came first and the city workers climbed back into their vehicles and went home, and pretty soon the protesters did too. Doc hitched back into town to help Ramona see about hiring the unicorns a lawyer. He asked me to stay and see if any of the beasts came back or new ones came. He said Randy and Jess were supposed to come back for us when they'd taken the unicorns safely off into the national forest on some of the back roads Randy knew.

It wasn't a bad wait. The water was so pretty and clear that even the turbulence of the river mingling with the still water couldn't mar its beauty. You could still see clear to the bottom, like in a mountain stream. And the reservoir was plenty deep.

It was getting dark by the time the truck returned for me, and it had started to rain. I picked up the lights all the way down the road and Randy parked and honked for my attention. When I stood up, Randy yelled, "We got to get back to your place. Jess wore himself out—he's running a fever and he's looking pretty bad."

But about that time there was a thump and a crunch of gravel and a splash.

"Where is he?" I asked, peering into the cab.

"Still in the back."

But he wasn't. His guitar was there. I ran to the reservoir. He was laying face down in it, the ripples still circling away from him in the pallid moonlight beyond the truck's headlights.

When I pulled on his arm, it was hot as a poker. Randy leaped out and helped me and did mouth-to-mouth and got him in the truck. I couldn't help thinking on the way to the hospital that it was a blessing this had happened. He'd apparently gotten delirious from fever, half drowned himself trying to cool off, and now we *had* to turn him over to someone else.

My relief turned to anger and dismay when they took him away from us into ICU, and not even Randy's friends on the nursing staff could help. Nobody but next of kin allowed. Randy took me home and I sat there crying and hugging my cats, waiting for a phone call to tell me my friend—my oldest, dearest love who was now my friend—had gone out with his boots on and was now, if Atlanta and Doc were right, on his way to unicorndom to be chased through a country where he had no real niche, even in the afterlife.

The call came at about six in the morning.

I scared all three cats grabbing for the receiver. "Hello?"

"Sue Ferman?"

"Yes?"

"Mr. Shaw in bed six wishes to check himself out now. He said to call you."

The damned fool, I thought, briskly brushing the tears away and cleaning my glasses so I could see to drive, he was determined to die here. I drove into the hospital lot and walked through the door, afraid of what I might see. What I saw was Jess arguing with an orderly that he didn't need a goddamn wheelchair, he could walk out on his own two feet.

"Susie-Q get me outta here, will you?" he said. "I thought I told you no hospitals."

"Yeah, well, you didn't tell me you were gonna drown yourself," I said, hugging him whether he wanted me to or not. He did. And to my surprise his hug was strong, and cool, if not as fragrant as usual. I took a good look at him. His eyes were tired and lined and he was still thin, but the pain was gone from his face and when he stood up to get into the car, he stood erect as he ever had, moving with an ease I'd almost forgotten he possessed.

He hung around another day or two to see if the unicorns returned but you know, they never did. We're still not sure why. Then he said, "Well, darlin', I love the audiences you got around here but I guess if I ain't gonna die, I'd better haul ass home."

I surprised myself by laughing, not even bitterly. "Yeah, we already know we can't live with each other."

He grabbed me and hugged me and kissed my ear rather sloppily. "I know it. But I sure do love you. I don't know what the hell you see in me though, I truly don't."

I returned his hug and kissed him on the bridge of the nose where I kiss my cat and where his horn would one day sprout if the present trend continued. "I don't either except that you're almost always interesting as hell."

"I'll stay if you want me to," he said, like he was going to make the ultimate sacrifice. "You damn near saved my life."

"Nah," I said, "I love you more than I've ever loved anyone but you get on my nerves. Go back and find some younger woman who's not got to cope with you and meno-pause at the same time."

And he did.

He's called every so often since then however, even though he hates the phone, just to stay in touch.

"How's our horny little friends?" he asked the first time he called back from the road in Boulder. "Do they miss me?"

"They must," I told him. "Since you led that bunch off that day, nobody's seen much of them. Do you suppose At-lanta was right and they were just on their way to some other place?"

"Either that or it was just the cosmic testing ground like somebody said and somebody else saw the test was failin'."

"Well, it's the city that feels it's flunked now," I told him. "Do you know, when they tested that water, even after the flood supposedly polluted it, they found it was free of all impurities? We had the taps turned on again right after you left. Three cases of hepatitis C, two cases of AIDS and several more cancers supposedly made miraculous recoveries in that time, but then, of course, the good water got all flushed out of the system. The city would *pay* the unicorns to come back now. But I guess you can't just have magic when you want it."

"Nope, which brings up somethin' I been meanin' to discuss with you. Do you know that ever since I got out of the hospital, I haven't been able to enjoy a good drink? It's like it turns to water the minute it touches me."

I expressed my sympathy with cheerful insincerity and hung up to take a couple of bags of daffodil bulbs out to the woods, just in case.

Scarborough Fair

"Yes, madam, I know very well *where* you are. I *asked* for your name," the taxi dispatcher said, patiently but firmly, as to a child or an intellectually challenged entity. Like an American tourist dumb enough to visit an English seaside resort at the end of October.

"My name is Scarborough and I'm also in the town of Scarborough. There's a connection there, see?" I was patient too, even jovial. I understood attitudes about tourists. I live in a small, charming Victorian seaport town on the Washington coast. Several times a year, and particularly in the summer and at Christmas, it becomes impossible to find a parking place or a seat in a restaurant in my own town. That's how overrun it becomes with people from other places in search of atmosphere, scenery and gifts (or so the Chamber of Commerce hopes). "Part of my family used to be English, see," I explained further, getting into the role so that her preconceptions about how shallow and trite I was would all be validated and we could get on with finding me a cab.

"The Prince of Wales hotel, was it then, Miss

250

Scarborough?" she asked quickly, afraid I'd tell her my life history and expect her to invite me for tea, no doubt.

"You got it."

"Heading where?"

"The beach I guess."

"The strand then," the woman corrected me haughtily.

"Look, lady," I said, tired of the game. "I'm not stupid. I speak English. I watch PBS. I know for an absolute fact that "beach" is a perfectly legitimate word, in England as well as America, for a beach. What are you, a taxi dispatcher or a—a—" I couldn't think what profession would possibly employ someone to be deliberately rude over two equally correct word choices.

"Ahem. The walk is actually quite pleasant, if you don't mind a bit of wind," a voice at my elbow said.

"Great. I like wind. I'll walk," I told the telephone, and hung it up. Then I turned to see who had spoken. A white-haired lady looked up at me with bright Delft blue eyes. She wore a navy coat with a silk scarf in a jeweled pattern draped over the shoulders, and a powder blue and white afghan in a lacy pattern tucked over her knees between the wheels of her wheelchair. It was one of the old fashioned wooden kind you used to find in VA hospitals. She was still very pretty, her bones fine as a bird's, the lines in her face delicately etched.

"Thanks," I said.

"Think nothing of it. I couldn't hear the other end of the conversation of course, but from your response it seemed like quite unprovoked rudeness. As is eavesdropping, I suppose . . ."

"My voice carries well," I said to cover her apology. "How far is it? To the beach I mean."

"Not far at all if you go down the road and across the bridge. It's quite scenic, even now. There's rather a steep hill but there are steps in several places and there's also the funicular."

"The what?"

"The little tram that goes up and down the hillside. It's called a funicular."

"Are you a local?"

"No, but I used to spend every summer here when I was a girl."

"I'll bet it was really beautiful then. I only saw a little coming to the hotel from the train but it looks like it's been a gorgeous place."

"Ah yes, it was before the war. When the baths were in operation, the gardens were in bloom year round, the promenade was always filled with strollers and evenings in the hotel dining rooms were like fashion parades."

"Just like Agatha Christie," I said.

"You're a mystery fan, then?"

"Oh, yes. And I only partly wanted to come here because my family has the same name. The other part was all those Christie mysteries where the whole family was returning from or going off on their hols at Scarborough."

"Just as we did," the lady said, then twisted slightly in her chair to greet another lady, somewhat younger, who was just getting off the elevator. Lift. "Oh, here's Daisy now. My sister, Daisy Jacobs, Miss Scarborough."

"Ann," I said. "Nice to meet you, Miss . . ."

"It's Mrs. Jacobs actually, but do call me Daisy," she said with a little sniff, after which she mopped her nose with a crumpled tissue. Like her sister, she was dressed for the outdoors, but she wore gray wool trousers and a beige coat with a little beige felt hat over her lightly tinted strawberry blond hair. She was obviously younger than her sister, her face rounder and her build sturdier. Her eyes were puffy and red-rimmed behind stylish big tortoise-shell rimmed glasses.

"Nice to meet you, Daisy," I said.

"And I'm Eleanor Porter," my new friend said. "Daisy, Ann is here for the first time, finding out about where her family comes from. Isn't that nice?"

"Pretty typically American, I guess," I said. "But you can't get much more direct. I mean, it's not like my name's Smith or something."

"No, Scarborough isn't awfully common," Daisy agreed. "There's an exhibition down on the strand but I don't know if it's open or not this time of year. We've never been at this time before. Only during the summer, for the fair."

"There really is a Scarborough Fair in *this* Scarborough then?" I asked.

"Naturally," they both said, a little puzzled.

"Well, I mean, I thought it was just a song. Then there's a Ren Faire in Texas by that name but . . ."

"A what fair?" Daisy asked.

"A Renaissance Faire, where they re-enact medieval times, only they skip the unhygienic bits," her sister informed her. "There was an article about it in the Sunday supplement. Do you know, Daisy, before we tend to business, I think it would be nice if we showed Ann something of the town. Do you think we might?"

Before I noticed that Daisy was looking doubtful I blurted out enthusiastically, "Oh, would you please? If you spent your childhood here, you'd know all about it. It would be so much more fun . . . that is, if you don't mind."

"*I* should love to," Eleanor said. "But I can't get about much these days without assistance."

"Well, I don't see why we shouldn't, if you're sure we wouldn't be imposing on your holiday, Ann," Daisy said. She sounded as if courtesy really were her only concern.

"Oh, no. I'd love it."

That settled, Daisy and I maneuvered Eleanor's wheel-chair down the handicapped-inaccessible entrance of the motel. A forty-year-old bellboy belatedly bestirred himself to help us, and then we set out down the grand promenade, as Eleanor called the thoroughfare which swept past dozens of once-stately Georgian edifices similar to our own hotel.

Our hotel and all of the others faced the sea and the cliffs leading down to it. The promenade followed the shoulder of the cliff, which was beautifully landscaped in deciduous trees now wearing their fall wardrobes and busily showering their gold and auburn leaves on the ivied terrace. A little path zig-zagged down the hill to the Spa and we stopped to look.

The Spa was an imposing building, even seen from above. It resembled a Victorian conservatory—lots of glass in the walls, a la Prince Albert's Crystal Palace, little domed towers at the corners and a large central tower in the middle. A red brick courtyard joined the building with a semicircular-shaped cloister and an oval domed enclosure surrounded by fancy tiles. At the far end of the brick courtyard lay an empty pool, large and round, with a tiled bottom. "Did they bathe there?" I asked.

"Oh no, that's only a fountain," Daisy said with a little cough. "The baths were in the central area. Of course, they were used most often by adults who felt in need of taking the waters for health reasons. The sea was much more ex-citing for us as children, though the water was very cold indeed."

"When you're young you don't seem to mind as much, though," Eleanor said wistfully.

"I know," I said. "The water in the Sound, where I come from, is so cold it makes my bones ache and I can only stay in a second or two, but the kids will run in and out of it all day long."

"It wasn't so much the swimming, really," Eleanor said. "It was that one met all of one's special summer friends year after year—the same families came to the same hotels and the same spots on the beach and did the same things. It was very—comforting. As if we had one life most of the year and an entirely different identity for summer. So many memories." She twisted in the chair to look up at Daisy. "Yes, dear, you do see why I don't mind staying, don't you?"

"I suppose, but I still don't see why you can't come to stay with us."

"You've no room, darling, and you know it. It will be just like the old days to be here again, only I'll not have to leave this time."

"I wish you'd reconsider. The hotels aren't what they used to be, especially the ones that have been converted for nursing homes. Some of them are desperately dilapidated."

"That's why you'll help me look until we find one that isn't, dearest. But I do insist it have a decent view of the sea and the promenade."

I hated to think of our hotel, with its one miserable lift, its seven stories of steps, and its one-bathroom-to-a-floor toilet facilities being turned into a nursing home. I was a nurse before I started my present profession and the thought of trying to tend to bedridden and incontinent patients under such conditions did not appeal to me. The places looked like fire traps and even our hotel, a three star one, was crumbling around the edges and in need of paint. "Are you unable to live by yourself now?" I asked. Maybe it wasn't polite to ask so soon after I'd met these ladies, but when you've spent several years of your life asking total strangers when they had their last bowel movement, questions about health no longer seem particularly private or personal.

The wind tried to snatch the scarf from Eleanor's coat but she caught the silken square and proceeded to tie it around her head. "I don't see why not, actually. I've been coping with life in this chair since the war."

"It's your blood, dear," her sister said, as if reminding her of something she surely needed no reminding. "The doctor said the clotting was very dangerous, with your heart condition, and that someone really must be around to watch you at all times."

"I can't feel my legs, you see," Eleanor said to me. "If I injure them by playing polo in my chair or something ridiculous like that, the medication I'm taking for my disorder could cause me great damage before some responsible adult took me in hand."

I nodded. "I've been a nurse. It does sound like a good idea for you to be with someone in case you need help." I still hated to think of her in those moldy old hotels though.

"So I thought, what better place for my personal elephant's burial ground than Scarborough, where we were so happy?"

"You said you'd been a nurse, Ann. Did you quit when you married?" Daisy asked her own untactful question, changing the subject.

"Oh no. I kept working after I got married," I said, not dropping a stitch or ignoring the implied question about my marital status. "My husband and I were building a cabin in the woods in Alaska. But about the time I got divorced, I decided to start writing."

"Do you really?" Eleanor asked. "What do you write?"

"Fantasy novels."

"For children then?" Daisy asked.

"No, for adults—or children in some cases. They're stories based a lot on folklore and fantasy and in my case, on folk songs. That's one reason I'm here. It's always tickled me that my name had a folk song about it so I wanted to see the place."

"Fascinating," Eleanor said. "I once had a friend who loved folk songs and told wonderful stories. Mostly about Ireland."

We strolled across the causeway, as the ladies called the bridge that topped the high stone wall separating beach from cliffside town. There were no swimmers out today, of course. A surfer or two with wetsuit and board, a lone sea kayak and the bright sails of two wind surfers showed against the white plumed silvery water.

The waterfront was a disappointment. Daisy and I eased Eleanor's chair aboard one of the funiculars and paid our ninety-nine pence. The little tram car then descended a track down the steep cliffside to beachfront level. Other than the seascape, only the architecture was wonderful—wrought iron edged awnings over a long boardwalk. The multi-domed, many-sided, red brick colossus that was the old Grand Hotel towered from beach front to high above the tallest buildings in the clifftop town, dominating the skyline.

"Of course, it's been so long since we've been here that I didn't have occasion to notice then," Eleanor said, "but the nice thing about being at a health spa is that so many things are accessible to wheelchairs."

"Except the hotels," Daisy said stiffly. "I didn't find them to be at all convenient."

"One can't have everything. I'm sure the ones that have been turned into nursing homes have been adapted accordingly. Daisy. Dear. I do intend to spend my last days here."

"Very well."

"There are a lot of video arcades here, aren't there?" I

asked. They were, I suppose, beachside fun for the kiddies, along with the shops selling cold drinks and ice cream and tacky souvenirs. It was no worse than places in the States, but I've never spent much time in those places. It seemed a shame to me to lure kids to the beach so they could turn their backs on the sea and sand for virtual battles with coin-generated foe. Oh well, it was supposed to be good for the eye-hand co-ordination.

"There do seem to be, don't there?" Daisy said. Eleanor was lost, looking out to sea again. "There didn't used to be but there was always something of the sort, though not so loud and with so many flashing lights." Clanging and flashing still issued from a couple of the places, though many of them sported "Closed" signs.

"No, it wasn't like this. It was lovely then, meeting our friends year after year. At night there were fairylights all along the strand. Remember, when we were small, how Eamon claimed the lights really were the lanterns of fairies?"

Daisy didn't smile.

"And later, when we were older, for those moonlit strolls . . ."

"You were older," Daisy said, with a sniff that wasn't entirely her cold this time. "I was still a child."

"It was so romantic, Ann, you can't imagine," Eleanor said. "Just the fairylights and the stars and moon shining on the ocean, the warm sand and a friend you'd known since childhood suddenly so very intensely interesting. Of course, when the war broke out, we couldn't have our fairylights any-more. In fact, we . . ."

"We stopped coming altogether then. I remember you cried for weeks when father said it was too dangerous," Daisy said, and began coughing hard. "Oh, dear. This wind is aggravating my cold I'm afraid."

"I'm becoming rather tired myself. You must excuse two old ladies, Ann. I understand there's some sort of historical exhibition here now—there—that Millennium thing. You'll probably enjoy that. And do try to see the main part of the town. It's a bit of an arts colony these days, I understand. But now I think we must go back and rest."

A taxi was passing then and I insisted on putting them in it and paying the fare in advance, thanking them for their company.

"Perhaps we'll see you at dinner," Eleanor said.

"I'll try to see the exhibition before closing time, that is, if it's still open," I told her. "I'll probably be going down for dinner about six."

"Lovely," she said, and their taxi drove away at a neck-breaking speed, as if the driver was so glad not to have to maneuver his way through crowds that he celebrated by pushing the edge of the envelope.

The exhibition was far down the beach, away from the rest of the attractions. Halfway there I was picked up by a shuttle bus with bright slogans and no passengers at all. The driver, a middle-aged man, looked profoundly bored, but in answer to my question said in a thick Yorkshire accent that aye, the exhibition had not closed and I might find someone there if they hadn't gone to tea already. We sped far down the beach, past all the businesses and the cliff containing the skeletal remains of the castle, to a fake Tudor cottage with its atmosphere destroyed by a large sign saying Millennium.

The door was open and I poked my head in. I didn't see anyone to sell me a ticket, and called out. Someone called back from the bowels of the building, "Go on round then and I'll catch you on the way out."

It wasn't exactly Disney World or even Madame Toussaud's but it was more interesting than I would have expected from what I'd seen of the town so far. Apparently we Scarboroughs had a Viking in the woodpile—one Skardi, as he was nicknamed for his harelip. I was glad they hadn't translated his affliction when they named the town. He founded the village, which became a center for pottery, a medieval seaport and a meeting place for tradesmen—the origins of the fair. There was more about the castle, though they didn't mention the murder of King Edward's gay lover there, an interesting tidbit I'd picked up in an English history class. A particularly vivid diorama featured the slighting of the castle by the Roundheads during the Civil War (I kept seeing boys in blue and gray even though I knew it was a different Civil War).

There wasn't too much about the fair after that, except that they said it continued. The most recent history all concerned the healing waters of the spa and the bombardment of the town by the Germans in 1914. It was rebuilt then and the posh clientele of the spa were joined by middle and working class people on holidays. The ladies were probably from a fairly well off middle class family, I thought. I paid on my way out and bought a few souvenirs, and could not stop humming the Simon and Garfunkle tune all the way home. I wondered if they had researched the original ballad, as I had, to know how appropriate the very old song was for an ancient Viking settlement.

It was dark out by the time I emerged from the exhibit and the wind was wilder and colder, so I popped back in long enough to phone a cab—I got a better dispatcher this time. I arrived just in time to go to my room, deposit my souvenirs, and rest my feet a moment before dinner.

Eleanor was engaged in a heated discussion with a waitress when I arrived. "That's ridiculous," she was telling the woman. "No one was seated at this table when I arrived, there

260

was no reserved sign and I wish to look out at the sea."

"You were assigned a seat by the wall over there, madam," the woman said.

I clucked my tongue as I arrived and pulled out a pad and pen, "Oh dear, my editor failed to mention this," I said, ostentatiously flipping over a page as if I couldn't believe what I'd read before. "A three-star hotel that assigns seats to its guests as if they were school children. I don't think so! That's probably worth the loss of two stars at least."

The waitress turned and glared at me and I gave her my biggest most American smile. "Hello, I'm Elizabeth Ann Scarborough. I've been traveling around England for the *New Yorker* Fine Dining supplement but there seems to be some mistake. I certainly don't think the *New Yorker* would give a high rating to a restaurant that denies the best seats to its diners when the dining room is entirely empty. And it might also appear to some critics that your wish to make this lady take a less desirable and visible table might smack of discrimination against her as a person of disability. The *New Yorker* would frown on that. A lot."

I said this in my loudest, ugliest American tones, throwing my not insubstantial weight around, and as I suspected, another woman, older than the one I faced and not wearing a uniform, hurried forward to say, "Is everything to your satisfaction, Miss Scarborough?"

"If I'm not to be arbitrarily assigned a table not of my choosing in this empty dining room."

"You may, of course, sit anywhere you like."

"Then I believe I'll sit here, and enjoy the lovely view at the table my companion has already selected. May we have our menus please? And some bottled water?"

They left and the older woman returned with both the menu and the water. When she'd gone again Eleanor and I

261

both allowed the giggles we'd been suppressing to sputter forth.

"Jolly well done," she said, patting my hand approvingly.

"Will Daisy be down soon?"

"No, poor dear. She came here to help put me in care and she could do with some herself. She feels much worse than I do." She picked up the menu and browsed. "I'm ravenous. Let's see, the lamb or the veal?"

"I'm sort of in the mood for anything with parsley, sage, rosemary and thyme," I said, half singing the last as in the chorus of the Simon and Garfunkle tune. She didn't react for a moment.

"What dish would that be then?" she asked when she had finished scanning the menu. "Sounds appallingly over-seasoned. Rather like tossing in the whole herb garden."

"It was a joke," I said. "You know, like the line in the song."

"I'm afraid I don't know," she said. "What song would that be?"

"Scarborough Fair," I said.

"There's a song about it? How lovely. You must sing it for me sometime."

That was perhaps the wrong thing to say, since I'm a shameless extemporaneous *a cappella* singer. However, I have always maintained that singing in conversational tones should be every bit as acceptable as conversation in conversational tones and no more intrusive to adjoining tables. Since there were no other diners at adjoining tables anyway, I sang her the song.

She brooded all through the soup course without saying anything, leaving us to sip and slurp in silence. Finally she patted her lips with a napkin and said, "I've been trying to place that song. It sounds so very familiar. Wherever did you learn it?"

"It's vintage Simon and Garfunkle! A monster hit in the sixties. I loved it because after it came out, everybody could pronounce my name. I'm surprised you haven't heard it before."

"We never listen to popular music, only classical. Perhaps it's only the tune I know and it was taken from something in a larger work?"

"Could be. Although actually, a lot of classical pieces have bits that were adapted from popular folk songs of the day."

"Is that so? How very interesting," but she sounded vague and she was staring into the distance again, as if ours was a three-way conversation. Then suddenly her eyes were back on me, and she was smiling, though her tone was surprisingly cautious, as if testing its weight on a shaky looking ladder rung, when she said, "A pity, really, that they put such modern words to it. They make no sense at all, do they?"

"Actually, they do," I said, warming to one of my favorite topics and pleasantly surprised to find such a sympathetic listener. "It's not really a modern song at all, just a modern version of a much older ballad that's collected in the Child Ballads as one of the Riddles Wisely Expounded. The original version was called "The Elfin Knight"—and various other things. And Scarborough isn't always the town, or even usually. But the theme is the same. The man asks a woman to do an impossible thing if she wants to be his true love and she thereupon asks him to do an even MORE impossible thing if he wants to be hers. Which didn't make much sense until I read about it in Wimberly's folklore book. Am I boring you?"

She had been looking out to sea again and could have been halfway to New York from the far-off expression on her face. But at my question, she returned her attention to me with a troubled-seeming smile. "Not at all, dear. I'm simply reflecting on how people are always putting riddles between themselves and their true loves. Not just in ballads either. People do that in real life all the time, don't they? 'If you *truly* care for me you'll do or won't do thus and so.' Tests, I suppose. Is that what your song is about? Because it's all rather sad. You can lose someone very precious by expecting them to jump hurdles that are too impossibly high."

I nodded. "The song about the Lady of Carlisle always struck me that way. She wanted her boyfriends to fight a lion to get back her fan. I'd have told her to take a flying leap if I'd been them."

"Yes, I can see the temptation. You've made quite a study of these songs then, have you, Ann?"

"It's a lifelong interest. I've written three books about the story songs, actually. And I promise not to go on and on about it until I make your eyes glaze over. But, since you really love this place and may end up spending the rest of your time here, I thought you might like to know the rest of what Wimberly had to say about the Elfin Knight."

"I would indeed. It had never occurred to me that the words might be riddles for that purpose, but it makes sense. When times are uncertain, as they so often are, bloody-minded young people feel they have some sort of right to ensure their mates are suitable. Possessed of the proper survival characteristics. Rather cold, that. But romantic love wasn't quite the consideration it is now I suppose, and it's quite practical to know if someone is loyal enough to play one's game, intelligent enough to understand the puzzle, and ingenious enough to solve it."

"That's true of some of the riddle songs—early versions of the False Knight of the Road have answering verses that are actual solutions to the problems so that the person answering wins the prize—either a lover or staying out of hell, depending on the version. And the Riddle Song I know from when I was a little girl has solutions in the song. But the riddles in "The Elfin Knight" are so hard they would have been impossible back then. And they're answered not with solutions, but with other riddles."

She laughed. "A bit like life then, always answering a question with a question. And so typical of people unsure of their ground. Throw up impossible obstacles and if your love can somehow magically overcome them, then you can be sure. But one never can be sure really, can one? Not until it's much too late. Why, oh why, are we so afraid of each other?"

Die-hard enthusiast that I was, I wasn't listening to the nuances in her voice, the longing, the regret, the sadness. Insensitive as any fan telling me what was wrong with one of my books, I took the opening she gave me and plunged ahead. "In the original of 'The Elfin Knight,' fear definitely entered into it. The Knight in the song is a supernatural figure who wants to carry a girl to the underworld. Wimberly says that according to another expert named Baring-Gould, this dates back to an old Norse or Teutonic tradition during a time when plighting a troth was such serious business that a girl owed her loyalty to her lover even after he was dead—so much that he could drag her back to the grave with him if she couldn't answer his riddle with a harder one. So she wasn't *trying* to be his true love, she was trying to escape being drug back to the grave with him. Kind of a *Fatal Attraction* sort of thing."

"Ah," she said and seemed to be giving it so much thought that I was wondering if I had a real folk music convert on my hands.

"It's really those impossible riddles that stay pretty constant in all the versions of the song," I told her. "And that's the difference between the Elfin Knight riddles and those in other riddle songs."

She sighed, deep and shuddering and looked very tired. I wondered if she was beginning to feel unwell again. "Pity," she said. "That the riddles are so impossible."

"Well, they were when they were dreamed up. These days I don't suppose they would be. What with new technology and so forth. If you just fudged on the interpretation a little. The shirt for instance."

"I beg your pardon?"

"You could make a shirt pretty much like it says in the song. Mind you, not an Armani or anything, but a rough upper garment by getting a length of cloth—I suppose that's what cambric would be and still available readymade, and tear it or cut it with a laser tool instead of a knife or scissors . . ."

"And what would you hold it together with? Staples, perhaps?"

I shrugged. "Hot glue. Then you could have it dry cleaned and it wouldn't have been watered or had wind blow on it— suppose you'd have to provide the cleaner's with the thorn yourself."

"And how about the acre of land the woman asks for?"

"Well, they reclaim land from the seas in a lot of places— it's expensive but it's done. As for the planting and harvesting, nanotechnology . . ."

"My word! You Americans!" she said.

"That's just my science fiction side coming out," I said.

That brought us up to dessert, or "pudding" as Eleanor called it.

Eleanor had changed the subject entirely, asking about my life in Alaska and my marriage. "Are you married?" I asked, when I'd given her the Cliff Notes version of that portion of my life.

"No, I never did," she said sadly. "I retired ten years ago

from the civil service. I was very lucky to find a position with my disability."

"So you've basically been a career woman then?"

"I was engaged once, before the war. But we parted over politics and—and then he was killed, you see. So many were."

"Yeah, Vietnam was kind of the same for women my age in the States," I told her.

She was quiet all through dessert, and then said, "I met him here, you know. We were children together, Eamon and I. You'd have liked Eamon, Ann. He was musical, like you. A lovely singer, one of those soaring Irish tenors. Sometimes I hear him still, in my dreams. We were going to be married. We meant to announce our engagement during the Fair here, when we were all together for the summer again. But then the war broke out and the Irish Republic declared itself neutral. Eamon's father had been conducting his business in London for some time, but chose to return with the family to Ireland at the start of the war. Father was furious. Although he had always said that Daisy and I might marry as we liked, he had never really approved of Eamon's family and called the Houlihans traitors. Eamon and I met on the beach, as our families were angrily packing to leave. He asked me to elope and return to Ireland with him. I demanded to know why he was running away to Ireland, why he couldn't join up and protect us from the Nazis like every other real man. He said he would defend me with his life but for reasons that should be obvious to me, he didn't care to extend his protection to my country. We had a horrible row and—that was the last time I saw him."

"What happened?" I asked.

She nodded. "Without telling me what he was going to do, he went right off and enlisted and was promptly killed en route to the front. I only learned of it months later. I was in uniform myself by then, driving ambulances and so forth. Until my jeep got hit. That was when I lost the use of my legs. Our parents were killed in the bombings in London. So you see, there was no use in falling out, no use in spoiling our last good time together here, and no use my giving up Eamon, for I never was fit to marry anyone else after, even had I wished . . . no, no, don't protest. You don't know. You've no idea what it was like."

I did, a little, having been a nurse in Vietnam, but I hadn't been injured as she had, hadn't lost someone I loved as much. I always thought of the English as being just an earlier, maybe a bit stuffier, version of Americans. I kept forgetting how devastating it had been for them to have both world wars on their doorstep, killing not only soldiers, but civilians. I reached out and laid my hand over hers and hoped she wouldn't think it terribly, gauchely American.

She didn't cry openly though there were a few tears. She must have shed so many.

"So that's why you wanted to come back here when you couldn't live alone anymore?"

She nodded. "Daisy hates the idea, but I keep thinking, perhaps if I become senile, I'll remain in the dream I have of seeing him again, of being here and young and in love . . . though I'd settle for old and forgiven. Ann, dear?"

"What?"

Her face was brightening. "You're so very clever, knowing about that song and figuring out how to solve the riddle of the shirt. Do you think we might, between us, do what you suggested and perhaps . . . I don't know. I just feel that I should like to do something of the sort."

"I was going to leave tomorrow to visit a friend in Romsey for Halloween."

"Of course, you must do as you think best, but it would

mean so much to me . . ."

The lady had had a very hard life and was getting ready to spend the rest of it in a mangy old hotel to be near the memory she wished to honor. What I had told her about the song had apparently given her an idea for a little ritual gesture that would give her a sense of closure on something that had caused her pain throughout her life. My friends at home in Port Chetzemoka are always doing that kind of thing, but usually for a lot less important reasons. I didn't figure it would hurt me and my friend Marjorie in Romsey really wouldn't care one way or the other. "Okay sure."

She sighed as if terribly relieved at my agreement and said, "One other little thing. I'd rather Daisy didn't know. She'd think I'm getting feeble-minded as well as just feeble. I shall tell her to rest an extra day tomorrow and that you have agreed to let me show you the town properly."

The fabric store had a bolt of white linen that cost the earth, but was the closest thing we could find to cambric, a kind of French linen, or the other fabric mentioned, Holland, which was linen from the Netherlands. This linen was made in Sussex, but it would have to do. When the woman began to cut off a piece, Eleanor bought the entire remnant, so that it wouldn't have to be cut.

"Now where would we find a laser knife in a Yorkshire seaside town, I wonder?" I said aloud.

"I've another idea. Could we not wrap a sort of shirt perhaps, since we've so much fabric? Rather like the Indian saris?"

And as soon as we got our hot glue gun at the local artist's supply store, that's exactly what we did, with Eleanor serving as model and me as draper-gluer, right there in the mostly deserted store. We were both laughing and swearing, me roundly and Eleanor with a surprisingly unladylike "bloody hell" once or twice. The sales clerk, a boy of about twenty who had previously looked extremely bored said, "I say, that's going to be a smashing mummy costume. You'll be the hit of the masquerade."

The draping and gluing accomplished, we had a shirt of sorts, and all we had then to do was persuade the local dry cleaners to ignore the unorthodox nature of our garment and to give us their extra fast service—a goal accomplished by an under-the-table ten pounds in addition to what they normally charged.

Before the woman hauled the "sark" across the counter, Eleanor said, "Wait," and stuck a thorn into one of the folds. "That's not to come out, now," she told the woman, who looked as if she'd like to put as much distance between herself and us as possible.

After that, we had a very nice stroll along the beach. The day was one where the sky changed every two minutes, the brisk wind whisking mountain ranges full of clouds across the horizon, then sweeping it clear until the next buildup. The air was full of moisture and ozone and the salty, fishy smell of the beach. Eleanor had a friendly conversation with the tinker man who offered the pony rides—his grandfather had been the one to offer pony rides when Eleanor was a child, she learned.

We enjoyed a late lunch of hot dogs, soft drinks and ice cream in one of the tacky little waterfront places instead of at our hotel. The plan was that we would then go back and pick up our "sark" before the dry cleaning establishment closed.

But Eleanor started to fade then. "I'd best return and check on Daisy," she said. "Do you mind picking up the sark yourself?"

I assured her I didn't and suggested she get some rest. The plan was that we would sneak away from the hotel at about eleven-thirty, after Daisy was asleep, and I would wheel Eleanor to the beach where she would present her offering. We were hoping for high tide to take it out right away. I felt slightly silly, but it was fun and I knew it would be a great anecdote to share when I wrote home.

Eleanor returned to the hotel in a cab but I took the funicular back up to the town and hired a cab out to the castle hill. Very little remained of the castle and the walk was too far and too steep. But the side trip occupied me until time to pick up the sark.

The thorn was still in it, and it was clean. The clerk shook her head as I held up the unlikely garment for inspection. "Halloween costume," I said. "Our mummy's very particular about her shroud."

I stepped back out of the cleaner's into a sudden, driving wind, flinging sheets of rain over everything. Fortunately, the sark was in a protective plastic bag. I ducked back inside, pulled my rain poncho out of my shoulder bag and slipped it over my head, then tucked the bag with the sark underneath it as well. Instead of battling my way back to the hotel, I headed for a restaurant I had seen around the corner. Hot dogs and ice cream left an empty place and I didn't want to battle the snooty dining room staff again.

Somewhere in the distance a siren announced A) that a speeder had been apprehended, B) that a fire was being fought or C) that someone was on the way to the hospital. I voted for C) in a town so full of nursing homes. I wondered which one Daisy and Eleanor would select. The rain hadn't lightened at all even though I took plenty of time finishing my meal and had dawdled awhile longer reading my tour book over tea. I called a cab, and fifty minutes later, it still hadn't

271

arrived. So I fought my way against the wind back to the hotel, sloshed my way to the lift, and on to my room where I hung up the sark, divested myself of my wet pants, shoes, and socks, which I arranged over the heated towel rack, and let the poncho drip into the tub. Then I fell exhausted onto the bed and let a pit of sleep close over me while the wind whistled around the building and rain assaulted the pane of my window.

I awoke, confused, in the darkness, to the sound of a knock at my door. "Ann dear?" came a whisper. "It's Eleanor. It's eleven-fifteen. Are you awake?"

I jumped up, pulled on my extra pair of trousers, and went to the door. My hair was still damp. Eleanor sat in her chair, dressed much as I'd seen her to begin with in her coat and scarf with her little lap robe.

"Maybe this isn't such a good idea tonight," I told her. "It's pouring out there."

"Nonsense, it's just a bit of rain."

I pulled the sark out of the closet. "Here it is. Now that you have it, can't you do what you want any time?"

"Spoken," she said. "Like someone young and healthy. Please, Ann. I've no idea how long I'll be able to do this. Come on now. There's a good girl. Stop whining and let's get on with it."

I knew it all along. I knew that I was nuts taking an elderly British lady, wheelchair bound and with a heart condition, to the beach in the middle of a storm at midnight on Halloween. It simply didn't seem like very good judgment, even at the time. But she wouldn't take no for an answer and if I hadn't gone, I felt sure she'd try to go alone. As it was, she couldn't have done any worse if she had.

"At least let's call a cab," I said.

But she shook her head stubbornly and I pushed her out

into the rain, then dragged the wheelchair backwards down the steps, a technique we'd used earlier in the day. I could hardly see and I really wished I'd brought mittens. My hands were already cold and numb on the handles of the wheelchair.

It was all downhill to the beach, however, and we had an excellent tail wind, my poncho making a kind of sail. The sark was tucked beneath Eleanor's lap robe. Except for the white mare's tales of the waves, the water was utterly black. The sky boiled with black on black on steel gray clouds and shimmered with the pelting rain when the wind pushed an opening for the clouds or the high, full moon. Dead leaves whipped wildly around us until we got to the beach, and then it was wet sand that sprang up to sting us.

Eleanor said nothing. The tide was high, as we wished, yard-high waves crashing onto the beach.

"You want me to put the sark in the sea for you?" I asked Eleanor.

"No, dear. Not yet. I want you to sing the first part of the song, about the sark. Would you do that please?"

No one ever has to ask me twice to sing so, though the wind tore every note from me before I quite had it out, I did as she asked.

I'd got to the bit about the "wash it in yonder dry well" part when I noticed someone walking out of the water, an aura of shining water still clinging to his outline. One of the surfers in his wetsuit, out for a highly stupid midnight surf, I thought at first.

I took a breath, meaning to wait until he'd gone.

"Ann," Eleanor said urgently, shoving the wheels of her chair to propel herself toward the man. Her scarf tore loose from her head and went flying, as did the lap robe, leaving the sark twisting in a ghostly fashion on her lap. *"Keep singing."*

"Guy's going to think we're nuts, Eleanor, singing in this kind of rain."

"Nonsense. Eamon's Irish. And he's been singing the same song to me in my dreams for years. That's where I knew it from, you see. Trust me, Ann. He will understand about the sark . . ."

But I couldn't remember any more. It didn't matter. The man was closer now, and I saw that instead of a wet suit, he wore a vintage military uniform. Just one stripe. As he drew nearer, the wind rose even higher and tore the sark from Eleanor's hand. She let it go, opening her fingers deliberately to let it fly at him. He caught it and let it fly out to sea like an oversize gull. He was almost close enough I would be able to make him out clearly, though his face was still in shadow.

Then, suddenly, a blast of wind roared between us, knocking me to my knees in the sand, and when I could look up, it was to see a huge wave come slamming down on us all.

I screamed and dived for the wheelchair, hanging onto it with all my might as I drank in seawater.

As the water drained backward again I scuttled toward the sidewalk, pulling the chair, but even before I could see clearly again I knew it was empty.

The waterfront, the road, the shops, all were totally empty of people and cars. I ran along the beach, trying to see, calling for her, but I never saw a sign, not so much as a hand or foot of her or the man she claimed was Eamon. Nor did I see the sark, except perhaps, unknowingly, amid the tossing white-caps.

Finally, when I'd called all I could and looked until I was certain she was beyond my help, I returned to where I had left the chair, to find that it too had washed away.

I half thought I'd wake in my bed at home, as if I'd lived through a particularly weird and exceptionally wet nightmare, but I was awake and shaking with all-too-real cold by the time I forced my way back through the gale, up the hill to the hotel, which was as close to other people and help as any other place. I rang the bell for the concierge, rang it and rang it but without response.

Daisy. I'd rouse Daisy, I thought. How would I tell her what I had allowed to happen to her sister? I didn't know, and I certainly couldn't explain about sarks and songs and strange military men. But I did have to get help, someone to search for poor Eleanor. Eleanor had told me their room number and I found it and pounded my frozen hands against the wood. The door opened immediately and the night clerk stood there. Beyond her I could see Daisy, sitting forlornly on the bed. "Daisy, I'm sorry, but we have to get the police. Something's happened to Eleanor."

The concierge just stared at me and I pushed past her to kneel beside Daisy, who seemed not to hear me. "You have to listen to me. Something terrible has happened to Eleanor."

Daisy shook her head and when she lifted it, I saw that she wore a sad little smile. "Not so terrible, really. It's spared her the indignity of the nursing home. I had no idea you'd be so upset, Ann, or I'd have made sure someone told you. Did you only just hear?"

"Hear nothing, I saw!" I said.

"You've been at the funeral home? Oh, I knew I should have kept vigil but I've been feeling so ill and Eleanor really had no belief in all that superstitious nonsense."

The concierge was glaring at me. "Miss Scarborough, I think you should return to your own room. I've just given Mrs. Jacobs the sleeping draught the doctor left for her this afternoon when he came to officially declare Miss Porter's death."

"Death? This afternoon?"

Daisy reached up and touched my sleeve. "Oh, you poor dear, did you think it had only just happened?"

"I did hear sirens," I admitted.

Daisy nodded and patted my hand. "It must be a great shock to you. Eleanor was enjoying your company so much. You couldn't have known how close she really was to death. Neither of us knew for sure either, of course, but I felt, when she asked to come back here, that it was almost time. Thank you for keeping her such good company on her last day."

How could I tell them that I'd been with her not an hour ago? That I'd seen—thought I'd seen—her carried away by a wave, and a man. I stumbled for the door like a zombie but Daisy said "Wait," and turned to the other bed, where she fumbled in an open suitcase.

She held out a worn black and white folder to me. "Scarborough Faire" the heading said. It seemed to be a little pamphlet advertising the event. "This was one of Eleanor's mementos. Since you were both so intrigued with the fair here, I think she'd like you to have it." She closed my hand around the brochure and I returned to my room.

I just lay there in my wet clothes upon the bed for hours, listening to the hammering wind and rain. At last, the pane of glass began to lighten just a bit, and the wind to subside, enough for me to hear what I thought were voices on it, a tenor and an uncertain alto, singing, "Then you'll be a true love of mine . . ."

About the Author

Elizabeth Ann Scarborough is the Nebula-Award-winning author of *The Healer's War*, which won the 1989 Nebula for best novel. Her most recent solo novel is *Channeling Cleopatra*.

Altogether she has 26 published novels to her credit, including the "Petaybee" series with Anne McCaffrey and the most recent three books in the *Acorna* series, also with Anne McCaffrey. Additionally she has written numerous short stories, including the ones in this anthology, and edited three anthologies.

She was born in Kansas City, KS and graduated from nursing school there. She went on to be an Army nurse serving in country during the Vietnam War. The army also took her to Alaska for the first time. There she spent much of her tour as head clinic nurse at Fort Greeley. She got lots of rides in ambulances, helicopters and small fixed wing aircraft transporting pregnant ladies to Fairbanks, helping with emergency rescues, and watching chopper pilots buzz the fort's buffalo herd.

She left Alaska briefly when she got out of the Army and

went to work for the Indian Health Service in Gallup, New Mexico. She returned to Alaska during the time of the building of the Alaska Pipeline to live with her then-boyfriend the romantic cabin-in-the-woods Alaskan dream. Learning that the reality was no running water, no plumbing and no electricity, she left the husband and the woods but remained in Fairbanks for 18 years altogether, counting her Army time. While in Alaska she worked at nursing off and on but also sold shoes and fine jewelry at J.C. Penney. She also started her own handweaving business, Howling Woof Weavers, which lasted a whole year.

After she started writing, she began attending classes at the University of Alaska, Fairbanks, receiving a BA in history with a minor in journalism. During that time she also worked in bookstores and in general was a very busy girl. In 1987 she moved to the Olympic Peninsula in Washington State and has lived there for the last fifteen years. During this time she was privileged to live part of three consecutive years in Ireland while writing the Petaybee trilogy with best-selling sf writer Anne McCaffrey. Today she lives with four cats in another cabin in a Victorian seaport town and writes full time with a small supplementary income from designing bead patterns.

The employees of Five Star hope you have enjoyed this book. All our books are made to last. Other Five Star books are available at your library, through selected bookstores, or directly from us.

For information about titles, please call:

(800) 223-1244

or visit our Web site at:

www.gale.com/fivestar

To share your comments, please write:

Publisher
Five Star
295 Kennedy Memorial Drive
Waterville, ME   04901